HALWENDE'S REDEMPTION

HALWENDE'S LEGACY
BOOK 1

JOHN WEGENER

Halwende's Redemption

Written by John Wegener.
Published by John Wegener.
Copyright © 2017 John Wegener.
Copyright © 2022 Cover designed by Fiona Jayde Media.

Fairy tales help us dream of what could be.

1

MAROONED

Sitting by the fire, I gaze up at the stars. A month has passed since my ship crashed on this god-forsaken planet. I had been traversing one of the obscure trade routes to Santori, avoiding unwanted attention and chasing extra cash for much-needed repairs to the ship, when I collided with the mother of all asteroids, far too big for my shields to deflect. The impact damaged my primary drive and caused my spaceship to spiral out of control. Suddenly a planet appeared where no planet should be. I was lucky to have sufficient power to land the ship and me in one piece. There's major damage to the ship, with breaches in the hull in several places.

When I rechecked the astrogation charts, sure enough the planet doesn't appear on the list. That worries me the most because it means I'm at the mercy of my distress beacon. Who knows if someone will bother to respond to the signal? Everybody will check its source and conclude it must be a mistake. That's what I would do.

The only good thing about this calamity is the site where I landed: a grassy knoll with plenty of surrounding edible vegetation and a freshwater stream nearby. So, I won't starve or dehydrate in a hurry. But the landscape is devoid of animal life, including birds and insects, and there are no fish in the stream — strange. No sentient beings threaten me or offer companionship. The silence is overpowering, and the loneliness of not knowing when I'll see a friendly face again, if ever, is lowering my spirits. Speaking of which, I yearn for a boisterous drinking bout with the other traders. I chuckle at the thought that I usually can't wait to return to my ship and speed away from prying eyes and ears for a few months. It's different now that I'm denied contact with humanity.

Accepting that I won't be getting off this planet in a hurry, I have started making a home for myself. The ship is still intact enough for shelter, even with its damaged hull. My living space is untouched and livable once I picked up the debris from the rough landing. I have built a lean-to shelter extending from the main hatch, which provides shade when I sit on my camping chair on the frequent hot, humid days, the place being in the planet's tropics. Fortunately, there's a gentle breeze as well on most occasions, making the outdoors bearable. I sit under my shelter now, my campfire burning and crackling in an enclosed ring of rocks. There's plenty of firewood to burn. It is peaceful watching the flames dance in the breeze.

In the month since the crash, I've explored most of the surrounding countryside. Dense, lush vegetation surrounds me — the bushes and twining vines hard to penetrate even with my laser knife. The forested region to the northeast is sparse and easy to traverse, so I explored that direction after I first landed. The trees are only a few meters tall there, and one species has succulent golden fruit hanging from the branches with a stringy texture inside, tasting of passionfruit. The stream flowing four hundred meters away in that direction provides plenty of water. It's a leisurely walk to collect it once a week when I need to top up my supply.

The jungle provides an abundance of fungi. My composition analyzer has confirmed they are edible and non-hallucinogenic. They have many flavors, giving me ample variety. There are amorphous dark brown ones with the flavor of freshly cooked lobster, circular black ones with dark green spots and the flavor of chicken, and many others with various meat and vegetable flavors.

My elevated position allows me to see a reasonable distance from my ship. Only forest extends downstream in the river direction before it disappears in a hazy mist, but a large, elevated landmass towers on the horizon on the upstream side. The jungle density prevents me from seeing further in that direction. A vast mountain range spans the humidity-hazed distance to the west, snowcaps plain on its peaks.

I don't trust the vegetation in the jungle, not since the day I ventured deep into it. The atmosphere was suffocating and claustrophobic. No noise accompanied me, not even a breeze to rustle the leaves of the trees, and yet I sensed danger. Maybe I was just being paranoid, but it made me uncomfortable, as though the jungle was enticing me, like the flower of a Venus Fly Trap. I retreated to my camp that day.

The major sun is descending in the sky now, its fiery orange-red glow disappearing below the horizon. At least that star and its accompanying minor companion are on the astrogation charts. The minor sun is further away and produces negligible light, like a moon in its brightness. It emits a chill, blue aura that bathes my surroundings in an eerie, steely blue sheen in the night sky. It disturbs me sometimes. My darkest moments surface when just that sun occupies the sky. In those moments, I dread a monster breaking from the jungle to attack me. I've set up a security perimeter to alert me of such an event, which gives me some peace of mind when I sleep.

As the forest and the river appear harmless, a week ago I began a trek upriver on a trip of discovery. I packed a rucksack with provisions to sustain me for four or five days. I knew the forest would contribute with plentiful food, although I packed extra in case things changed along the way. I set off northeast until I came to the river, then continued east upstream. The walking was easy. On the first night, I camped on a sandy protruding bank. Plenty of dry driftwood was available for a fire. Lonely and frightened, I almost despaired that night of anyone ever rescuing me. The lifestyle of a trader was a deliberate choice I made that has enabled me to leave behind past regrets and inquisitive eyes. But I am unsure of the wisdom of it now. I came out of my self-imposed pity and settled for the night, listening to the gentle flow of water running past me. A chirping cricket would have been welcome, but running water was the only sound I heard.

The next morning, I packed up camp and continued my exploration along the river. The scenery remained the same, and I pitched camp in a soft grassy patch of the forest. Changes appeared in the scenery the following day, which I was thankful for as I had been considering turning around if nothing altered soon. As the forest thinned, I approached a lake from which the stream issued. A cliff face only four or five hundred meters away reflected on the lake's crystal smooth surface. It was a beautiful sight. A waterfall cascaded from the cliff, deepening the scar caused by the erosion eating into it. The roar of water serenaded me like the greatest symphony ever produced, delightful after so much silence. I turned to the right and kept walking along the edge as the gentle waves lapped the shore. Soon afterward, I came to another river flowing from the lake. It was a wider river than the one I had traveled. A vast grass-covered plain stretched out on the far side, enticing me to cross over to it. After an hour, I found a spot where the river broadened and became shallow enough for me to ford it. I grabbed a stick and stepped into the water, poking in front of me to test the depth. The water rose to my waist before subsiding and leading me to dry ground again.

Cliffs rose from the plain's far extent, which was flat and verdant, lush with grass and peppered with the odd tree. Flowers bloomed in pockets of red, orange, and gold in some places and blue and violet in others. I took a deep breath, infusing the panoramic scenery into me. If I died now, I thought, I would at least die having seen this paradise. I walked toward the cliffs to study them before the sunset required me to make camp for the night.

No food grew there, so I took rations from my sack for my dinner, consisting of fruit that I had collected along the way and preserved meat, chewy and dry but delicious. Before I retired for the night, I sat by the fire and started humming a song I remembered from my childhood. There was no reason for this except to break the silence that surrounded me. The words are lost in my subconscious, but the tune has always stuck in my mind. It is a cheerful song, one I would sing when frightened as a child. My humming continued until I reduced the volume to a whisper and stopped. I felt at peace after that and slept a sound and dreamless sleep.

The next morning, I followed the cliffs back to the lake and the waterfall. The torrent of water cascaded from more than a hundred meters above, crashing onto rocks, my skin dampening with the engulfing mist it produced. Several holes pierced the cliff face, large enough for a man, but I refrained from exploring them as I wanted to return to my ship. I retraced my path across the river and then set a direction straight for the vessel, aiming for the ship's beacon.

At nightfall, I found a small clearing and set up camp. The next day I returned to my ship. I pondered what I had discovered and whether any of it was useful to me. After deliberation, I decided I wanted to explore the caves soon.

2

I AM ALONE, OR AM I

The wind has picked up as I close my eyes, attempting to sleep. There is usually a gentle breeze in the evening that lingers into the night, rustling the leaves of the trees within earshot unless a storm breaks. When this occurs, the wind can become a battering ram, stripping away the vegetation as it tries to protect itself against the turbulence. The assault soon passes, and the silence and humidity return to torment and haunt me again. The wind's tone changes into myriad sounds of birds chirping, animals mouthing their distinctive calls, and even whispers, but I put it down to the oppressiveness of my isolation. I even wonder if those fungi are hallucinogenic after all. I drift off to sleep under the stars and the whispering wind.

Another day dawns as the brighter double star rises above the horizon in its majestic orange glory to beckon the leaves and flowers to open to a fresh day of growth and productivity. I remain at my ship for the day. Something disturbs me, but I can't put my finger on it, so I push it aside and continue with my industrious monotony. I gaze toward the jungle, seduced by its green lushness. My expeditions have avoided it, as I've always felt unsafe and watched. It's a foolish thought as only vegetation grows there. It has no eyes or other senses to detect my presence, yet I sense a closeness engulfing me when I trespass its bounds. Not today, though. I resolve to enter the mysterious realm tomorrow and see if I can discover different fresh fruits or vegetables to eat, a succulent fungus even, one that I haven't tasted yet. I will prepare for the trek in the morning.

The wind picks up again as I doze in the twilight of my slumber. I swear I can hear birds, animals, and whispers again before the wind swirls into random chords of chaos and I enter the coma of dreams and rejuvenation.

The morning chores completed, I prepare for my excursion into the jungle. I pack food and water and a few other necessities and head west. The light dims as I venture further into the forest. All at once, the vegetation changes, becoming wilder and unwelcoming, as if it resents my intrusion into its domain. The trees tower overhead, the buttressed trunks keeping them in place. Purple, blue, and sometimes orange-colored vines entwine in the branches above, only to cast tendrils below as if groping for something on which to feed. Dead vegetation carpets the ground consisting of leaves and twigs that have fallen from the branches and vines that have lived past their use-by date, and various other fungi and mosses, all fermenting into rich compost for the next generation.

It's lunchtime, so I look for a place where I can sit and eat the food that I brought with me. I find a slight clearing in this maze of flora and eat and ponder my learnings from my expedition. Not much at present, I conclude. I discover no other fruit or fungus that is edible. I console myself with knowing that at least I now know.

Sleepiness overcomes me after my meal, so I doze for a while, waking with a start as something gentle rubs my shin. A vine tendril has encircled my ankle. Jumping up in a panic, I hack the probing tentacle off with my machete. I scan my surroundings and note that the jungle has crept in around me while I slumbered. Does it know that I am here? Is it interested in me for curiosity's sake — or as a food supply? It might be both. I resolve to return to the ship, only to discover the path blocked by thick jungle, the machete unable to hack through it. After a futile search for an easier detour, I fetch my laser knife and start hacking away at the barrier. It is slow work in the beginning, but it gets easier after a few minutes as if the jungle knows that I can slash through its delicate life and it dreads any further injury, withdrawing for my exit. I finally smash through and dash back to camp. As I glance back, I can barely see my exit route, as if the jungle has closed in after me, signaling its displeasure at my intrusion and forming a blockade against any future incursion. I'm just glad to leave the dread behind me.

The day's effort has exhausted me, so I prepare supper and settle for the night. Whispers waft past again before I sleep. They are too soft for me to make any sense of them.

I wake and resolve to explore the caves and the expanse of land before them. I pack supplies for a few days. As I know my route, the trip will be shorter, and exploring the caves won't take long.

On reaching the larger river in the late afternoon the next day, I cross at the ford. The caves loom before me, but I set up camp nearby for the night. I slip into the fold-up sleeping pod I brought with me and drift off to sleep. Whispers torment me again. I jerk my eyes open and glance around but see nothing, no one. I'm imagining things. That surprises me, having been alone longer in the past without hallucinating. The alien environment might be affecting me more than I realize. I decide to do my relaxation exercises over the next few days, but not tonight. The hike has made me overtired for such activities now. I fall asleep, still hearing the whispers but ignoring them.

As I wake, refreshed, the morning greets me with chilled air. This is unusual given the tropical climate I have experienced so far. The season may be changing. I go to the stream and wash my face, gulping a copious amount of water. My breakfast is next. I cook bacon and an egg on the small fire — it was a challenge getting the egg here in one piece, but I did it. I boil water and make coffee. With breakfast finished, I pack and head for the caves.

On entering the cave on the right, I turn on my torch as the natural illumination dims. The walls are rugged and dimpled. Water, long since diverted to easier courses, has carved them. It is sandstone or something similar, judging by the surface texture. A branch angles sharply left twenty meters into the cave. As I gaze along it, I realize it leads to another entrance as a strong white light penetrates through to me with only a minor effect on the cave's illumination. The cavity is thirty meters wide and ten high. It is dry but humid. I keep walking deeper into the cavern, throwing my light from wall to wall, inspecting my surroundings. It is silent — eerie, but natural on a planet that has no fauna to create noise, no bats to resent my intrusion, and no rats to scurry off seeking food.

One hundred meters further into the cave, the walls start to close in on me. As I shine my light further into the abyss, they are only fifteen meters apart now but run parallel. An alcove cuts into the left wall after twenty meters, contrasting with the rest of the cave surfaces. I walk over and illuminate the cavity. It is ten meters deep and the same wide. The walls are smooth, and the back wall is flat and unnatural in its construction. It looks like someone has built it. It is obsidian to the extreme, devoid of any reflective quality. I lift my light in front of me to study the wall in more detail as I step closer. A meter away, I wave my light over it to find any blemish on its surface. I lean closer, squinting to gain even more detail and gasp. I jump back and drop my light — the wall surface just changed; I am sure of it.

Quickly grabbing my light again, I hyperventilate, trying to regain my composure. I'm not sure what to do. Should I run out? That seems over-dramatic. I probably imagined it anyway. I remind myself that imagination can play strange tricks on people in isolation. I calm myself and think. I know no one else is here. From what I've seen, the planet is devoid of any animal life. If I've experienced a phenomenon, it's of a natural origin, so let's just figure out what I just encountered.

I shine my light at the wall again. It is mirror-smooth and ebony. I take a step forward. Nothing changes. The wall is two meters away now. I step closer. It stays the same. My palms perspire, as I know the next step may cause the change. The non-reflective surface amazes me. I gulp and step closer.

The wall is now less than a meter from me. It illuminates and displays text, but it's nothing I have ever seen, and yet it's familiar. This is unnatural. I do not need the light to read the text. It is self-illuminating. I reach out to touch it but am repulsed by a force field that won't let me. It doesn't hurt me; it just exerts a greater force the more force I use. I step away. The wall returns to blackness. I step closer. The writing reappears. Is this a portal? If so, why can't I touch it?

"Why are you here?" comes an ethereal voice from nowhere speaking my language. I drop my torch again and pick it up just as fast.

"I am stranded." Why did I reply? This frightens me now. Is there an unexplainable presence here, or is isolation turning me insane? It's a strange thing for me to imagine if I'm freaking out. Then what? I'm momentarily unsure what to do but then decide. I will return to my ship and ponder my predicament.

Rushing from the cave, I escape to the safety of my ship.

3

CAN YOU HELP US?

Making sense of yesterday's surprise is frustrating. There is no explanation. I've experienced nothing like it, and I've been absent from civilization before for much longer than this. I've seen nothing like that wall in my travels, either. Is it a portal or a tombstone? Who is it for? Why is it on an uninhabited planet? Did I really hear a voice speak to me? The questions are perplexing and are giving me a headache. I go back into my ship and rummage through my secret stores where I keep my alcohol, finding a bottle of rum. I drink it straight from the bottle, the fiery liquid burning my throat and dulling my senses. Half the bottle is gone before I replace the cap. I stash it away again, retire to my bunk and lose consciousness to an alcohol-hazed sleep.

When I wake in the late afternoon, a slight hangover thumps in my head. *I need to drink more; I'm out of practice.* I will need to produce the stuff here, too — if I survive. It won't last forever. I cook something to eat and ponder my experience again. Did I imagine that voice? I mean, I had been wondering why I was there, so maybe it's not real. That must be it. I'm still doubtful, though.

It is dark now, and my usual light illuminates the awning. I peer into the jungle at nothing in particular as I sit outside in my self-made lounge seat. The various scents of the flowering trees waft past me in the breeze. It smells pungent tonight. I doze off, my head nodding ...

"Can you help us?"

I sit bolt upright. What was that? I turn around and jump from my chair. Two children are standing behind me, scruffy-looking but with a dignified stance. One is tall and looks about twelve years old, male. He has blond hair and green eyes. The other is shorter and about ten, female. She has green eyes and brunette hair. They look alike, like brother and sister. After considering they could use a bath, I realize that they must have just rubbed dirt on themselves because they are otherwise well-groomed. They wear pants and a shirt of advanced manufacture. I've seen nothing like it in my travels. Where did they come from? I've lost it. I'm imagining people now. "What?" I ask, not knowing why. Why am I talking to my imagination?

"Can you help us, please?" Their eyes plead like malnourished waifs. Why would I imagine people in such an impoverished condition? I'd rather dream of people in splendor and plenty to contrast with my predicament — a young, voluptuous woman perhaps.

After breathing deep, I close my eyes tight and open them again. Nope! They're still there. I play along with my hallucination. It might be enjoyable to entertain my presumed madness. "Where did you come from?"

"From the city," the boy says.

"What city?"

"The city you were in yesterday."

"I wasn't in any city." What is he saying? I explored the caves. But I didn't see any city. I must be delirious.

"Yes, you were. You just couldn't see it."

I'm even more puzzled now. I walk toward them. They aren't frightened of me. I reach out and touch the boy.

"What are you doing?" he says, jumping backward and staring at me indignantly.

"Sorry. I want to see if I can hallucinate touch."

"Hallucinate? What are you talking about?"

I've confused them both.

"Don't you think we're real?" the girl asks.

"Well, consider it from my perspective. I crash land on a deserted planet that shouldn't exist and has no animal or sentient life, and you kids appear from thin air talking my language. How do I explain that?"

They glance at each other and sigh.

"He doesn't understand," the girl says.

"No, he doesn't," the boy agrees.

"We will need to start with the basics and explain everything to him."

"Must we?"

"He won't understand otherwise."

The boy sighs again. "You explain it. I don't want to."

The girl looks at the boy with daggers in her eyes, "Typical." She looks at me. "It's simple. We've cloaked ourselves so that we're invisible to the casual observer. The animals and the buildings and the structures where we live are all cloaked. The whole planet is cloaked. Don't ask me why; it's just how it is. This cloaked space is including you now, so you can now see us and, if you listen, you will hear noises of animals."

As if by the girl's magic, I listen and sure enough, crickets chirp, and other animal noises become discernable.

"We have a situation, and Sigmund and I believe you can help. You look like a brave person to me."

Even though I don't believe any of it, I decide I may as well play along with this little charade of my perception for a while longer. "What is your name?" I ask the girl.

"Frieda."

"And you are brother and sister?"

"Yes."

"And you have a 'situation'?"

"Yes."

"Why do you consider me brave?"

"Loneliness doesn't worry you, and you explore without weapons to protect you."

"I don't need weapons if nothing can harm me, do I?"

"I suppose not. But how do you know nothing can harm you? Something scared you when you walked into the jungle and fell asleep."

"Have you been spying on me since I got here? You seem to know everything I've been doing."

"Not all the time. We didn't notice you at first, and we sleep and do our chores too. But it was hard not to notice you coming through our city."

I think for a moment, staring at Frieda and Sigmund. What a bizarre trick my brain is playing on me. I've studied the effects of isolation, but this conversation with children is a novel experience.

"What's that wall in the cave for, and what's written on it?" I ask to test them. If they can come up with a plausible answer, maybe I'm not hallucinating.

"We're not allowed to talk about that," Frieda replies after looking at Sigmund for guidance and getting a slight shake of the head.

"Why not?"

"It's taboo. Ask something else."

I shake my head, uncertain of my sanity. The children appear physical. Sigmund felt real when I touched him.

"What do you want then?"

"We want you to return to the city with us."

"What for?"

"We can't tell you."

I laugh in disbelief. "You want me to travel to a city I can't see to a situation you won't explain and do something you can't tell me? Forget it!"

"I told you he wouldn't," Sigmund says, looking at Frieda. "He's not as brave as you thought he was."

"Yes, he will. He just needs time."

"Sigmund's said the only sane thing in this entire conversation," I interject. "I'm not going anywhere, not tonight anyway. I'm going to bed."

Sigmund and Frieda glance at each other, confused about their next move. Not my problem. I go back into my ship and grab the half-empty bottle of rum and start drinking it again, figuring I just need a sound sleep to rid myself of this hallucination and get back to my lonely existence. I stand in the hatch to the ship, staring at the children as I swig the rum, getting increasingly drunk. They return my stare with quizzical expressions as if asking me what they should do next. I retreat into the ship, finish the rum, and fall asleep, hoping they've disappeared when I awaken.

4

THE CITY

I wake the next morning to a brilliant sunrise that I should be in no fit state to appreciate. But despite my hangover, I find the reds, oranges, and yellows on the horizon truly spectacular. I feel overjoyed to be alive — until I see Sigmund and Frieda standing in the exact spot where I left them last night. I can't believe what I'm seeing. How could they have not moved all night? Surely, that's proof I'm imagining this. With a shake of my head, I stare at them in disbelief, anger, and resignation — two specters taunting me to peer into the spiritual realm. I sigh. "Have you stayed there the entire night?" I ask them.

"Don't be silly!" Sigmund replies, in a childish matter-of-fact way, implying that my question is absurd. "We haven't stood here the whole night. We returned home when you went to sleep and have just returned. We figured you'd sleep until about now. And this is the best spot to study you from."

"He's not very intelligent," Frieda observes to Sigmund.

"Hey! Hold on a minute," I protest. "There is no need to be insulting."

"I may be wrong," Frieda concedes without conviction.

"I told you last night he wouldn't help us," says Sigmund. "He is too selfish."

These two imps are annoying me now. How dare they tell me I'm too selfish? Sure, as a lone trader, I need to make sure no one short-changes me or hijacks me or places me in sinister predicaments, and tormented thoughts do trouble me — hence the drinking. But that's far short of being selfish. I glare at the two sprites, fuming with indignation and resentment. Why do these brats infuriate me? I gasp for breath, regaining my composure. It won't hurt to see if these two speak the truth. Did I really walk through a cloaked city by those caves? What are their actual intentions? Why can't they tell me? I reach a decision. "OK then. I'll go with you to this wonderful city I can't see," I say. The snideness is obvious, although if I told the truth I would admit that the thought of my isolation being over is an attractive one. "But first, I am having breakfast."

Delight and satisfaction appear on both their faces.

"She will be so pleased," Frieda says.

"You can eat breakfast in the city," Sigmund says.

"No! I'm having breakfast here, and then I'll follow you to the city."

"If you insist."

They approach me and hold my hands, Sigmund my left and Frieda my right, to show their appreciation. I let them, and the warmth of human closeness threatens to overpower me. They let go, and I go into my ship to prepare my breakfast. I decide on ordering bacon and eggs from my food constructor. Sigmund and Frieda stare in fascination as the machine produces the food. I order an orange juice and black coffee too, the coffee with a delay of ten minutes, so it doesn't cool while I eat.

The children gaze at the food and wrinkle their noses.

"How can he eat that?" Frieda asks Sigmund.

"He must be used to the blandness," Sigmund replies.

I glance at them, resenting their impudence. "You have better food then?"

"Ours is fresh and flavorsome. You should have come to the city to have your breakfast," Frieda says.

I ignore her, take my food to the table I set up outside and start eating. The visitors follow and study me. Once I satisfy the first pangs of hunger, I ask, "Why did they send you two?"

Sigmund and Frieda glance at each other. They do not respond.

"Well?"

Silence.

"The cat got your tongues?"

Eventually, Sigmund responds, shifting in discomfort, the first time I've seen any crack in their confidence. "No one sent us. We just thought you could help us."

My fork stops just before it enters my mouth with bacon impaled on it. I return the fork to my plate. "What do you mean, no one sent you? What'll happen when you return to this city I've never seen with me in tow?"

"We will explain to the others. They will understand," Frieda says.

"Great," I reply sourly.

As I resume my eating, thoughts of the various ways I could die flit through my head. I should bail out now. But curiosity impels me to go with these strange children. I need to find out what this cloaking technology is because — if I'm not dreaming the whole thing — it's far more advanced than anything I've seen before. I drink my juice and take the dirty plate and glass back into the ship, placing them in the cleaning unit. The coffee has poured, so I grab that and return to my seat at the table. The smell of fresh coffee tantalizes my nostrils, and I revel in it. As I sit back, I sip my coffee and contemplate the children. I wonder what lies ahead.

A thought comes to me. "You said last night that I walked through your city. You can't have been the only ones to spot me. There must have been others. And how can I walk through everything?"

"He isn't intelligent, is he?" Frieda says.

"Give him a break," Sigmund replies. "He doesn't understand our technology and how it works. The cloaking makes–"

"You can't tell him that," Frieda butts in, fear radiating from her.

"I'm not going to," Sigmund replies crossly and then turns back to me. "As I was saying, the cloaking makes us disappear."

My jaw drops. "You can't be serious. That is impossible."

"Believe it or not. It's up to you."

"You still haven't answered my question. Why doesn't anyone else see me?"

"They may have. They may have thought you were a visitor from one of the other cities."

"What? One that walks through buildings?"

"Stranger things have happened."

I lose myself in thought. "Who is she?"

"What?" Frieda asks.

"Before you said she'd be pleased. Who is she?"

"Oh. It doesn't matter. You will meet her in due course."

I finish my coffee in silence after that. After returning to the ship, I put my cup in the cleaning unit and go to my armory — careful that the children don't see me — where I collect two small weapons, which I conceal on my wrists, and a maser pistol I place in a holster strapped around my waist. I return to the children, raise my arms from my side in submission and say, "Lead the way."

The children walk toward the river at a diagonal, so we reach it after a kilometer. We walk in silence, which suits me. I don't know what to expect when I reach the lake — the cliffs and waterfall? To my surprise, a scooter awaits us at the river.

"What's that?"

"It's a scooter," Frieda informs me.

"I know, but what's it doing here?"

"We'll fly it to the city."

This is getting bizarre. The scooter has room for four people and operates using antigravity thrusters. They are common and easy to use, even for children. I recognize the spot from my exploration, so I know it wasn't there then. We hop in the scooter, Sigmund driving, and we dash forward upriver, traveling along the bank, the wind whipping our hair into our faces as we go.

After half an hour, we approach our destination, the countryside changing in a way different from last time. I stare in shock as we pass a copse of trees. A farm spreads out before me with cattle, sheep, and people tending them. They weren't there before. I find it difficult to continue my journey. This can't be happening. Are the children telling the truth? Frieda grabs my arm and smiles at me in support.

As we round a bend in the river, past the receding treeline, a city sits where none existed before. It sprawls over the plain, hemmed in by the river and the cliffs. I can't see where it ends. The city is unlike any I've ever seen in my travels. It covers the entire plain's expanse, and many bridges cross the river to access it, ornate and glowing with a multitude of colors. Past the bridges are houses, all low density and white — nothing fancy from what I can see. The housing density increases as one looks further afield, changing into high-rise apartments and condos. Massive towers near the cliffs soar above the suburbia in the foreground, displaying magnificent transparent panels in the design of their architecture. Near the waterfall stands a set of buildings, at odds with the city's décor. One building is circular with three-pronged towers at the top, joined by a platform halfway up. I smile. It looks like a pineapple. "What is that?" I ask, pointing to it.

"That is the palace," Frieda informs me.

"Who lives there?"

"The 'Most Imperial Ruler of the Kingdom'," she says in a sarcastic, mocking tone.

"Oh. I take it he's not your favorite ruler."

Frieda looked at me bemused, "You are perceptive."

"Don't mock me," I say, indignant.

"I am sorry. I did not mean to," she replies, repentant.

We keep traveling along the river for a distance until we cross the last bridge before the landscape returns to farmland and native vegetation. I suddenly realize something that has been bothering me the closer we have come to the city. There are many creatures everywhere — insects buzzing, and animals, small and large. Fish swim in the water when I glance in as we cross the bridge. These once familiar sights and sounds have been denied me since my arrival.

As we move into suburbia, the houses are mundane and similar: one story, white walls, flat roof. It seems wasteful of space, but high-density accommodation mustn't be necessary. There appear to be no makeshift huts or slum areas where people eke out a living. Other scooters pass us as we travel to our destination, traffic flow increasing as we move further into the city and thinning out as we fly toward the cliff on the city outskirts. We arrive at our destination, a nondescript house butted up against the cliff, with nothing to distinguish it from the other houses nearby.

"We are here," Sigmund announces as he lands the scooter.

5

WHO IS THIS?

"Where are we?" I ask.

"At our home," Frieda says, puzzled that I had to ask.

"You didn't tell me where you were taking me. I wanted to know," I say, affronted that she thought it a stupid question. "So, why are we here?"

"You will find out," Sigmund says as he alights from the scooter. Frieda follows him, and I oblige and dismount.

I gaze around me. The street — just a pedestrian path with spaces for scooters and other airborne vehicles — is clean and empty of people. I look more closely at the other houses nearby. At first, they appear the same — one-story, white walls, and a flat roof. But now I notice differences. They have unique designs for their entablatures and the jambs on their grand front doors. I wonder what they mean. Could they be indicators of the owner's lineage or another rune of identity?

We hear the whirr of motors approaching our position from the air. Sigmund and Frieda become agitated.

"Quickly," Sigmund calls, "get inside now!"

"Why? What's happening?" I ask.

"Security Patrol. Quick! There is little time."

Sigmund pushes at me as Frieda opens the door. We go inside, Frieda closing the door behind us. I am confused. Why are they frightened of the Security Patrol, and why hustle me inside so urgently? My suspicions of these sprites' intent start agitating me. They listen to the patrol outside as Frieda stands guard against the door. I see them both relax as the sound fades into the distance.

"What's with this Security Patrol, and why does it frighten you so much?"

Sigmund replies, "We live under a very strict ruler who watches everything that happens. The patrols spy on us, so if you want privacy, you hide from the patrols."

"But there must be other means of spying — fixed cameras, satellites?"

"We did away with fixed cameras long ago. They kept 'malfunctioning' and people could trick them. We only use them for specific functions ... What are satellites?"

I'm puzzled. They have advanced technology, and they're human, but they have never heard of satellites. They are not indigenous, so where are their spaceships? What is their origin? I'm dying to ask, but I know I'll get the same response from these children as to my earlier questions, so I wait. "So, what now?"

"Come with us."

"Where are we going?"

"To meet someone."

We walk along the hallway and turn into a lounge room. It has two lounge chairs, a holovision set, and other furnishings of family significance, but it includes a study desk and other workplace-related items.

"Wait here," Sigmund says and disappears somewhere else. Frieda stays with me on guard duty.

I have nothing to do, so I sit in a lounge chair and wait. Fifteen minutes pass in silence. Frieda is unusually reticent. I study her. She's so young to be traveling around the countryside collecting derelict shipwrecked spacers for mysterious purposes. She stands by the lounge doorway, alert and peering through the window and toward the entry door as if expecting trouble. I dislike her alertness. It smells of danger.

Moments later, Sigmund returns with someone. They appear through the doorway. The companion comes to a halt and looks at Sigmund. Tall and lean with braided hair that flows to his shoulders, he wears clothing reminiscent of camouflage fatigues as if he is in an army. He has a short, well-kept beard and an intelligent face, but his expression is hard and menacing, and there is a scar on his left cheek. "This is him?" he asks.

"Yes, the person I said who can help us," Sigmund replies.

I eye Sigmund suspiciously.

The stranger looks at me and back to Sigmund. "He's an outsider."

"Exactly. They can't trace him. He isn't in the databases. He can slip through surveillance."

"Silence! You are saying too much," the stranger says, chastising Sigmund.

Sigmund blushes and drops his head in submission to the stranger. He is silent as instructed.

The stranger looks at me again. He saunters into the room, inspecting me like a prize bull. He says nothing as he observes me from every angle.

I am frustrated, so I say, "Do you have a name?"

"Not your concern at the moment," he replies.

I stand. "I'll be leaving then," I say, disgruntled with the secrecy and rudeness.

"Sit!" the stranger commands. "You cannot go outside at the moment."

"Why should I?" I shout, getting annoyed. I am not used to having people giving me orders except debt collectors.

The stranger studies me further. He decides something and smiles. "My name is—."

Pounding resounds from the entry door. The stranger looks

around in alarm, as do Sigmund and Frieda. "Open, by the order of the emperor!" a voice yells.

"Quickly, follow us," the stranger calls to me as the children run from the room.

I believe it wise to follow the stranger's order, so I say, "Lead the way," and walk toward him.

The stranger turns and rushes in the opposite direction to the pounding as it gets louder and more emphatic. I follow on his heels. An old woman passes us as we make our escape from danger. "I'm coming, I'm coming," she shouts, as she waddles toward the door. "No need to break it down." She looks around to make sure we are leaving and continues toward the door, disappearing from sight as we turn out of the passage and weave our way through a maze of rooms. We enter a room matching the living room with lounge chairs, a table, and cabinets. It has a fireplace too. An animal statue stands next to the fireplace. The creature is reminiscent of a unicorn. The stranger grabs the unicorn's horn and twists it once clockwise and then counterclockwise. A click sounds and the fireplace slides sideways, revealing a tunnel. He turns to Sigmund and Frieda. "You need to stay here. Your scooter is out front."

"But they will take us away," Frieda protests.

"Relax. Stay calm. Just answer their questions, and your friend was never here. OK?"

Sigmund and Frieda look nervous but obey. "OK," Sigmund says.

"Come with me," the stranger says to me.

I stare at Sigmund and Frieda, not wanting to leave them. As odd as they are, I've grown accustomed to them.

More loud noises cascade from the front of the house.

"I'm coming. I'm coming," the old woman shouts in the distance.

There's no choice but to obey the stranger. "OK." I follow him into the tunnel. The entrance closes. I see Sigmund's and Frieda's worried faces disappear as it does so. It is dark once the door is closed, but lights blaze seconds later, blinding me. I hold my hand to my eyes so they can adjust to the change in illumination. As my sight returns, I survey my surroundings. A bare tunnel tapers off into the distance, darkness returning two hundred meters away.

"Come," the stranger says as he walks away.

I follow him at a steady pace. "You were going to tell me your name?" I remind him.

"Later," he says as he picks up the pace. "We need to hurry."

I walk faster to match his speed. Lights turn on up ahead as we progress. I glance behind me and see lights extinguish in the distance. We walk for half an hour before we get to the end of our mysterious journey to safety, or so I assume. We approach a barrier to our path. The stranger places his palm on a projecting stone, and a panel opens. We enter a tiny room with one door, and the panel closes behind us. The stranger gazes at a bartender lounging behind the bar next door. Once he spies us, the bartender scans the bar and nods. The stranger leads me through the door. The lighting is dim. We venture to a table in the bar's shadows. The bartender delivers two beers without us asking.

I pick up my beer and have a long draft. I hold it up to the light, inspecting its color, although the light's too dim to see through it. *A fine brew*. But not enough to quell my frustration. "Will you tell me your name and what the hell is happening, or won't you?" I demand.

The stranger picks up his beer and sips, staring at me with skeptical eyes. He studies me, looking for I don't know what. He finally decides. "Call me Sentinel."

"OK, Sentinel. I'm glad we cleared that up. I'm Halwende. Now, why the hell am I here?" I say, raising my voice.

"I'd lower my voice if I were you unless you want to attract unwelcome attention and an early grave."

On pausing, I peer around to see if anyone noticed. "I like my life, and I'd prefer to keep it a while longer, so I'll heed your suggestion, but please answer my question," I say in a whisper.

"It is a good question. I don't know the answer. The children believe you are of value."

I sit back, confused. The children? I take it he is referring to Sigmund and Frieda. What does he mean by 'of value'? I recall events from when I first met the two imps. I work out a line of questioning that I hope will enlighten me, but I'm not holding my breath. "What is happening here?"

Sentinel stares at me, assessing. He burrows into my eyes. I'm uncomfortable and self-conscious but stand my ground and keep eye contact. "What's happening is we are waiting for the children to arrive."

"Why are they so important?"

"Why? So, they can tell me why a hermit from nowhere interests them. I don't see any value in you."

I am offended. "What is it about you people? You don't seem to be big on charm."

"This is very serious business here, and we can't afford risks. We need talent, courage, and endurance. I don't see that in you. Look at you. When did you last wash and shave?"

I'm stunned by his reprimand but recover quickly. "Listen, I crash-landed on this godforsaken rock that doesn't exist and is bereft of any animate life and then two children appeared from nowhere. I am hallucinating. You aren't here, so why should I care?"

Sentinel moves at the speed of light, pinning me to my chair with a grip simple but effective. I can't move or cry out, and the pain radiating through me is excruciating. "Is this an illusion?"

"What are you doing?" Sigmund demands as he walks into the room with Frieda. "Leave him alone! We need him in one piece."

Sentinel glares at Sigmund with fire in his eyes but relents and lets me go. "You collect obnoxious specimens."

"Don't be silly," Frieda says. "He is vital to our plans."

I listen to the conversation but understand none of it. "Can someone please tell me what is happening?" I whisper in exasperation.

Frieda sighs in displeasure. "In time, Halwende, in time."

"How do you know my name?" I ask, surprised. "I didn't tell you."

"Do I have to explain everything to you, like a child?"

The insults from every quarter are starting to infuriate me — my questions go unanswered and now I'm being treated like a child *by a child*. I fold my arms across my chest in a huff and glare at Frieda and Sigmund. They are colluding together, but why are two children calling the shots and not Sentinel? I say nothing and gulp another draft from my beer, waiting for someone to say something that makes sense.

Sentinel gets up and walks away, disappearing into the rear room. The children sit with me, patiently waiting, oblivious to my frustration and anger. Whatever I ask gets ignored or deflected by insult.

I try one last time while we wait. "Can you tell me something ... please?"

Frieda looks at Sigmund and then at me. "We can't tell you very much. When Sentinel returns, we will go somewhere safe. We will tell you what you need to know then. What we can say now is, we have studied you, and Sigmund and I believe you can help us."

I am placated for now. At least she replied politely. "OK. I'm prepared to wait, although I don't have a choice, do I?"

"Not at the moment, no."

I resign myself to waiting and return to sipping my beer.

Sentinel returns after twenty minutes. I had finished my beer by then but decided that it wasn't worthwhile to ask for another.

"Let us go," he says.

"Where are we going?" I ask, naively expecting a sensible reply. I am met with a wall of silence. No harm in trying.

"When we get there," Frieda says.

The children stand and usher me to follow Sentinel. I obey in resignation. We re-enter the back room from where we emerged. Sentinel opens a different secret door on the room's opposite side, revealing a tunnel. When he enters it, I follow. Frieda and Sigmund bring up the rear, and the door closes. We walk for more than an hour and a half, passing various side tunnels, but we stay in the main corridor. We finally come to the end of our journey. Sentinel opens another door, and we enter an underground city. I stop in my tracks to stare at it in amazement. It is incredible. The vault is vast, the ceiling hidden by the intensity of the overhead lighting. Single-story buildings litter the space, and a multitude of people hurry past to fulfill their duties.

Sigmund gives me a nudge. "Not much further."

I come out of my trance and return to where I am. I follow Sentinel again. People stare at us as we pass. Several acknowledge Sentinel and the children with respectful nods. We pass into a corridor separating the buildings. It is straight, narrow, and long. I walk as a prisoner with Sentinel in front and the children behind, and I avoid eye contact. We walk at a brisk pace along the street. The buildings are similar in design as if part of a refugee camp or a hastily assembled haven. We arrive at the street's end, revealing an entrance, whether to another tunnel or the entrance to a building is unclear.

This door is unlike the others. It has retinal scan and brain-wave comparison locks. Sentinel stands in front of the scanning bay and allows the machines to do their work. I hear a click after a few moments, and the door opens. Sentinel turns to me. "Come." He walks in, and I follow. The children bring up the rear. The door slams shut.

We walk through a short corridor into a small but impressive chamber. The structures are spectacular, still only single-story but spectacular. A miniature palace stands straight in front of me with a bold white façade and steps leading to an enormous doorway blocking the entrance.

"Move," Sentinel says as he walks straight ahead to the doorway.

We step across the threshold. Trepidation overpowers me. I am usually braver than this, and I've been in tighter scrapes, but I can feel that a momentous event is imminent. We enter a hallway and come to another set of doors guarded by six soldiers, three on either side, weapons ready in defense. Sigmund steps forward to a scanner. He allows it to scan his eyes. The doors swing open. He returns to his position behind me, and we walk forward. We enter an enormous room with no furniture except a throne right in front of me. Banners and other tapestries hang on both sidewalls, and thick drapes cascade behind the throne, concealing whatever might be behind them. They depict historical scenes that I do not know or understand.

We walk forward as a group and stop in front of the vacant throne —
and wait. I assume a king is about to arrive.

The drapes flutter and a female emerges dressed in a bright red
battle outfit with black boots. Her hair is blonde and braided. Her
green eyes blaze with flames of fire. Confidence and a dancing
amusement linger in them as she surveys us. I'm mesmerized by her
beauty as if beholding God's glorious creation for the first time. I
gulp, nervous at the proximity of this goddess.

Sentinel kneels on one knee with his head bowed. The children's
reactions stay hidden behind me. As I don't know this person who is
so important to Sentinel, I stand at ease waiting for an introduction,
and hoping she can't tell that inwardly I am not the least bit at ease.

She approaches us with regal poise, the same confident smile still
on her face, though tinged with a query. She stops before us. Her left
hand rests on the throne's backrest, and her eyes stab mine with
shafts of lightning. "Who is this?" she asks Sentinel.

6

DINNER AND EXPLANATIONS... OF SORTS

"This is the one I told you about," Sigmund explains from behind me.

"Interesting," the vision in front of me says. "Does he know who I am?"

"No, Princess, he doesn't."

I hold my demeanor of cool indifference.

The princess removes her arm from the throne and walks toward me, keeping her eyes on me as she does so, inspecting me like a prize horse up for sale. I shuffle to my other foot, uncomfortable at her examination.

"Don't worry, I don't bite," the princess says.

"Why should I worry? You look harmless enough," I say coolly, determined not to appear intimidated — which I am.

The princess laughs, a sparkle of challenge in her eyes.

"Do you have a name?" I ask, tired of being made to feel insignificant.

Sentinel goes to rise. "Don't," the princess says to him. She turns to me. "Yes, I have a name. I am Princess Adala, daughter of King Abelard of Helheim. You can call me princess."

"Well, Adala, I know nothing of your king or Helheim. I presume

Helheim is the name of your planet. Everything else is a mystery to me at present, I'm afraid."

Far from taking offense at my cheek, she seems amused. "I may have to educate you in our history," she says with teasing eyes as she stands straight in front of me, challenging me to become more intimate with her.

I gulp with confusion. It isn't the behavior of a princess. She should be aloof and arrogant, annoyed at my informality with her — but she is almost ... normal, sensual. "... I'd be most interested," I hear myself say.

She laughs again. "Will you relax? I am interested in you too. Sigmund and Frieda are superb judges of character." Adala becomes sober, "We are in desperate times, and we need a game-changer. My stepsiblings tell me you are the one. I am impressed so far, but you're an unlikely candidate for the position."

"I didn't think I was being interviewed."

Adala laughs at the flippant remark. She looks at Sentinel and says, "You may rise, Uncle Ranulf. I don't understand why you kneel. It's flattering, but you don't need to be so formal with me."

I glance at Sentinel — *Uncle Ranulf*. He must be royal too.

"I swore an oath, Your Highness, and I prefer formal recognition even on informal occasions," Sentinel says as he rises, his head still bowed.

"I appreciate it," Adala replies with humility. "Now, have you eaten, Halwende?"

"How does everyone know my name?" I ask in weary frustration. "I had breakfast."

"Very well. We shall eat and talk." Adala claps her hands, and people appear from behind the curtain. "Prepare the dining room." They disappear again.

"That's impressive," I venture to say.

"One perk of my position. I prefer not using it, but they get upset if I don't," Adala says brightly. "Come with me."

She leads and I follow. The others come behind me. We venture behind the curtain into another world of private accommodations.

After striding along a hallway, we arrive at a dining room large enough to seat twenty people.

"Expecting company?" I ask.

Adala turns with that same twinkle in her eyes. "Not today. This is an intimate dinner."

I balk at the implication but stay impassive. I don't believe that my restraint deceives her, though. She's very observant. I continue to follow her to the table. She motions for me to sit in a seat and gestures for the others to sit as she directs. I settle at the end of a long table. She sits at the head next to me. Sentinel sits on my other side, and Sigmund and Frieda sit opposite me. I feel trapped. Adala lounges in her chair, still watching me with razor-sharp eyes. She places an elbow on the table and cradles her head in her palm in silence, looking at me as if trying to penetrate my soul.

People appear from behind doors, carrying food and drink for the meal, placing it on the table in front of us. They place a tureen filled with a spicy tomato soup between us and a large plate of still-warm bread rolls, their sweet smell wafting across my nose, encouraging me to salivate in anticipation. A plate of various cuts of cured meats, with another of cheeses, sits on the table too. A servant pours soup into bowls and places one in front of each of us. They distribute water and wine around the table, the water in tumbler-shaped glasses and the wine in gold-rimmed goblets of glass.

Adala fetches her wine glass and holds it in front of her. As she stares at me with that same gleam in her eyes, she says, "To a fruitful rendezvous."

I look at her, suspicion and a million questions in my smile back to her. I take my glass. "And answers."

Adala laughs. "You may not like what you hear."

"I won't know until I hear it."

I marvel again at how enchanting she is as I sip my wine. She sees me looking at her, and I sense she knows what I'm thinking by the sudden raising of her eyebrows in surprise as she smiles another beguiling smile. But I sense an emerging shyness as if she has realized something important for the first time since we met. Her eyes dart away, breaking the spell between us; a slight flush to her cheeks is unsuccessfully hidden by her hand and goblet stroking her face. She turns back to me with regained composure, "We had better give you answers then."

I replace my glass. "After we eat," I say with an impish grin.

"As you wish."

We keep to small talk as we consume our soup and nibble on bread, meats, and cheese. The servants come and go, clearing our plates away and bringing out roast lamb and roast vegetables — potatoes, carrots, beans, tomatoes, and a whole host more.

"You're sure you're not expecting company?" I tease.

Adala laughs, relaxed. It's as if she now has one less worry in the world. She has removed a barrier between us. "I am sure. They indulge me. And they get to share the leftovers later."

We continue selecting our food and eating in relative silence, partaking in the wine as we wish. The meal ends, and I am bursting. I haven't eaten such a sumptuous meal for a long time. 'The path to a man's heart is through his stomach,' the saying goes, and my stomach says to be sociable.

Adala grabs her glass and stands. "Come," she says as she moves off toward a door. I stand and follow with my glass of wine. Sentinel, Sigmund, and Frieda follow me. We enter what appears to be a den or library. Shelves with tomes of ancient books cover the walls, many chairs are scattered throughout the room, and a side table with a variety of wines and liqueurs stands against the wall. Adala motions to me to sit in a leather-bound and comfortable chair. The leather's aroma relaxes me as I snuggle into it and place my wineglass on the side table. The others sit in pre-assigned chairs. Adala goes to the wine table and pours something into two glasses. She returns to me, handing one glass to me while keeping the other. She sits in a chair opposite to me, a meter away. "So, what questions do you have?" she asks openly, a seriousness that I haven't seen before masking her face.

Nerves tense my stomach, but it's necessary to understand what they want with me. "What is this place?" I ask. "I mean, the city and everything."

Adala leans back and concentrates for a second, gathering her thoughts, and gazes at me again. "As I mentioned before, I am the daughter of the King of Helheim, which, as you guessed before, is the name we give our planet. We are in the city of Heimstadt, the capital. There are many cities on the planet. We thought we were a peaceful monarchy until two years ago when the Grand Commander of the armed forces, Egon, staged a coup and took control of the government, imprisoning my father. I narrowly escaped, thanks to Ranulf, Sigmund, and Frieda here. We have established a resistance movement to rescue my father and take back the kingdom. There is little love for Egon, but he holds onto power. This camp is the center of our operations."

"You didn't mention one thing, Your Highness," Sentinel interjects.

Adala blushes. "Sorry, Ranulf. Egon is trying to capture me so he can marry me and legitimize his rule."

I try to absorb all this information. Then I ask what, for me, is the burning question, "How does this cloaking work? I mean, I crash-land on this planet, and I find nothing here but vegetation. Then, Sigmund and Frieda appear, and I see farms, a city, and people everywhere. I have never seen this. Why do you need to cloak your existence?"

"I don't understand what you say when you say you crash-landed, but the cloaking is a historic development. My understanding is, we were in danger of being annihilated by an enemy on the other side of the planet — the details are vague — so we developed the cloaking as a defense, disguising the existence of our cities. We cloaked the animated life forms, as an added deterrent. From what I have read, it was life or death for us. That is why you couldn't see us and now you can." Adala relaxes into her history lesson as it progresses.

After considering where I want the questioning to lead, I ask, "Did you see me crash?"

"Sigmund and Frieda did. They were scouting and saw you fall. They thought someone had flung a projectile from a far place. Then they spotted you wandering the forest, lost."

"I landed on a planet that doesn't exist."

"What do you mean, we don't exist?"

"Our charts say nothing is here, and yet I'm here."

Adala pondered the revelation. "Maybe that's part of the cloaking, to remove the planet's existence entirely from the others. I don't understand you when you say other planets exist ... and other people. We believe we are the only living beings in the universe. You change things — if you're telling the truth."

"Telling the truth? How do you explain my spaceship?"

"It could just be a terrestrial ship."

I sit nonplussed, staring into Adala's eyes to discern if she's joking. But I see she is serious. "I'd ask you if it looks like it's from the other side of the planet, but you haven't seen it."

"I have seen images of it, and ... its form is alien. It is disturbing. It changes what we think of our existence and our place in the cosmos."

"Why don't you have satellites?"

"Satellites? What are satellites?"

"Mechanical things orbiting the planet in space for communication and other purposes."

Adala grins with a near-condescending look as if she is tolerating a tall story a child is telling her. "That's impossible. There is no atmosphere in space. How could the satellite fly?"

As I roll my eyes, I say, "I'll have to give you a science lesson."

I disturb Adala for the first time since we met. "There is nothing you can teach me. We know everything of science."

I change the topic. "What is that portal, and why does it resist people getting too near it?"

Sentinel glances at Adala, alarmed. The question catches Adala off guard too. "Do not talk of that!"

"Why not?"

"Because we don't talk of it."

"OK, then. Why am I here?"

"We want you to save us."

7

I'LL HELP

I stare at her, dumbfounded. How on earth can they want me to be their savior? I am just a trader. They know nothing of my past, and they would abhor me if they did. I've even tried to hide my past from myself.

Any remnant of regal arrogance disappears, replaced by a scared girl begging someone to help her, pleading. An air of expectation strangles me in its throttling grip. I drown under the weight of their request. Embarrassed with my response, I deflect my gaze. "I cannot," I say as I glance back at Adala. "I'm just a trader, not a superhero that can apprehend an evil villain."

Adala lowers her gaze in disappointment and hurt, even betrayal. "Well, we had little hope," she says, shrugging off the disappointment. "You tried your best," she says to Sigmund and Frieda.

"I told you," Sigmund says to Frieda.

"I am an excellent judge of character, and I know I am not wrong. But I admit I am wrong for now," Frieda says, insulted by the others' distrust.

Adala sighs, "Regardless, Halwende has refused to help us, and that is his prerogative. You need to return him to his ship."

Guilt weighs heavily on me, but what they are asking is impossible. Adala has deflated in stature and dignity, like a balloon that has developed a pinhole. This fills me with remorse more than anything, but I can't help them. I'll just get myself killed for nothing. I must consider my survival until someone comes to rescue me from this godforsaken planet. But Adala ...

"Come," Sentinel says in his most formal manner.

"Where are we going?"

"Back to your ship. I will escort you to the house where you arrived. The children will take you back to your ship."

"Oh." I follow Sentinel back through the complex and back through the tunnels. Sigmund and Frieda are right behind us. We arrive at the old woman's house after an eternity of walking. I could use a sleep.

Sigmund and Frieda lead me back through the front door. I glance into the room before the door closes. Sentinel is standing there, a look of bitter disappointment on his face. I don't understand. He was skeptical from the start, so why is he so disappointed now? The door closes. We mount the scooter and start the return trip.

An announcement blares from a loudspeaker only moments before we re-cross the bridge over the river. "*This is a District C-12 of Heimstadt inspection. Transportation must shut down. We will shoot anyone who does not comply at once.*"

Fear grips Sigmund and Frieda, their eyes darting to seek a route of escape. We are too far from the bridge. A patrol ship hovers in the distance, giving us no alternative but to land. I sense we are in grave danger. Sigmund lands the scooter before they shoot.

"What's happening?" I ask.

"An inspection," Frieda says, eyes wide. "They are looking for people they suspect are friendly toward the resistance. They may have learned of our presence. We are in danger and not near a safe house. They will imprison Sigmund and me if they capture us. You, they may shoot, having no identity."

I gulp. Frieda speaks no deception, and she may be right. It is too much of a coincidence. "What do we do?"

"We'll need to sneak our way to a safe house. It's not that far," Sigmund says.

Frieda looks at him as if to say, 'Yeah, sure. Just a short walk.'

We jump from the scooter and edge our way forward under the cover of awnings to hide our presence from above. Sigmund is in front, I'm in the middle, and Frieda brings up the rear.

"Where is it?" I whisper.

"Five blocks that way," Sigmund says, pointing at a concourse running through a small business district, shop fronts facing the street, and owners' residences in the rear.

"That is in the center of their inspection zone!" Frieda exclaims, alarmed by their intended path to freedom.

"It is our only choice. The others are too distant," Sigmund replies, his eyes dilated as his body tenses for flight at any moment.

We reach an intersection, and Sigmund glances in both directions. There is no one there, so we dart across it. Patrols fly overhead, and I am thankful for the awnings. They are flying in the same direction as we are traveling, though. We cross another two intersections but hear noises — shouting, cries of fear and pain, and shooting.

"How much further?" I ask.

"Two more blocks," Sigmund says. "The princess might send reinforcements to get us to safety."

"Don't count on it," Frieda advises. "That would be suicide for our operations' security."

"I know."

We come to the next intersection. Sigmund glances around the corner and retracts again. "They are close. We cannot run across without someone seeing us."

"We cannot stay here either," Frieda says.

"Retreat is our only choice."

"No. We cannot. We'll just have to chance it."

"I am game if you are."

"Me too."

I stare at them, perplexed. They are discussing our dilemma as if discussing their strategy in a game of tag instead of the risk of capture or worse. "Do I have a say?" I ask.

"No," Frieda says. "You do not know what is happening. Get ready to run."

"On three," Sigmund says. "One ... two ... three."

We sprint across the intersection. I glance at the scene developing to the left. It is mayhem. People are being kicked and pulled by the hair from their houses. I see several shot on the spot, loved ones screaming in despair at the loss of their kin. Misery is everywhere. The world freezes as events unfold in front of me, and I recall a scene from my past ...

I AM CROUCHING over the monitors in the command center, studying the advancing enemy. There are too many of them. I see my units slaughtered, together with any civilians in the way. People dart around the room in a panic, going somewhere, but I sense nowhere. They are directionless, leaderless. My eyes stare in horror. People enter buildings, only to have them collapse on top of them. Soldiers bring up the rear, searching for survivors and executing any they find.

Someone comes up behind me. "Orders, sir?" he asks in a strident voice.

I straighten my stance and turn. It is my Second-in-Command. Despair crushes me, sweat falling from my face and onto the floor. I open my mouth and close it again as words fail me. I meant events to end differently. They shouldn't have known we were there, but they have found out and have sent troops in force, surpassing our numbers three to one. And the carnage they are reaping is like the devil and his cohort stripping the flesh from those who fall toward him; the devastation is complete — men, women, children. They are taking no prisoners. I have no answer for it, no answer for him.

"Orders, sir?" he asks again, this time with an air of hopelessness and contempt. He knows what I am thinking. I must retreat. They've cut off even that. He knows they will annihilate us, and he knows I lack the courage to lead them into a last stand so they can die with honor.

I glance at him. "We must retreat to the rendezvous point and regroup." It is cowardly to leave so many unprotected when it was us that placed them in this danger.

"Yes, sir." He looks away in disgust at the order and leaves.

Facing this outcome is unbearable. I must run, escape, and hide. My family is dead. My home does not exist, the home my wife and child stayed in, believing my promise to protect them no matter what. I have failed them, and I'm failing the people now. My self-respect is shattered. To die with dignity is an honorable thing, but I cannot bring myself to do the honorable thing. My survival instinct is too strong. I run, knowing I am a coward. But I run regardless, past scenes I cannot describe — blood and murderous desecration everywhere. The stench of death violates my nostrils. The quiet, once the maelstrom has passed, unnerves me the most. Not even the moaning injured disturb the silence. I strip off the markings of my authority and keep running until I find a place to hide. I sit and wait in isolation as the sounds of war and bloodshed fade in the distance, finally creeping from my crypt and looking around me.

There is rubble and destruction everywhere. Not one building stands as far as the horizon. I cry for losing my family, for losing so many good people, for losing my soul.

MY WORLD JUMP-STARTS AGAIN.

"Hey, you!" someone shouts as we disappear behind the intersection's far side buildings. They have seen us. We hear more shouting and running as people approach us. We run away. Four armed men reach the intersection and spot us again. They run after us. It is useless. They are much faster. A shot ricochets off a building above our heads, spraying splinters of wood and stone over us.

Sigmund slows and stops. Frieda does the same. I think they realize they can't escape and prefer to surrender than get killed. I must join them, but I get a sense of déjà vu. The remembered shame fills me with rage. I still carry my weapons. I don't know why they didn't disarm me when they took me to Adala, especially the maser. Maybe these weapons are unknown to them.

The men catch us up, weapons drawn, and push us to the ground. They are especially rough with the children.

"Who have we here?" one of them asks. The others laugh.

Two of them lose interest and slouch, viewing the street.

Their ambivalence sets off a rage that won't let my past repeat itself. As I point both arms at the two that guard us with weapons trained, one wrist at each, I fire my wrist lasers straight through their heads. The buildings behind them are visible through the holes I make. They collapse. The other soldiers, realizing something is amiss, glance at us — too late as I fire again. They have matching holes.

Sigmund and Frieda stare at me, mouths open in dismay. You could fit a lemon in each mouth, they are open so wide. "What ... what was that?" Sigmund asks, finding his voice again.

"Did you think I'd go with you unarmed when I came here? When I see people, my first reaction is to defend myself."

They get off the ground, brushing the dirt from themselves as they do so. We hear more gunfire from around the corner but of a different timbre. It is an exchange of weaponry. Someone is fighting back.

"Our troops are here," Sigmund says. "We had better go."

"No," I insist. "We need to help."

"We have no weapons."

"I do."

"You will get killed. There are too many of them."

"Why are your people fighting them then? What is the point if they'll get annihilated?"

"It will allow as many of the civilians to escape as possible. That's why."

"Well, let's see if I can improve our odds then." I run back to the corner and glance around it. Three vehicles reminiscent of troop carriers descend to the ground. They have imperial markings on them. I point. "Are they on your side?"

"They are the Imperial Guard, not our people," Frieda says, a spark of fire in her eyes as she inspects me with a mien of confidence.

Retrieving my maser from its holster and aiming at the nearest carrier, I press the trigger. That carrier no longer carries anything anymore. It doesn't exist. I continue with destroying the other two carriers. The fighting stops as everyone looks up at the falling detritus, wondering what created it and what happened to the carriers. They look my way, but I hide behind the corner again. I am not a coward. But I just want my identity and firepower hidden for now. Moments later, the fighting restarts. When I glance again, the rebels are taking advantage and the troops are retreating. "Let's get out of here," I say as I stare at Sigmund and Frieda. The same gaping mouths greet me. I shake them from their shock. "Come on, let's go!"

Sigmund moves first, and we arrive at our destination moments later. We enter the premises and retreat to a basement where Sigmund finds a concealed opening to the tunnels. As we enter the tunnel, the door closes behind us, and we stop to catch our breath.

"We won't be able to take you to your ship now for a few days," Frieda says.

"Forget the ship. Take me back to Adala."

Frieda and Sigmund stare at one another, shocked at first, but then knowing smiles appear. "With pleasure," Frieda says.

We start back to the rebel base, through tunnels unfamiliar to me at first, but we eventually enter the main arterial tunnel we had traversed earlier. Exhaustion threatens to overcome me by the time we enter Adala's apartments.

I cannot see Sentinel anywhere. Maybe he is out fighting. We enter the throne chamber again and wait.

Princess Adala comes through the curtains five minutes later. A raised questioning eyebrow sketches her face.

I gaze directly into her eyes. "I'll help."

She produces a smile, the radiance of which eclipses any sun I've ever seen.

8

A TALK IN THE GARDEN

Princess Adala looks at the three of us. We are a scruffy lot; our clothes dirty from the rough treatment we suffered before the excitement started. "What have you three been doing?"

"They quarantined District C-12 for inspection, leaving us stuck in the center," Frieda explains. "They captured us, but Halwende killed the four who surrounded us. He then blew three troop carriers from the sky with a strange gun. I've never seen such a device. We reached the safe house, and he wanted to come here." Frieda concludes the debriefing with pride.

Adala stares in wonder as the amazing story unfolds, her spreading smile revealing her excitement in exploring my future potential. "That is interesting," she says, looking at me with admiration and respect. Fire returns to her eyes and the tigress I had seen before starts pacing the floor. Shyness lies beneath the surface too. I avert my eyes, not wanting to explore my emotions for fear of what I may find.

"Your weapons interest me," Adala says with a hint of seduction in her voice.

I glance back at her, trying to discern her intent. Her suggestive-ness confuses me.

I eventually say, "I might let you inspect them one day," trying to be suggestive and seductive myself.

Adala laughs with a sparkle in her eyes.

We hear a disturbance behind me, and I turn. Sentinel has entered and walks toward us. Dust and deposits of battle smear his clothing, medals of honor for his uninjured state. Fatigue escapes his eyes. He glances at me with questioning suspicion but returns his gaze to his princess. He bows before her.

"Rise, Uncle Ranulf," Adala says, annoyed at the formality. "What is your report?"

He rises to his feet, head bowed. "We rebuffed the imperials with effort and loss. A miraculous event occurred that defeated many of them while still airborne. We haven't seen the likes of it before today." He looks at me, suspicion in his countenance. "I fear they will not refrain from another purge soon."

"You have done well, Uncle. You may go freshen yourself."

"With Your Highness's permission, I'd prefer to stay and discover what caliber of weapon this man has that we cannot detect with our scanners."

"As you wish." Adala stares at me again. "I wish to know the nature of these weapons too."

I throw my hands in the air. "Do you think I would have followed Sigmund and Frieda here unarmed? I may not be the brightest person here, but I'm not stupid. From what I see, you only have kinetic weapons. What happened to your laser-based weapons?"

A frown paints Adala's brow. The others look confused too. "Laser? What do you mean?" Adala asks.

"What science do you still understand?" I take my maser out and show it to the others. "This is what I used to destroy those troop carriers."

Ranulf goes to take the maser from my hand.

"No. You're likely to blow a hole in the wall or worse," I say as I place the maser back into its holster. I pull up one of my sleeves and point to the weapon strapped to my wrist, "And this device is a high-powered tight beam laser."

Adala stares open-mouthed at the magical devices in front of her. She looks from my wrist to the holster and back again.

"You'll catch a fly."

"What?" she says, coming out of her unbelieving stupor.

"You'll catch a fly if you don't close your mouth."

She bursts out laughing. "Your mouth can be a weapon too, I see." She paces the floor in thought, returning to me again once she reaches a decision that only she knows. "Do you own more of these?"

I'm reluctant to say yes. I don't believe they can safely use them, but she will detect my lie if I say no. "I have a few, but your people aren't ready to use such weapons. And if they were to fall into your enemy's hands, you would be in grave danger."

"What you say of our danger is true. But how do we gain the advantage in this stalemate otherwise?"

"Did you not say that I was a game-changer?"

"Yes, I did."

"Why am I so valuable?"

"You have no identity, so they cannot trace you with the city scanners, making you invisible."

"Frieda said that they'd shoot me on sight because of that."

"There is always that risk, yes."

"Great! You want me to conduct a continuous suicide mission until I'm eliminated."

Adala looks hurt at my comments. But there's pain too in her expression as if she would suffer a great personal loss if I died. As if more is at stake than regaining her realm.

"I'm sorry," I say. "I didn't mean that the way it came out."

"No, you are right to suspect our intentions. You should be angry that we wish to use you in that way. It is I that should be sorry. I don't wish to mislead you. Yes, it will be dangerous if you still wish to help us, but I don't wish to lose you." Adala looks directly into my eyes as she says the last words.

I can't draw my eyes away as I gaze into heaven. I finally say, "I don't want to lose me either."

Adala smiles, suppressing another laugh. Then she sighs. "Leave us," she says to the others.

Sigmund and Frieda move to leave. Ranulf does not budge. "I cannot leave you alone with this person without protection," he says.

Adala looks at Ranulf with a steady stare. "I am protected. Now go. I will be fine, Uncle."

"As you wish." Ranulf leaves the room with the others, reluctance still in his composure.

I watch this exchange in confusion, perplexed by what is happening. Why is she sending everyone away? I wait, intrigued.

The doors close behind us.

I glance at Adala, questions in my eyes.

"Come," she says as she approaches me and wraps her arm around mine.

I comply. We walk in unison through the curtains and along many corridors until we reach a door. Adala opens it and sunlight shines through to us. I blink to adjust to the change in illumination as we enter a garden that is lush and vibrant. It resembles the mythical Garden of Eden.

"Where are we?" I ask.

"My private garden. Few know of its existence. I retreat here to think and contemplate and when I wish time for peace."

"It is beautiful. Which is it this time?"

"Thank you. A bit of both."

I say nothing more. I take in the scenery. Trees tower overhead with verdant foliage cascading from their branches. Flowers of red, yellow, and blue decorate them. There are paths to walk along, and we stroll up one of them. Flowers and shrubs in every color of the rainbow populate the promenade. We walk deeper into this garden and a waterfall cascades before our eyes in an unceasing musical crescendo as the water strikes the rocks at its base. The music sounds familiar, but the tune escapes me. A meadow, lush with grass, opens before us as we turn a corner. A park bench stands nearby, silently inviting us to sit and marvel at the view. The waterfall creates a lake before the water escapes to lower realms. Blossoming flowers release their sweet perfumes and birds twitter in the trees. Insects attack the flowers for their nectar with rhythmic precision.

"Let us sit, Halwende," Adala says as we approach the bench.

I don't answer as I am in a dream. But I obey and sit. She sits next to me, making me uncomfortable, her perfume wafting past me. It stirs a memory in me I want to suppress. I realize an emotion I am unsure of exploring. She holds my hand but then releases it again and places hers in her lap. I become flustered for no reason. What is happening? What does she want?

We sit in silence before I ask my pressing question, the one needing an answer. "What is on your mind?"

Adala looks at me. "This sedition of Egon's gives me headaches, and I worry over my father's state of health. I haven't heard of him in ages. They keep him in tight security." She gazes at her folded hands in her lap. "And you."

"Me?" I ask, surprised, glancing at the side of her bowed face.

"You are an enigma. I have so many questions for you, and yet I sense I've known you my entire life." She looks at me again. "You are so fresh and honest. You don't tiptoe around me for fear of upsetting or angering me."

"Maybe I'm too naïve to understand how angering you might affect my life."

"Ha! I believe you could withstand my displeasure. But sadness lies within you. What troubles you?"

"Nothing," I say abruptly, looking away from her and at the waterfall.

"I'm sorry. Please forgive me for prying."

I sigh. She is opening doors I wish to keep shut, but I sense the time is nigh for them to open again soon. "That's OK. You are too observant," I say, looking at her again. "I sensed that the moment I set my eyes on you. It was as if you could smash right through the façade I display."

"I have that talent or curse, depending on how one sees it."

We both turn and gaze at the waterfall in silent contemplation. I am uncomfortable again, not because she threatens me, but because she takes me to places of unbearable loss and loneliness, awakening hope again, and that scares me.

"Tell me of up there," Adala says, pointing to the sky.

I glance at her, wondering what she wants to know. I start somewhere and learn where she wants me to go. "A vast empire rules star systems — the Rigel Empire. The greatest empire ever to exist, comprising thousands of planets populated by humans. I come from a planet called Eridu. We travel between star systems in spaceships. Mine is just a small one. The larger ships are gigantic, requiring thousands of people to run them.

"The worlds are like Helheim, I suppose, with vegetation and animals of various kinds. They have vast cities with populations ranging from hundreds of millions to billions of people even."

Adala's eyes widen in amazement as I paint the scene. I see she is unsure whether to believe me. She displays childlike enthusiasm and wonder as she imagines an unlikely truth. She returns to her present reality. "But how is this possible? There is nothing there. Our scientists have proven it."

I shrug my shoulders. "Explain me then. And my ship."

"I cannot," she admits, retreating into the blush of a shy girl again for a moment as she looks away, embarrassed by her awkward behavior in my presence.

We ruminate for a while, absorbed by our own thoughts.

"Where is your family?" Adala asks, innocent eyes searching mine.

Great sorrow spreads over my face as I try not to remember my loss. "I have none."

"Oh. I am sorry," she says, reaching out and touching my forearm.

A tingle rushes from her touch to my head, making me light-headed for a moment. Cheekiness blossoms in me, and I don a suggestive grin. "Are you?"

Adala taps my shoulder. "Don't." She laughs and reclines on the bench, stretching her head back with eyes closed.

I gaze at her in profile and my passion stirs as I scan her majestic body and face. Her eyes open and watch as I inspect her body's form. I notice her attention and redden. "Sorry." I look away.

"Don't be," she says. It is her turn for playful behavior. "Life is lonely and sorrowful. Anyone else would worry I'd chop their head off saying the things you say and eyeing me the way you do."

I glance at her, appreciating the demands of her role. "It must frustrate you being a princess. I'm glad I can help you relax for a change."

"So am I."

We sit in silence again until I ask, "What is it you want me to do?"

Adala touches my forearm again, both concerned and protective. "Do you really want to get involved?"

"Yes, I want to help. I am remorseful now because I did nothing many years ago. I don't want to keep running from myself. And I can help you regain what's yours. To be frank, I have nothing else to do. I doubt anyone's coming to rescue me for a while. So, my choices are to sit and rot by my crashed ship or help you change things. I saw those troops tormenting and murdering those people. It is not right. I don't care if the people were doing wrong. It's no way for the government or anyone in charge to treat people." My speech becomes more passionate than I intend.

Admiration is on Adala's face. "That settles it then," she says with a saucy smile.

"I suppose so," I say, calming to a relaxed state again.

"Our goal is to rescue the king, but we've had no success so far because they constantly watch everyone."

"I don't get it. If Egon watches you, can't he just search for you and capture you?"

"We shield this complex and the tunnel entrances from the monitoring network. Tracking can only happen in the city. And they only know someone is there, not the person's identity."

"I see. But getting the king doesn't solve your problem. You still need to wrestle Egon from power."

"You're right, but with the king able to make announcements and speeches again, we can undermine Egon's position."

"That's too slow. He can devise other plans to keep his position and keep suppressing your rebellion until he defeats you."

"Well then, I don't know. That is our only chance," Adala says, depressed at my negative reception of her plan.

"What has been happening so far?"

"What you observed today. Sometimes they come in and sweep a district clean. Other times we repel them until we can remove our people to safety. We are at a stalemate and need a fresh approach, unexpected. We hope you'll surprise them." Adala's sadness deepens to the point of despair.

It is my turn to touch her forearm, to comfort her, but I do not expect what I feel when I do. Her skin is so smooth and warm. The touch sparks up my fingers and arm to my head again. I blush with emotion but finally speak. "Don't worry, I'll think of something."

Adala looks at my hand and then into my eyes. She blushes too but says nothing. With reluctance, I retract my hand, seeing disappointment when I do. She gulps for breath. "What should we do first, then?"

I think. "Show me the layout of the city and this refuge. I need the palace layout too. Then I can consider our options."

"I am so happy. You give me hope."

"Don't get your hopes up yet. I am only one man against an entire army."

Adala's disposition and demeanor display not only joy and hope, but somewhere deep a spark of love. It scares me. Her smile beams like the sun's rays. "We had better return. They might search my quarters trying to find me." She develops a wicked smile, "They may think you've captured me and taken me away." She stands.

I stand too. "I might just do that."

Adala laughs with glee. "You make me so happy," she says and hugs me. Her warm body curves press against me. It stirs me to embarrassment, but I don't let go. My heart races as if I've sprinted somewhere when she releases me. I see she is panting too. She takes a few deep breaths. "Let us return."

9

RECONNAISSANCE

Sentinel wants to educate me on the city and environs. We intend to make a reconnaissance of several sites, so we pack a few items to prepare for our mission. My itinerary means the trip includes a night away.

"Take care," Adala cautions both of us while gazing at me.

"We will," Sentinel responds. "And I'll take care of Halwende."

Adala blushes.

I'm surprised how close together just one talk in the garden has drawn us. My face reddens. Sentinel's knowledge or at least suspicion of our blossoming relationship surprises me. "Let's go," I say to break the awkwardness.

Sentinel and I stride from the base and into a tunnel unknown to me.

"You have impressed Princess Adala," Sentinel says in a droll, matter-of-fact way as we walk together.

When I glance at his face, he shows no emotion or malice. "I have agreed to help. I suppose she is thankful."

Sentinel looks at me. I see unbelief or a knowingness that means he doesn't believe I've told him everything. He turns his head forward again. "Do not hurt her."

"I won't."

We continue walking in silence for a distance.

"How did you get the name 'Sentinel'?"

"I guard the princess. Always have since she was born."

"Why? I mean, it's a worthy thing to do, but why? What was — is — your motivation?"

Sentinel is quiet for a time before he replies. "Adala's mother was my sister. She died in childbirth. It shouldn't have happened, but it did. I always suspected that she didn't die of natural causes, but I could never prove it. King Abelard had his own suspicions and was full of grief. He loved her dearly. I swore to King Abelard to protect Princess Adala with my life after that."

"You think Egon was manipulating events even then?"

"Not Egon. Another." Sentinel lapses into silence.

"Where do Sigmund and Frieda fit then?"

"They are the children of King Abelard's second wife. She died too."

"Being married to the king is a dangerous pastime," I say drily.

"You could say that."

We continue through the rest of the tunnel in silence. It takes over two hours to reach the end.

"How were the tunnels made?" I ask, puzzled.

"There were old caves through here. We extended and braced them so we could use the passages."

Sentinel opens a door, and we pass through the entrance into a storage room, with boxes and loose packages of household goods stacked on racks of shelving. He motions me to silence as we creep toward the door on the opposite side. He presses a button by the door and waits. Minutes elapse before the door opens and a person ushers us through. We stand in a large hardware store, having left one of its many storage rooms. Sentinel moves further into the room, and I follow. We make ourselves busy looking at the displayed items before we exit the store into the open air. A promenade extends in both directions. From the memorized city map, we are to go right. We walk and come to a public scooter station, one of many scattered throughout the city. Sentinel hires one, and we are on our way.

Sentinel cautions me after half an hour. "The main security compound for the city is ahead. Be sure you do not draw attention to yourself."

I nod. A few moments later, I ask, "Won't they think it strange that they can see two people, but only one shows up on their monitoring network?"

"They will just assume we're standing too close together to register as two."

"Oh."

We pass the compound in silence, being as unobtrusive as possible. Little activity is occurring with only two patrol craft passing us for an unknown location. Fifteen minutes later, we reach our first destination, an elevator to take us to the top of the cliff and onto the plateau. Adala and Sentinel have informed me that the people installed the elevator to gain access to the plateau for pleasure and farming. They discovered various resources there, too, inland from the cliff face.

Sentinel lands the scooter. We dismount, and he pays the required fee to ascend the elevator. We enter the elevator chamber, and it rises, giving us a view of the city as we gain height. Twenty seconds later, it stops, the doors opening to a covered concourse and the plateau beyond it. We exit and wander a frequented path before veering to the cliff face overlooking the palace compound.

A forest stands nearby, and we agree Sentinel will wait there while I reconnoiter the city below the cliff face. Someone might come to investigate why anyone is visiting that spot if Sentinel accompanied me. He remains busily fussing over his photographic equipment to avoid suspicion.

I scamper off on my own, creeping up to the cliff face ten minutes late. It is at least a one-hundred-meter drop to the palace grounds. I presume they have denuded the landscape of any trees here for a hundred meters to allow easy surveillance of the surroundings. The space is lush with grass.

I retrieve my data plate and take video footage of the palace below from four or five different angles to study later. The main palace with its entrance stands on the right. An opulent tree-lined avenue runs from the entry gates to the raised dais at the palace entrance for official entry to the principal building. As I scan the palace walls, I see few other entrances.

A large, tall building is to the left of the palace with a lower, longer one abutting it. Unsure of their purpose, I make a mental note to ask Sentinel later. I sit and study the scene before I'm satisfied that I have seen enough. Sentinel will wonder where I am. I return to the forest and find him. He is still having fun with the photographic equipment and takes a quick photo of me, which I palm off in annoyance. I get a smile from him.

"Enjoying yourself?" I ask, mocking.

"Yes. I enjoy the outdoors and studying the effects of light on photographic subjects. I seldom have the time." He doesn't notice my sarcasm or chooses not to react to it. "Seen enough here?"

"Yes. Let's go."

We retrace our steps to the elevator and descend back into the city. We hire another scooter and fly to our right, through the center of the metropolis. An enormous cathedral looms closer as we ride.

"What is the story with that?" I ask Sentinel.

"It is the cathedral of the city. It is a historic building now. We no longer have an organized religion. There was one thriving in the distant past — worship of the stars, I believe — but it faded away as people lost interest. They only use it for official regal occasions, weddings, and coronations."

"Its demise could've coincided with the lost knowledge of the universe."

"Maybe."

Three buttressed spires tower at one end of the cathedral, corresponding to three chevettes or chapels. A long nave extends to a larger tower with a half-crescent sail extending to the sky. This is the narthex and tower end of the building. It's impressive and must have been a hive of activity in years gone by.

A gigantic skyscraper is the next building of note on our right as we continue our ride. It rises as high as the cliff face itself. I ask Sentinel the building's name.

"That is 'The Spire,' nicknamed 'Egon's Tower.' Egon has massive business interests on the planet. It is one of the pet buildings he has constructed as a monument to himself."

"Over the top."

"Yes."

Another ten minutes and we arrive at our destination, the hotel we intend to stay at for the night. It is friendly to the rebellion, and Sentinel has used it often. By the time late afternoon comes, we are both worn out. We check into our rooms and go to the bar for refreshments.

The bar overlooks the palace wall and the gated entrance to our left. We sit at a table so I can study the wall as we eat and drink. We chat casually so as not to draw any unwanted attention, acting like two friends catching up and watching the sunset as we sip our beers. I may hit the harder stuff later. A hunch tells me Sentinel can keep up with me. We will have a good night.

I study the palace entrance, wondering whether it has any security weaknesses. I can't discern any, but I have a full mental picture of it now. Sentinel doesn't talk much, and that's fine with me. I prefer not to talk in social environments too. Companionable silence allows me to watch and examine the world around me instead.

A disturbance resounds from the bar's entrance. Two security officers enter, looking at identification chips. I stare at Sentinel, anxious. He reaches into his pocket and produces one, hidden in the palm of his hand. Discreetly, he places it on the table in front of me. I reach out and take it as he removes his hand.

"Stay calm," he says. "That will avoid suspicion for now."

I nod, take a breath, and place the chip in my pocket. I consider retreating to the restroom but decide against it, fearing it would appear suspicious under the circumstances. Instead, I stay sipping my beer as I gaze out over the city and palace, ordering a fresh beer when I finish the glass.

The security officers progress to our table.

"ID," one grunts.

I peer at him, looking displeased at this interference in my drinking session. Resigned, I reach into my pocket for the chip Sentinel has given me and give it to the officer. My pulse is racing, but my expression does not betray me. He places the chip in his scanner. It gives a beep and green light after a few seconds, and the officer removes it, gives it back to me, and moves on to the next table.

I glance at Sentinel. He gives me a nod of approval, displaying minimal change on his face. I release my breath on the inside before I take my beer in my hand again and sip.

A few minutes later, a disturbance erupts from across the bar as a patron tries to run for it, but the officers quickly immobilize him. They leave with the detainee, and the bar returns to its usual atmosphere not long afterward. We continue drinking late into the night. Sentinel matches me drink-for-drink. At the end of the night, we wrap our arms around each other's shoulders and stagger out and to our rooms.

The morning comes too soon for me. My head throbs, but I decide Sentinel is a suitable drinking partner.

I meet Sentinel at breakfast and discuss the day's activities. We intend to travel to the parkland next to the lake and waterfall on the west side of the palace grounds. I'm interested in the protection the palace has at that point. We set out after breakfast and hire a public scooter, circling the palace wall.

"Don't look now," Sentinel says, "but we are being followed."

I resist the urge to glance behind me. "What do you suggest we do?"

"Nothing. They aren't after us. It's probably one of Egon's special forces checking up on people from the bar last night."

"Special forces?"

"Yeah. You don't want to meet them. They are not pleasant people."

We continue without interference from our pursuers, but they do not get bored with us either. After we arrive at the parkland, we make our way to the lake, landing on the grass next to it and next to the palace wall. We amble along the edge. "Are they still with us?" I ask.

"Yes. They're hiding well. I'm surprised that they haven't introduced themselves. They must be undecided about our identity."

"Why don't they check then?"

"That would give away their cover before they are sure."

We sit by the lake and watch the water flow by for a while. I hazard a peek at the palace wall and the interface between that and the lake. There isn't any protection from an attack, but I suspect it's still protected or Adala would've attempted it.

"What is protecting the palace from incursion by enemies using the lake?"

"There's a force field there. You can't get through it. We have tried to our remorse."

"Surely you would've known before you attempted an attack?"

"We thought we could circumvent it, but we were wrong." Sentinel looks embarrassed at his admission of failure.

"How high is the field?"

"It surrounds the palace on every side but the cliff. They only isolate in sections when people and equipment need to enter."

I ponder Sentinel's advice. "Why de-isolate the lakeside field then?"

"To gain access to the lake."

I find the snippet of information interesting and file it away for later use. "Let's go back then. I'm finished."

We return to the scooter and travel back to the nearest scooter depot to the tunnel enclave entrance, and to safety, satisfied we've lost our tail.

10

IS THAT YOUR STRATEGY? REALLY?

At Adala's invitation, I enter the meeting room, choosing a seat in the room's shadows where I will be unnoticed unless asked to contribute. These people intrigue me, and I'm interested in understanding them. Whatever they consider their strength is, it's not working from what I can fathom. I sit and wait for the others to arrive.

Sentinel is the first to enter. He spies me from the corner of his eye, turns his head, and nods. I nod back, and he proceeds to the conference table. The table is solid wood, deep brown, and rectangular. I estimate it can seat twenty people with comfort, three on the ends and seven along the sides. Adala didn't tell me the number of participants for this meeting, so I don't know whether the table will reach capacity. I hope not. They'll never decide on anything if that's the case. Sentinel sits on the far side of the table facing me. He might want to see my reaction to the unfolding discussion. He stares at me and looks away but says nothing.

I am silent, too, happy to bask in my own thoughts for the moment. I am surprised at my present general happiness since I should be the epitome of misery, stranded on a planet that shouldn't be there. My life has been one of wretchedness and despair, self-loathing even, caused by painful memories and my determination to hide from them. Now I'm amid a battle, like before, but there's a second chance, a chance of redemption for my past failings. I'm fighting a personal battle as much as the one I've entered.

The door opens and someone I do not know enters. He does not see me, pressing on to the table and seating himself opposite Sentinel, his back to me. He is tall and self-assured. His back is erect as he sits, and his shoulders straight. He is in uniform. I assume he is a general or of similar rank in Adala's defense force. His stance suggests a driven man. "Good morning, Ranulf."

Sentinel nods to him.

Another tall man enters, more elderly with gray hair, but with a similar air of confidence. He, too, wears a military uniform. He sits next to his compatriot. He nods good morning to Sentinel and the person next to him. They greet him with a nod in return.

The three sit in silence while they wait.

Sigmund and Frieda enter next, chatting and sniggering in their usual childish manner. They both spot me and wink as if I am playing a game of hide-and-seek, except I am hiding in plain sight for anyone to look at if they cared. I give a slight grin back at them and nod. Adala must have warned them not to draw attention to me. They caper to the table, rounding it to sit on Sentinel's left, Sigmund next to Sentinel, Frieda next to him.

A short and overweight man enters the room next. He wears a poorly fitting charcoal gray business suit, and he's balding and pretentious in his gait. His eyes stare directly at the people at the conference table. When he arrives at the table, he sits next to the elderly general and looks at the others. "Prince Ranulf, Prince Sigmund, Princess Frieda, General Ernst, General Tancred."

Each one nods as he greets them, Frieda with a look of distaste. She says, "Chancellor Korbinian."

At least I know the names and titles of the players at the table. An interesting assortment.

Princess Adala enters a few minutes later by another door. She, too, wears a military uniform of the same style as the two generals, but of higher rank, judging by her shoulder insignia markings. Those present stand as she enters. I do not. She glances at me with the faintest of smiles before she focuses her attention back on the others. The table is far too large for her to station herself at its head. A ludicrous position and she knows it. She sits next to Sentinel instead. It is an excellent choice, as he is the most able to protect her. She reaches her destination and nods to everyone before she sits. The others sit in response, waiting for Adala to speak. She looks at them before she begins. "My intel informs me that the usurper gains strength daily. We barely repulsed the attack the other day, and we lack adequate countermeasures. Defense is our entire strategy so far. We need to do something different. We need a game-changer to gain the advantage. Any ideas?"

The chancellor is the first to speak. "Your Highness, I consider your criticisms are too harsh–"

"Too harsh?" she interrupts, blood rising to her face. "Tell me one inroad we have made in the last six months."

"Your Highness, please hear me out. We have rebuffed every concerted attack that Egon has made and prevented the discovery of our location and network of operations. This is a significant start."

Adala stares at him with contempt. "Do not mention that name in my presence. And your suggestion for the future? The same? Let me hear how we will regain my father's throne."

"We must move forward with caution. Too many risks will lead to them discovering us, and we will lose everything. We must increase our defenses until we see a crack in his."

Adala stares at the chancellor as if blasting him with lasers from her eyes. "Our weapons are being whittled away. Our ammunition supply is getting low. What do you suggest, Generals?" She changes her focus of attention to them.

They look at each other. I expect they are checking which one should speak. After deciding, General Tancred responds. "Your Highness, you know our suggestion of staging strategically planned attacks. As you have highlighted, we are running low on munitions and need to restock. We consider one of the remote security compounds our best choice. But, every time we suggest this action, our esteemed chancellor countermands our arguments by saying they are too risky and endangering your safety for no reason. Still, we both strongly recommend adoption of this plan."

"Your Highness," the chancellor intervenes, "We have reviewed this many times before and concluded it is best not to undertake such a perilous exercise. We must continue with our current strategy."

"Where will we get the firepower to continue our course of action then, Chancellor?" Adala asks.

"We are collecting the leftovers from our battles and making do with them. Factories are being set up now to manufacture our own. This will suffice."

Adala says nothing in response, but I can see she is fuming.

Sentinel wades into the conversation. "And where will we continue getting the bodies to use these magically appearing munitions, Chancellor?"

Sentinel's question stuns Chancellor Korbinian. He's affronted by the audacity of even asking such a question. "Volunteers will always fight for the cause."

"Will they? You might lead one of the defense teams to show your dedication?"

The chancellor is quick to respond. He resents Sentinel's gall at even suggesting placing a person of such obvious importance as himself in direct danger. "I am best able to contribute to the cause in my current capacity."

"Maybe you are." Sentinel eyes the chancellor with a wicked sense of satisfaction as if justifying his opinion.

I suppress a laugh with difficulty, as I want the strangers to remain ignorant of me unless Adala wishes my discovery. The generals' lack of influence in strategy for regaining the kingdom perplexes me. It's as if the chancellor has them spellbound. The children's lack of influence isn't surprising, and Sentinel seems more a moderator than an instigator of ideas, although I am sure that he has many. I discern two schools of thought as I spy on the interaction between the parties at the table. One, the chancellor's stance, is to defend the status quo. Why he believes they can repossess the kingdom for King Abelard in this way is beyond my understanding. The other, forwarded by the generals, is an aggressive attack strategy. This has a better chance of success, but they've developed no detailed plans to achieve their goal. I sense another game being played, one subtler than displayed at the table, more sinister even. The prospect makes me uneasy, and I wonder whether the others have the same foreboding.

"We are getting nowhere," Adala says in frustration, her hands flaying in the air for effect as she sits back in her chair. She stares at the generals and the chancellor, waiting for a sensible suggestion for a path forward.

"Your Highness," Chancellor Korbinian continues, "My intelligence suggests that the usurper's forces are losing morale for the fight. They are becoming uncomfortable mistreating and killing their kinfolk, and dissension is rising within the armed forces. We need only stay resolute, and this coup will collapse on itself with the desired result."

"And what desired result is that?" Sentinel butts in with a dry acidic tone.

"The return of the kingdom to its rightful rulers."

Sentinel eyes the chancellor. It is clear he does not trust him. Given that fact, I don't understand why the chancellor has maintained his powerful position. The chancellor's suggestion is absurd. He is naïve if he hopes the coup will die of natural causes in his lifetime, which may be shorter than he realizes.

Adala sits in silence, doodling on the table in front of her with her finger as she ponders what they say. She stops her imaginary drawing and looks up again, directly at me, a cunning smirk covering her face. "And what is your opinion, Halwende?"

I jump in surprise at being included in the enclave of tacticians. I am not prepared. The chancellor and the generals freeze as they realize Adala is talking to someone behind them. Everyone turns to discover who the intruder is.

"How did he sneak in here? Has this spy listened to our plans?"

Chancellor Korbinian demands, the eyes of a hyena gauging my threat level and inspecting me for vulnerabilities.

The generals just raise their brows and look back at Adala.

"He is not a spy, and I invited him here. He is our game-changer. I'm sick of sitting here doing nothing like a scared mouse waiting for the cat to pounce. Heaven knows what condition my father is in or even if he is still alive." Adala's face reflects deep grief. "We need something different, something to tip the scales in our favor. Halwende, what do you think?"

A plea for direction flows from her to me. My heart stops in sympathy for her. I arise and move over closer to the table, the better to address the group.

"Is that your strategy? Are you for real? You are intent on a strategy of eventual defeat. Any experienced campaigner will tell you that. You've lost sight of your goal. Your current goal is survival, not repossession of your kingdom. I'm sorry, but that is my observation. If you're serious about regaining your kingdom, if you intend fighting to the death for it, get real, make plans to get yourself one step closer to that goal and then the next plan and the next one until you achieve what you want." I am out of breath, but I have made my point. The generals smile, and Sentinel winks at me. The children sit up straighter as if responding to an authority that they respect. Adala has a smile that I cannot fathom. It seems to be a mixture of newfound hope and determination. Korbinian wears a scowl of disapproval.

"How can this person know our circumstances? What is his history? How do you know you can trust him?"

Adala redirects her attention back to him with ice in her eyes. "He comes from somewhere we only ever dreamed of and has technology we did not know existed. Sentinel has been with him the last few days, and he informs me he trusts Halwende with his life."

I jerk my head toward Sentinel in surprise, not realizing I have made such a strong impression on him. I thought he had the opposite opinion. An uninterpretable blankness covers his face as if to say, 'You didn't hear me say it.'

"As for our circumstance, you just heard what he said. He has a far better appreciation of our position than we do. Now, Halwende. Any suggestions?"

I look around, unsure where to sit. I decide not to bother and sit on the table near General Ernst to collect my thoughts. "My understanding is you're short of munitions." The generals all nod in agreement. "How do you move your troops?"

"We use the tunnels where we can and walk or use whatever scooters we can when we are out of the tunnels."

Korbinian and the two generals sit, attentive to my words. "We need troop carriers–"

"What?" Korbinian exclaims in disbelief. "We can never hope to capture one of them."

Out of the corner of my eye, I see Adala smile but stay focused on the others. "Not one — we need four … and we need serious ammunition and weaponry. Where can we get them?"

Korbinian stares at me as if I'm mad. I can see the cogs moving in the generals' heads as they dissect what I just said with wistful smiles.

General Tancred speaks first. "They store the troop carriers in the main security compound by the cliff elevator." He pauses in thought. "But I suggest the easiest place to get heavy weaponry and resupply of our normal ammunition is another compound, the one next to the Raunenstrom by the Wilmar Bridge. Our constant suggestions for this have fallen on deaf ears." He looks to General Ernst for confirmation, who gives his approval with a nod.

Korbinian's face turns red and blue in indignation at the suggestion that he has been an obstacle, but I ignore him. He is not relevant to me anymore. He is a sycophant and a conniver. I do not know what his aims are, but I suspect they do not align with Adala's interests. "Suggestions on attacking this armory?"

Both generals scratch their chins. "It won't be easy," Ernst says. "They protect it well. We need to review the defenses and develop a plan. We cannot detail this now, as we need to consult with our staff and may need reconnaissance of the compound."

"OK. Go. Brainstorm alternatives for discussion and start developing plans to attack this main compound while you are at it. We will need detailed layouts inside too. Inform Sentinel when you have something to discuss."

"You will need to keep me informed," Korbinian says, a squint of conspiracy in his eyes.

There is something in the way he makes this request that unnerves me. "We will tell you what's necessary for you to know," I say. "Well, that's it then." I clap my hands together. "We have work to do." I glance over to Adala, whose angelic face has a look of adoration. That unnerves me even more.

"As you said, Halwende," she says, "we will meet in one week."

The generals and Korbinian file out. The rest of us stay.

"I do not want Korbinian at any of our strategy meetings," I say. "I don't trust him."

"He fancies himself as a great diplomat and politician, but he is harmless," Adala reassures me.

"How come he has manipulated you into inaction up till now then?"

Adala cannot respond and looks away, pondering, as does Sentinel. It is the first time the children have remained silent in my presence.

"You could be right," Adala says. "Let's go to the garden and talk."

11

FOLLOWED

I t takes a week to complete a workable attack plan that achieves the desired result and minimizes the risk to the resistance forces, and yet something bothers me. General Ernst, General Tancred, and Sentinel are with me as we discuss the options. I sense they are uncomfortable with the plan as it stands too.

"Everything's worked out except one thing," Tancred says. "We can't develop an acceptable plan to get inside the compound without raising the alarm. The plan depends on quick execution. If delayed, we will fail. They will get reinforcements before we can gain entry."

I consider this for a moment. "I'll just knock on the door."

"What?" they say in unison.

"I'll just knock on the door. Say I hold vital information."

Sentinel smiles and shakes his head at the audacity of the suggestion. "That's so crazy it might just work."

"But how will you subdue the guards without raising the alarm, even if they believe you?" General Ernst asks.

"Let me worry about that. How many will be in the guardhouse?"

"Protocol demands two."

"That shouldn't be too difficult then."

The generals stare at each other, dumbfounded by my confidence.

They shrug their shoulders. Tancred says, "If you can achieve that, then you can switch off the gate shield and open it for us to go ahead with the attack."

"That's it then," I say with a cheeky grin. "We'll organize it for tomorrow evening just before sunset."

"Our forces will be in position, ready to storm the compound."

"I will keep Halwende in order," Sentinel reassures the generals.

We laugh.

We then rest and prepare for the morrow. I trudge back to my allocated accommodation, tired and ready to collapse.

Adala is waiting for me.

"Hi. What brings you here?" I ask, cheer and warmth returning to me, my fatigue taking second place. "Shouldn't you have a guard with you?"

"What? To protect me from you?" Adala asks, an amused smile on her face.

I match her bantering tone. "You never know what I might do."

"I'll take my chances." She laughs with delight.

I am swept away by her cheer and charm. She sees my gaze and looks away, embarrassed but delighted, I can tell. "Seriously, you shouldn't walk around without protection."

"You're talking like Ranulf now."

"Somebody has to protect you. Why are you here?"

Adala turns shy as she finds the words to answer me. "I just wanted to visit you ... and wish you luck for tomorrow."

I don't believe the last phrase. "We'll see each other again tomorrow. Well, let's not just stand here. People might talk. Do you wish to enter? View how the lowly people live?"

Adala smiles at my words, but sadness penetrates her smile too. "If you lack anything, you need only ask. Let us enter."

I unlock the door and let Adala enter my dwelling first. I follow closely behind her, so close I can smell her fragrance and that makes me uncomfortable. It smells of the freshness of apples. I close the door behind me, and Adala whirls and kisses me passionately. Shocked by the unexpected move, my eyes widen. Warmth flows between us as I wrap my arms around her and feel not just the closeness of our bodies but also our souls. We part, out of breath.

"You should've warned me. I would have washed."

"Ha! You are OK as you are."

"You know what I mean. Where are your guards?" I chastise her like a parent. She is taking an unnecessary risk for someone in her position.

She senses my disapproval and pouts for a moment before conceding, "You are right. I am unwise coming alone. But I just had to see you."

"You could have called for me ... You're here now. Take a seat." I indicate a chair.

She moves over to it and sits, watching me with eyes of mischievous intent. I stare back at her, confused. "Why did you really come?"

Adala lowers her gaze, her hands playing with themselves in her lap while she considers her answer. She looks back at me. "Two reasons. I am afraid for you and what you intend to do tomorrow. I wanted to tell you to be careful."

She pauses. I am waiting for the second reason. "... And?"

She looks at me, frightened. "I fear there's a spy among us. I wanted to go where no one would overhear us."

Given the pending mission, her suspicion alarms me. I stare at her and then pace the floor, thinking. I stop and face her. "Why are you suspicious?"

"The random inspections that the security forces spring are not random. They target areas where my key operatives live. I am losing too many valuable people."

I scratch my head for a moment. "It must be a member of your inner council. Only they could identify your key men." Korbinian comes immediately to mind. I don't trust the man, but I'm reluctant to name him without evidence.

Adala looks at me pensively before she speaks. "Yes, it would have to be."

"So, who is it? There aren't many to choose from." I want her to be the one to name him.

"I don't know. I chose them because they are beyond reproach, but I am losing people." She looks perplexed and worried. She looks like a child, too young for the knowledge or experience of her responsibility.

"I cannot consider this now. I have tomorrow's mission to internalize."

"That worries me. What if someone has compromised it, and you are walking into a trap because the spy has tipped off Egon's forces?"

Precisely my worry — and I'm only too conscious I'm rusty and need to recall my combat experience quicker if I want to stay alive. "We have a contingency," I say to allay her fears. I haven't convinced her or myself. But I need time to consider a backup plan. Adala needs to be out of my presence so that I can concentrate. "You need to go."

Adala looks offended. I turn, not wanting her to think I'm demanding she leave. I gaze into her eyes again. "You distract me, and I need time to think." She blushes at the implication. I can't retract my words now and am not sure that I want to, unsure of their truth, but I suspect they are indeed true. I glance at her, apologetic.

She stands. "OK. I will go. But you must promise me you will visit me before you leave tomorrow."

"I promise." I glance at her in confusion, hesitant for fear of saying too much. And then I just say it. "Tomorrow's attack couldn't go ahead without seeing you again beforehand." Embarrassed, I glance away, but it pleases me I've told the truth. I return my gaze and see that she is smiling. She walks over and plants another passionate kiss on my lips. I oblige her with equal zeal.

We part and she walks to the door. "Godspeed for tomorrow," she says as she opens it and disappears, closing the door behind her.

I touch my lips, still feeling the warmth of hers on them. I need to grab that feeling and place it in the vault of my greatest treasures. Her warning returns to me like a sledgehammer. *What is my contingency if someone has betrayed us?* After grabbing a beer, I sit on a chair by the table and ponder the problem. Sentinel and the others need to stay hidden until I'm sure we are not entering a trap. If trapped inside the compound, they could slaughter us at their leisure. We have publicized the timing. Even Korbinian knows, to my disappointment. I'll delay it an hour at the last minute so only the attacking team knows. We'll pay attention to any unusual movement beforehand. That just leaves me to consider my vulnerability. I am most exposed when I approach the guardhouse and ask to gain entry. That is still my best choice, but I should retrieve another gadget from my ship as a backup in case the attack turns sour. I decide to grab Sigmund or Frieda in the morning to take me to the ship. With nothing more to do tonight, I retire to bed and sleep.

The next morning, I wake refreshed, the usual tension before a mission building within me. That feeling's been missing for ages, and it feels good. I head for the regal buildings after breakfast, intent on finding Sigmund to return to my ship.

After entering the main doors, I find an assistant in the foyer and ask him to fetch Sigmund. I wait and Sigmund comes half an hour later, walking up to me in large childlike strides, full of self-importance. His face carries the mien of absentmindedness as if he's elsewhere and his body is on autopilot. "You wanted to see me?"

"Yes. I was wondering if you could take me back to my ship. I want to collect an item I might need for tonight."

Sigmund looks around to check who else is within earshot and sees that we are alone. "That is difficult for me at present. I have matters I must address."

"Well, is there someone else that can take me, Frieda or someone? I can't drive a scooter on my own."

"No, you cannot." Sigmund rubs his chin. "Stay here. I will ask." He turns and walks back the way he came.

Adala walks up to me ten minutes later. "Let us go then."

I balk at her statement. "You're not taking me."

"Why not? You can protect me." Adala has a mischievous smirk on her face.

"Adala, you're much too valuable to place yourself in such potential danger. Is Sentinel aware of this?"

"Relax, Halwende. Ranulf knows. He took convincing, but he saw reason, and he trusts you."

"It's not a matter of him trusting me. I don't know my way around the city. What if an inspection occurs again? They will be warier this time, and your identity is hard to conceal. Anyone capturing you would receive a handsome reward."

Adala becomes impatient with me. "Halwende, I can protect myself, and if I don't escort you, no one will."

I stare at her in protest but relent with a sigh. How can I refuse her? She could convince me to jump off a cliff for her with those eyes. "OK then. Let's get moving." I turn to leave and Adala does the same, walking by my side. Her closeness out in the open where we could be seen by anyone makes me uncomfortable. Gossip about the extent of our relationship could easily spread. I don't know why, but that bothers me. I want to protect Adala's reputation, and her being seen alone with me might jeopardize that.

We leave the main cavern and enter a much-used tunnel, arriving at the familiar house just over an hour later. Distracted, I engage in scant conversation. Adala is likewise reticent.

A great commotion occurs at the house when Adala exits the tunnel, but she calms their fuss over her. We traverse through and mount the scooter, shooting out of the city as fast as Adala dares to propel it. She requires no direction, and we arrive at the ship a half-hour later.

"How did you know my ship's location?" I say as Adala settles the scooter next to the wreck.

"Sigmund showed me. So, this ship travels in the void. Doesn't look very special," she teases.

"It crashed," I say, annoyed that she's poking fun at me. "It's normally in one piece and sealed. I'm lucky to be alive."

Adala looks at me, relenting but seductively. "I am too."

I blush but enter the ship before she notices. She follows me. Her fascination with where she is and what it implies distracts her. I rush to my armory while she is looking elsewhere to retrieve what I want, hiding it in one of my pockets. "I have what I came for, so we can return."

"What's the rush?" Adala is not ready to go.

I see she wants to inspect the ship, so I resign myself to showing her. "Do you want me to explain what everything does?"

Adala looks at me, inquisitiveness oozing from her with the naivety and innocence of a child. "Please do."

I begin showing her around when we hear another sound from outside the ship. We stare at each other, fear noticeable in Adala's eyes. "What is that?" I ask.

"It sounds like a scooter."

"We left ours in plain sight. They'll know someone is here. Did someone follow us?"

"I do not know. I didn't see anyone."

"Stay here. I'll go check. Whatever you do, stay out of sight."

I retrace our path to the ship's entrance, stopping at a gap in the hull where I can peer through and spy. A scooter has landed next to ours, and a man steps off onto the ground. He looks thirty years of age, tall, athletic, and black-haired. He wears dirty work clothing and appears unarmed. I watch his movements.

He strolls to our scooter and looks in, inspecting its layout. I wonder if he wants to steal it. He searches for people. His eyes settle on the ship, and I can swear he is looking straight at me, but I know he can't see me. He walks toward the awning I constructed at the ship's hatch. "Hello? Is anyone here?"

I am undecided what to do. He looks harmless enough. He's probably just a passing inquisitive bystander who saw the ship and stopped for a closer view. I shuffle a few items, making a noise as if I am walking to the entrance. His ears prick in response, but I don't detect any movement toward a weapon. I walk to the entrance to show myself. "Hi. Who are you? What brings you here?"

"Oh, hello. I was out hunting and passing. Seeing this ..." He points at the ship. "And the scooter, I stopped for a closer look."

He shows genuine interest, but I can't take any chances with Adala nearby. "Yeah, well. I pulled together rubbish over time and build myself a shack. Been inventive in the hovel's design."

"It's different. I've seen nothing similar. That's a scooter from the city, isn't it?"

"Yeah, I live there. I escape here when I want to relax."

"Interesting. Good for anyone who can afford it in these tough times. Me, I struggle to get the basics on the table for my family."

"I'm lucky, I guess." I stand by the entrance, barring any idea he might have of entering for a closer inspection, as he makes me uneasy. An instinct sets off alarm bells, and I need to get rid of him. "Well, I have things to do. Anything else?"

The visitor looks around, reluctant to leave, but then decides. "No, I suppose not. Good to meet you. Might see you around sometime."

"Yeah, you might."

He turns and remounts his scooter, starts it up, and disappears through the foliage after a few seconds. I stand where I am, pondering the intrusion. Something isn't right, but I can't put my finger on it. I shrug and turn to go inside, almost bumping into Adala. "Oh!" I exclaim.

"Sorry, did not mean to frighten you," Adala apologizes. "That person was not just passing. He's from Egon's Security Agency. He followed us here."

"But how did he find us? It was a last-minute decision, and I didn't tell anyone but Sigmund and you."

"That's my point. I trust Sigmund, but he may have mentioned it to another without realizing it."

"Well, we had better get back. I need to secure my ship better, though. Something tells me someone may come back to snoop, and I don't want people looking inside without my permission."

Adala changes her manner to one of coyness and mischief. "Why? Is there a woman stashed in here?"

"Ha! I wish. Your reaction might be of interest if you met each other."

"What do you mean?" Adala asks defensively.

I snigger. "Nothing, but I sense jealousy?"

"In your dreams." Adala huffs. "Let's get back." She walks away to the scooter before I can continue the conversation and waits there for me to join her.

I return to the alleyways of my ship and my compartment of

goodies to retrieve another couple of devices. I set up one device, a security network, to alert me of anyone approaching the ship when I am away. The other device is much more sinister. It will activate on my command, vaporizing its target. I can communicate with it through the same network that alerts me of an intruder approaching the ship. I hope I will not need to use it. Satisfied I have secured the ship the best I can, I seal the hatch and go to join Adala to journey back to the city.

12

ATTACK ON THE ARSENAL

Evening comes and I prepare to join the others for the journey to the security compound. I have my weapons ready but concealed, including the device I collected from the ship if things go horribly wrong. We reach the Security Compound and I approach Sentinel.

"Is everyone in position?" I ask.

"Yes. We await your signal."

"Which is?"

"You will open the gates and throw out a rose."

I quirk an eyebrow. "A bit melodramatic, don't you think?"

"We need something only known to you and me. That's what came to mind. Anyway, what's wrong with a rose? Aren't you romantic? Adala seems to think so." Sentinel chuckles at his own joke.

I chuckle too before I get serious again. "I don't want your people walking into a trap. It will be awful enough if I get captured. Your capture would be far worse. At least I know very little of your operations." My mind returns to a period long ago and the cowardly behavior I displayed at the fall of my planet. I shake my head to return to the present and gaze into Sentinel's eyes where I see a solidness of spirit as strong as the cliffs behind us, a lion's determination as it awaits a kill. I nod. "Let's do this."

"We will be ready."

With two deep breaths to steady my nerves, I walk out from our cover, keeping to the shadows as I head toward my goal. I want to stay out of sight. They can interpret that in two ways. One is I'm hiding because I'm doing something criminal. The other is that I'm going to betray someone and want my approach to stay secret. I hope they interpret my movements as the latter. I arrive at the compound next to the guardhouse and take more breaths to steady myself. This is it, I realize, but I am ready for it. It's been a long time since I broke from the cocoon that I wove for myself. I tidy my clothes and walk into the open street, sneaking up to the guardhouse window. I press the button to attract the guard's attention. Tense moments pass.

"What do you want?" blares from the intercom speaker.

I study the street, pretending to scan for prying eyes. "I have information and I must talk with you."

"What is it then?"

"Not here. I don't want anyone to see me. Please let me in."

There's a moment's silence while the two guards confer. "What information?"

"It is vital. It involves an impending attack by the rebels."

Again silence. Moments later, the personal access door to the guardhouse opens and a guard motions me to enter.

I glance around and spot Sentinel out of the corner of my eye and chance a quick smile. I cower and slink through the door. It closes behind me. I glance around the guardhouse, and it's as described. Only two guards occupy it with the described layout.

"And what is this vital information?" one guard sneers at me menacingly.

Bent, I appear submissive, as if defeated by the guard's air of authority. "Well, it's like this ..." My two arms come up, each pointing at one of them. My wrist weapons, set to stun, fire. Surprise highlights both guards' faces before they collapse from the overload to their nervous systems. I kill the internal camera, as Sentinel instructed me, and search for the controls that work the force shield protecting the compound, the external cameras, and the main gate's opening mechanism. I find them and switch off the cameras and the force shield. And I place my finger on the switch to open the gate.

"Why is the shield off?" the intercom speaker blurts.

In a panic from the unexpected interruption, I can't locate the microphone straight away. After locating it, I push the speak button on the desk. "There's a delivery incoming, sir."

"We are not expecting any deliveries tonight."

"Well, one just arrived. They have the correct paperwork."

"Damn Supply. They couldn't even stick to a sleeping schedule if they had one. OK. Make it snappy."

"Yes, sir." I take my finger off the button and breathe a sigh of relief. Their dispatch delivery is unreliable. *It must be a frequent occurrence.* I press the button to open the gate and exit the booth through the door inside the compound. As I stand at the gate entry in full view, I throw my rose signal for the attack to begin and return to the booth to supervise proceedings.

The rebels burst through the gate like someone has opened a dyke, bodies flowing in every direction once inside the compound. I wait, watching the monitors for any trouble. Gunfire assaults my ears a few minutes later as the rebels meet the first resistance from the troops.

"What the hell is happening there?" the commander asks over the intercom.

"We are under attack, sir," I say, barely able to keep the irony from my voice.

"I'll have your skin for this. Sound the alarm, will you?"

"Yes, sir." I can't believe that he thinks I am one of his men. I have no intention of sounding any alarm.

As I gaze outside, I see Sentinel is directing the rebels' movements as they capture and disarm the soldiers trying to fight back. Several people lie on the ground, either wounded or dead. The rebels are a tight-knit and well-disciplined force. They make quick work of their mission. It is impressive.

A noise grows louder from overhead and an incoming message on the comm. "Incoming backup in five."

"Shit," I say aloud to myself. *A troop carrier is coming in to help. I wonder who called them? Did someone inform on us?*

I go outside to search the air, trying to spot the carrier as it approaches. It comes into view. I'm relieved there's only one, but it will cause a problem for Sentinel. I call him.

He responds, huffing from the exertions of the fighting, "Yes?"

"There're incoming troops."

"That may cause an issue for us."

"Leave them to me."

"What are you going to do?"

"I'll think of something."

There should be a platoon of thirty soldiers on the troop carrier, adding significant strength to the existing soldiers in the compound. I could destroy the carrier like last time — I have my maser — but killing so many soldiers upsets me. I regret what I did the last time.

The carrier is now positioning itself for landing. It seems the soldiers won't be abseiling to the ground. This gives me the opportunity to use the device I collected from my ship earlier, so I start for a strategic point to use it, making sure that I keep myself out of sight of anyone wanting to take a shot at me.

In position, I have the device out and primed for activation. I wait. The carrier is five meters from the ground and descending at a smooth and decelerating rate. It touches the ground. The first men from the troop carrier exit, and I point my device in their direction. I press the button, and they collapse to the ground, squirming in agony. The others still inside the carrier react the same way. The device emits a signal that interferes with the nervous system, causing such a severe case of pins and needles over the entire body that the affected person is incapable of thinking. They soon lapse into unconsciousness but with no lasting effects. The beam is unidirectional, so one must aim accurately. The carrier motor still idles, but the pilots are unconscious too.

I wait until I am positive that they are unconscious and then stop the beam. The fighting lulls inside the other buildings. They must have noticed the incapacitated troops from the carrier. Turning in that direction, I see the defenders surrender to the rebels who round them up and disarm them. Sentinel comes into the yard with a person in front of him — the person in charge, I presume. Sentinel glances my way with an inquiring look. I shrug. The rebels guide the soldiers to a room to contain them. This takes another ten minutes before we can safely move around the compound. On glancing at my chronometer, I see we have fifteen minutes left in our window before we need to vacate to safety.

With the prisoners contained, Sentinel moves toward the armory and unlocks it. He talks on his comm. Two trailers hover in at speed, parking next to the armory doors. They load the weapons and ammunition onto the trailers, including heavy munitions.

I walk over to Sentinel's position and see that the armory is empty. The trailers prepare to leave, and the rebel footmen congregate to do the same.

"That was excellent work," I say.

"Yes. Casualties were low. We only lost a few, with several wounded." Sentinel points to the soldiers on the ground. "What happened to them?"

"I hit them with a nerve disruptor beam. They will start waking in half an hour. We should take the carrier with us."

"It's tempting, but it will be too easy to trace. It has transponders too difficult to disable. Next time," Sentinel says with a wicked grin, one of the few I have seen him display.

"Well, let's get out of here then."

"Yes, let's."

The trailers start up and return in the direction they came. Sentinel motions his band to move out and disperse. I follow him into a nearby tunnel entrance.

We both emerge from the tunnel two hours later, greeted by a cheering crowd. Others from the raiding party have arrived before us and announced our success. We progress toward the regal complex to inform Adala of the details. She is standing on the front dais with a satisfied smile as we approach.

"Your Highness," Sentinel says, kneeling as we stop in front of her. "We have succeeded in our undertaking."

"I have heard," Adala replies. "Please rise and dispense with the formalities. Let us go to the cabinet room for a debrief." She looks directly at me with a sparkle in her eyes. "Come."

13

BETRAYED

Sentinel and I enter the cabinet room after Adala. The other members are waiting: General Ernst, General Tancred, Sigmund, Frieda, and Chancellor Korbinian. They are excited, except the Chancellor. He has a watchful reserve. We sit, and Adala starts the proceedings.

"Celebrations are in order for an outstanding success today. We have captured a significant supply of weaponry for our battles ahead. We should thank Sentinel and Halwende, particularly, for the positive outcome of this mission. Let us hear the details of the events."

They turn to Sentinel and me. I leave the talking to Sentinel, who proceeds to debrief the council on the events that occurred during the raid. At my plea, he leaves out the detail about the incapacitation of the backup. I don't want attention drawn to the unexpected power that I can wield. I sense Adala knows that a detail is missing by how she looks at me, but I keep my face expressionless and nod to what Sentinel is saying. The others ask questions, we give answers, and then the meeting is over. Sentinel looks exhausted by the recitation, and I am no better. I need sleep.

The others leave. Only Sentinel, Adala, and I stay.

"What did you not tell us?" Adala asks.

Sentinel looks at me.

"I may have helped more than what Sentinel told the others, but that's mere detail. Your followers did the hard work."

Adala's eyes sparkle. My diversionary response intrigues her, but she decides not to pursue the issue further for now. "You're both tired. You may go, Sentinel. I wish to discuss a matter with Halwende before I allow him to rest."

"Your Highness," Sentinel says, bowing to the ground as he leaves.

I groan, not because I wish to leave Adala, but because I'm tired and envy Sentinel's release.

Adala notices. "I will only keep you as long as you wish."

The multitude of interpretations one could place on her statement unsettles me, leaving me speechless. Part of me yearns to stay with her until she tires of me, but the rest of me is frightened. "I am yours for now," I venture, not sure where my lead will end.

Delight transforms her face, a smile of pure bliss to me. These moments remind me of why I stayed to help. I stayed for her approval as much as the sense of redemption I need for my past failings. Adala rises and comes over to me. She strokes my hair as she moves behind me, massaging my shoulders with her hands. I groan again but with pleasure this time at the release of tension.

"Come. Let's walk," she says finally.

I rise with a protest from my muscles. Adala holds out a hand for me to grasp. I take it and we walk out of the conference room and toward her private garden. We do not talk. I enjoy the silence and closeness as we stroll. Evening has fallen as we enter the garden, and the chill of night encroaches. We walk over to her favorite bench and sit, basking in the scenery's beauty as the plants and animals prepare for the night ahead. It is peaceful and serene, a sharp contrast to the day's events.

"What do you want of me?" I ask.

Adala stares at me, the light filtering into the secluded glade reflected in her eyes. She looks unsure, vulnerable. She lowers her gaze. "I am in love with you."

I glance away with a rapid jerk of my head. The response is unexpected, one I do not deserve. I think.

"You are just infatuated with this unworldly figure that has appeared in your life. I'm no one. I am especially not deserving of a princess even if I felt the same way." A lump rises in my throat as I know I just told a lie. My need for her is more than it has been for anyone since I lost my family, but I cannot allow myself the same thoughts. They will probably snatch her away from me, or me from her, and the resulting loss would be too much pain for me.

She is not fooled. She grabs my forearm. "I know you don't mean that. Look at me and repeat those words."

I just shake my head, as I know I can't do as she demands. We sit and stare at the scenery.

Adala finally says, "What you did today has helped us immensely. I thank you for that, as you did not have to help us."

I bite my lip while I consider a reply. "You are wrong. I had to help you. My life cannot suffer a second tragedy. I couldn't forgive myself, ever. I haven't forgiven myself for the first one yet."

Adala looks puzzled. "Why? What has happened to you? Where are you from? What is it that's so terrible?"

"Not now. I may tell you another day. Your opinion of me will change if I do."

"I see a courageous man before me, someone who cares for justice and will sacrifice himself for it. That is a quality worthy of respect. That is a quality I admire. It is a rare quality in men."

"Even Sentinel?"

Adala chuckles. "Ranulf is a very special person. Yes, he has the same quality. That's the reason you two connect so well. He has a past regret too."

I stare at her in surprise. First, I didn't think anyone as self-contained as Sentinel would ever feel regret. Second, I am surprised that he would have anything to regret, certainly nothing like my past sins. "I can't believe that."

"Shh." Adala has decided she doesn't want to talk anymore. She moves closer to me and leans her head on my shoulder, wrapping my arm in hers.

Her warmth seeps through me, giving me a sense of peace again. We sit in that position, like statues. The light fades as evening turns to night. The creatures retire to their slumber, and the chill of the night air takes hold.

"We must go," Adala finally says with a sigh. "Before we leave, I must tell you that it comforts me greatly when you join me here. I come here for comfort, but often it feels so lonely."

I choke, not knowing what to say. "My pleasure," is all that comes from my lips.

It seems to be enough. She looks at me with a contented smile. "Thank you."

We both rise and leave the garden. We say our goodnights and go our separate ways.

As I walk from the makeshift palace back to my accommodation, Chancellor Korbinian confronts me. "I'm glad that I caught up with you," he says. "I wish to thank you for what you did today. Do you have time for a celebratory drink with a few friends of mine? It will be quick, and you can retire then."

I stare at him. This is unexpected and unwelcome. I haven't lost my suspicions of him, but I don't see how I can refuse him without insult. I sigh. "OK. I can oblige. Where are we going?"

Korbinian looks pleased. "It is not far. Follow me." He scans the surroundings, which unnerves me, but I dismiss my alarm as a product of too much excitement for one day.

We exit the underground fortress, and he takes me by scooter to the bar where Sentinel and I went on our scouting mission. I relax, as the place is familiar. We order drinks.

"How were you able to carry out such a task with such skill without knowing of our existence if you come from an external locale?" he asks after taking a sip of his drink.

"People behave the same throughout the galaxy," I say curtly, knowing I have made a mistake coming here with him. Moreover, I have left my weapons behind, which leaves me defenseless.

"You possess special talents unavailable to people here. Where did you learn them?"

"Your people deliberately closed themselves off from everybody else in the galaxy. I don't know your reasons, but if you were more communicative with the galaxy, you'd have our technology ..." I glance around and add, "So, wasn't this supposed to be a celebratory drink with friends, not an inquisition? Where are they?"

"They will come soon."

I finish my drink and order another. Korbinian doesn't care. My drink comes and I take a sip.

A ripple of silence traverses the bar, starting from the entrance. I glance over and see a security detail enter. It unsettles me.

They continue their normal duties as if they were just conducting a routine check, but when they come to our table they ask, "Is this him?"

Korbinian nods and they grab me.

"I hope there're no hard feelings," he says.

I struggle as I realize I have walked into a trap, and Korbinian has betrayed me to the enemy. He must be the spy. As I realize the futility of my struggles, I allow the security detail to do their duty, but they display a show of force despite my surrender. One punches my stomach, my chest, and, as an encore, my face with increasing ferocity. My eyes swell and my face bleeds from my nose and mouth. Breathing is difficult. I hear a protest from Korbinian, "You didn't have to do that here." The chastisement has no effect, as the officer punches me again for good measure.

I struggle to stay upright. The security detail drags me from the bar. There's no point in resisting these two; they have forced any fight from me. I'm barely conscious. My head swoons, and I'm confused about where they are taking me. I have a vague sense of being dragged from the bar and onto a scooter or similar means of transportation. A period of movement ensues before they throw me onto a floor. I have no idea where I am, but I am conscious of them stripping me naked and hosing me with icy water. My body shivers as its temperature plummets, and I curl up into a fetal ball. They laugh at my expense. One guard gives me another couple of kicks for good measure. Then they leave.

Time passes, and my nakedness and the temperature combine to allow hypothermia to start. My body refuses to stop shivering. I pass out at one stage and wake again. A puddle of urine stains the floor. It seems I must have relieved myself while unconscious.

Footsteps come closer, but the beating has fused my eyes shut. I sense someone staring at me in silence. "Give this animal clothing. Turn up the heat. I don't want him dead. He can't talk if he's dead," the anonymous person says.

"Yes, sir," a reply comes from a distance, the tone deferential.

Footsteps recede as the person leaves again.

Minutes later, they throw me clothing. Heat seeps into my body as the temperature in the room increases soon afterward. I grope for the clothes and pull them toward me. I can just make out the shape of each garment, so I uncurl, shards of pain shooting from my extremities. Remembering that I am lying in urine, I move to a dry spot on the floor. I should wash, but my injuries prevent me from discerning the services available in the cell. I stop shivering as the heat soaks into me. After a while, I can unlock my joints. They work without too much pain. I sit and pull a shirt on and pants over my legs. Not feeling stable enough to stand, I crawl over to a wall and sit against it. *What have I gotten myself into?*

I am left in peace except for food deliveries. My bruised eyes settle well enough for my sight to return. After eating, I gaze at my surroundings and see I'm in a room five-meter square. Spacious, considering they meant it to be a prison cell. A bed stands in one corner with a table and chair at its foot. A toilet and shower are in an adjacent corner. I see into it from where I sit against the cell's back wall. I could run a shower. Maybe later. The front of the room appears open to the corridor. I toss a pip from the fruit they gave me at the opening and confirm that there's a force field there, preventing my escape. The scorched pip bounces onto the floor toward me. After crawling to the bed, I gingerly rise and place my rear on it. It is firm but soft, a mattress cushioning me from the hardness of the base. I let out a sigh and rotate until I lie on the bed. My body collapses and descends into blissful sleep. My last thoughts are that this treatment is very unusual for a supposed criminal.

14

INTERROGATION

A noise from the corridor wakes me from my slumber. My body still aches from yesterday's treatment. As I open my eyes to slits, three guards approach my cell. They look bored and eager for excitement. I hope I am not on their agenda. One of them touches the wall. The force field at the front of the cell turns off and the others file through, walking to my bed. They shove me to the floor and kick me.

"Get up!" one of them orders. "This isn't a hotel." He kicks me again, chuckling with satisfaction.

Struggling to regain my breath, I rise to my feet before they inflict any more violence on me. They spin me around and place cuffs around my wrists. The senior guard then grabs my upper arm and says, "Come with us."

I do not resist and walk as best I can with them. They walk me through various corridors and descend an elevator. We arrive at a brightly lit room where they shove me onto an ominous-looking chair that has straps for arms, feet, and neck. I am getting a terrible feeling. Why am I surprised? The guards leave and I wait … and wait … and wait. At least eight hours pass. I am hungry and thirsty and dying for a piss. At this rate, I may be prepared to bargain with them to visit the toilet.

An unknown person enters the room and walks around my chair, examining me. He has a black uniform on, a pockmarked face, and is overweight. I wait for him to speak. I can't do much else except piss myself, which I'll do soon regardless of my predicament. He speaks from behind me. "You are not as I envisaged you."

I am confused. "I didn't realize you expected me."

He chuckles. "You are an unexpected addition to the skirmish we have with the princess and her tribe of deluded followers."

"And you are?"

"Sorry, where are my manners? I am Emperor Egon of Helheim."

"You don't look like an emperor. Any chance of a toilet?"

"No. You'll just have to disgrace yourself where you are."

"What do you want then?"

"I will ask the questions, and you will answer them. What is your name?"

"Halwende."

"What is your place of origin? You are not from around these parts." Egon walks around to my field of view again — I presume so he can gauge my reactions to his questions.

I am undecided how to respond. I do not want him to learn of my ship and its contents. It would be a disaster for Adala, although they can't activate most of it without me. "I come from far away."

"I can see that, but where?"

"It's complicated."

"Try me," Egon says, becoming frustrated at my evasiveness.

I try finding the words and settle on a half-truth. "The sky above your head is full of stars. I come from one of those stars."

Egon lets out a laugh, amused beyond belief at my suggestion. "Do you take me for a fool? There's nothing beyond the sky. That is something our scientists can agree on — if nothing else. Now tell me or suffer the consequences."

"It is the truth."

"Well, how did you get here then?"

"In a ship that could contain me and keep me alive and can travel vast distances. I crashed. The landing destroyed the ship."

Egon rests his hands on the arms of the chair and plants his face centimeters from mine, "You will tell me the truth sooner or later." He pulls away and turns from me, "Now, on another matter, where is Adala's hideout?"

"I do not know."

"You must have seen it. They must have taken you there. Describe it. Or were you blindfolded the whole time?"

I'm in a bind. I will not give away Adala's location, but it confuses me. Why isn't he aware of her location? Korbinian has betrayed me to Egon. Why hasn't he told him, or why hasn't Egon forced it from him? "I wouldn't tell you even if I knew."

"So be it. You will tell me in the end." Egon stares at me one last time with a monster's face, deranged by his passion for power. "She is mine. She will come to understand that." He walks out.

With a sigh of relief, I sit alone, waiting. Moments later, two men come in and undo my shackles. They pull me from the chair and throw me to the floor. I try to get up, but they kick me to the floor again. Unable to last any longer, I piss. They kick my face and head, puffing up my eyes into near blindness again. One of them grabs my wrist and starts dragging me from the room, a slick of urine trailing behind me. I gag from the winding of the attack but try to stand so I can at least walk to my destination. As soon as I try, they kick my feet from under me again. We travel through various corridors until we get to an illuminated cell block. They drag me to another cell. Another person occupies an adjacent cell. He is watching me with interest.

They throw me into the space. I roll with the inertia of the push.

"You best clean yourself. You smell," one of them advises.

The other one walks over to a panel and turns a switch. A wall of humming light extends from the roof of the cell to the floor, making the fourth wall. I open my eyes to check what the guards are doing. They laugh at me. "Wait till you see what's in store for you. Our boss has devised interesting torture methods if nothing else. We haven't used them for a while."

I shiver at the implication. They turn and walk away. The cell is much worse than the previous one. It has a bed made from hard plastic, a small receptacle for body functions, and a small basin for washing — that's it. It is only three meters square. I shuffle to the basin and wash the stale urine off me the best I can and then go sit on the bed, pondering my predicament.

"Are you from the resistance?" I hear from the cell next door.

I tense. It is the person I noticed when I entered. Wary that he might be a spy planted there to trap me, I answer, "I am aware of it."

"Have you seen Adala? Is she well? Please tell me." Eagerness for news of her tinges the tone of his voice.

"What is she to you?" I shuffle over to the wall closest to the voice's source.

He sighs. "She is my daughter."

"You are the king?" *King Abelard is in the cell next to me.* They should treat him with more respect.

"Yes, I am, or at least I was until that traitor Egon usurped power from me."

"She is well, but are they not listening in to our conversation?"

"No, they cannot. There are no secret passages here, and they are not anywhere nearby."

"Aren't there listening devices planted in our cells, though?"

"Listening devices?"

"Yes. Listening devices. Microphones. Cameras even."

"No such instruments exist in this section. No, they cannot hear us. Where do you come from?"

Tired of explaining my origin, I sigh as I tell the king. "I come from a distant star." There is no immediate response. I wait for the usual disbelieving reaction.

The king eventually says, "I have read of such places in the ancient writings of our library here in the palace. My great grandfather talked of such places too. As a child, he remembered people visiting. But something happened, and our forefathers removed us from the galaxy. You are the first visitor since then."

I listen with fascination at the history lesson and am relieved that someone believes me at last. "How have you forgotten what is out there beyond your planet?"

"I understand they suppressed it, and they spread misinformation to make the populace believe only this planet exists. There are fantasies and fables still told to the children. I shall show you the histories in the library if we ever leave here alive. I am surprised that you found us. Our ancestors cloaked us from the outside world."

"I hit a space rock and crash-landed here. I didn't realize this planet existed. Nobody does. It's not on any astrogation charts. I'm worried that no one will come to investigate my distress beacon. They will think it's a false signal and dismiss it."

"Well, I hope for your sake that someone does. The world is lonely enough without being separated from your loved ones."

"That isn't a problem. I don't have any loves ones."

"... I am sorry."

"Since you know more than anybody else, what's the portal I spied in the cave?"

"You saw the portal?"

"Can't everyone?"

Abelard is silent before he speaks again. "Few see the portal, and no one can enter it. Visitors to this planet installed it in a long-lost age from my reading of the histories. The writings state that only the blessed can use it. It must still sense an aura in your presence it recognizes."

"Are there more? What is it meant to do?"

"The ancient writings are devoid of any description of it as if they have removed the history from our records."

I ponder the insight Abelard has given me.

"You must escape and leave here," he says, interrupting my thoughts.

"I can't leave Adala. I promised to help her if I could."

"You are no good to her here."

"True, but I have no options."

"We shall see."

I lean back on the wall. "I have to think."

"Well, don't think for too long. They have interesting means of torturing people, and it won't be too long before they start on you."

Abelard's warning sends another shiver through me.

Five minutes later, the guards return. They saunter toward my cell and switch off the force field. I look at them warily, knowing I can do nothing.

"We have a treat for you," one of them says. The other chuckles but does not speak.

They cuff me and lead me away. I try to look behind me to see the king as we leave, but they pull me toward the door, making me face that instead. We walk along a long corridor and through several doors before entering a sinister-looking room.

A chair stands in the center. This one has prongs extending from the headrest, curving to encompass the head. I shudder to think of their use, but I suspect I will find out soon. The guards push me toward the chair and force me to sit, strapping me into it. Now they place a strap around my forehead and position the prongs so that they touch my temples. I cannot move my head one millimeter before they pierce my scalp inflicting pain. The guards laugh as they leave the room. I wait.

Another person enters the room moments later and goes to a control panel in the corner. I can just see it from the corner of my eye. He presses a button, and something whirrs behind me and clamps on my head. The person comes over to me to inspect his handiwork. He nods and smiles at me, "This might hurt." He moves away, a remote-control unit in his hand.

As he looks at the unit, he presses a button, and more pain surges through me. My body cramps to escape the bonds of the chair, my teeth clamp shut, and my eyes fuse in response to the agony infusing my entire body. The pain relents several seconds later. "Good. It works perfectly," the man says, nodding his head, pleased. Blood dribbles from the wounds produced by the prongs, a drop getting in my eye, the rest continuing on their path.

"Who are you?" I ask.

"I will ask the questions. Who are you? The emperor says that you believe you come from outer space, or so you say."

"I do."

"Yes ... yes." I don't think he believes me.

Pain wracks my body again. I try to keep my eyes open, and I see him turn a knob, increasing my pain. An eternity passes before he turns the unit off and relieves my pain. Perspiration floods from my forehead like a squeezed sponge releasing its contents, mixing with the blood from the prong wounds.

"Now, where is your home?"

"I told you. I come from a far-off star."

Pain again surges through me, threatening me with unconsciousness, but he turns the switch off before I can pass out. My head would loll if it could.

"How did you get here then?"

"In a spaceship."

"A spaceship? And where is this spaceship now?"

"The crash destroyed it. I just escaped before it exploded."

"Where?"

"Out somewhere in the forest. I was wandering there for many days before I found the city."

"Were you at the Wilmar Security Compound yesterday?"

"No."

Pain streaks through me for several seconds and then stops.

"Your answer proves your duplicity. You'd be unaware of the compound if you weren't there."

I castigate myself for my mistake. I must think faster. "Yes, I was then."

"Who accompanied you?"

"A gang I met. They wanted weapons, and I observed the compound and advised them how to break into it. I helped them." I hope that the confession doesn't get me killed.

"Does this gang have a name?"

"They didn't tell me."

"Why help them?"

"They gave me food."

My interrogator thinks for a moment. I doubt he believes a word I've said.

"What is your name?"

"Halwende."

"Do you know the princess?"

"Who?"

"Princess Adala?"

"Never heard of her."

He turns the switch on again. This time he doesn't turn it off, and I pass out.

When I regain consciousness, I am still strapped to the chair. My arm is strapped into an unknown device that has my forearm clamped at either end. There is a hinge in the middle and a ratchet connected to both sides. The device has various instruments attached. A person stands before me, and I see that Egon has returned.

"Good to see that you have woken up," Egon says.

The experience has dulled my senses, and I take time to regain awareness of my surroundings. "Your minion shouldn't put me to sleep."

A sharp pain penetrates my head again, but Egon puts an immediate stop to it. "Not yet. We have to talk first."

"Now, where were we? Yes, we were discussing your involvement with the rebels."

"What rebels?"

Egon becomes angry. "You lie. We have seen you with many members of the rebel rabble, including the elusive one called Sentinel."

"You've mistaken me for someone else."

Egon nods and an instrument on the forearm device activates, moving to my elbow, and three razor-sharp pointed blades appear.

They lower onto my flexor muscle and penetrate the skin, causing intense pain. Blood drips from my arm onto the armrest and the floor.

"I will ask you again, where is the rebel headquarters?"

"I do not know."

Egon gives another nod, and the blades move along my arm, shredding my muscle. I scream in agony, blood now pouring from my arm. "Where?"

"I don't know," I pant out as I hyperventilate with large gulps of air, trying to bear the pain. The blades keep moving and stop halfway. They retract. My heart races with adrenalin and sweat drips from my face.

"Where is it?"

"I don't know. Are you deaf?"

Egon nods again, and a shaft moves into place, bisecting my forearm. It just touches my skin. The ratchet lifts the two ends of the restraint, my wrist and elbow moving with them. The shaft presses hard against my arm until the bones flex. I scream again and pant to stay as composed as possible.

"Where?"

"I ... don't ... know," I get out through clenched teeth.

Egon nods, and the ratchet moves. I hear a sharp crack as a bone shatters. The device unwinds. Egon sighs. "You are a stubborn man. You will tell me everything in due time." He looks at the other person. "Give me that and clean up his arm."

"Yes, Emperor."

Egon presses the button and turns the knob to the peak setting. I pass out.

15

ESCAPE... OF SORTS

I wake, not knowing how long I've been unconscious. My cell reappears as I open my eyes. A terrible headache throbs, so I continue lying on my bed. I close my eyes again and rest. On recalling what happened to me since my imprisonment, I realize the torture will continue until I give them what they want or what they think they will get. I will no longer be an asset to them anymore, and they will then extinguish me to free up the cell and reduce their costs in keeping me. I contemplate my chances of convincing them to let me go and snigger bitterly to myself. My eyes open again, and I look at my arm, which is now swollen, bruised, and lacerated but roughly patched. Stabs of pain radiate from it when I try to move.

I must escape. But how? I should talk to the king and see if he can help me. He mentioned a library in the palace with information on the portal. He said that no secret passages existed behind these walls, implying secret passages must exist in the palace. How do I find them, and how do I gain entry to them? I need to talk to the king. I notice a plate of food sitting on the small table and realize I am famished. How long has it been since I ate? How long have I been here? The king will tell me how long it has been since I returned from my interrogation.

With effort, I sit, then stand and shuffle to the table, bearing the throbbing pain in my arm as best I can. Bread and what resembles stew sit on the plate. It doesn't look very appealing, but it's food ... A spoon lies next to the plate, so I pick it up with my good arm and start shoveling the stew into my mouth. It is only just what one might call food. Still, it fills my empty stomach, and that's what matters now. I grab the bread and mop up the remaining liquid with it, wiping the plate clean. A metal cup filled with liquid sits on the table. I taste it. It is water, so I gulp the contents to quench my thirst.

"Are you there, King?" I hear a shuffle getting closer to my cell wall. I move over to the wall too.

"Yes, I am here."

"How long since they brought me back in here?"

"Oh, maybe ten hours."

"That long? That machine whacks a punch."

Abelard chuckles. "I presume you mean the Nerve Stimulator. Yes, it 'whacks a punch' as you say."

"I've been thinking. I prefer not experiencing that again or have other bones broken and muscles shredded. And I suspect there're other interesting means of extracting information, and I don't want to give your daughter away. She is too valuable."

Abelard remains silent until he says, "Do I detect a slight hint of affection for my daughter?"

"Don't get the wrong idea. Yes, I like her. She has guts, and we've had interesting talks together, but that is as far as it goes. I don't want you ordering my execution for touching your daughter."

Abelard chuckles again. "Adala is an adult and can resolve unfortunate circumstances on her own. I'd support her, though, if she asked for help. That was not what I meant. I was just surprised she's allowed you close enough for you to have feelings for her. She has been very protective of her feelings ever since she was a child — I think to shield herself from not having a mother."

I sense a twinge of sadness in Abelard's voice when he speaks the last sentence.

"I've been thinking that I need to escape before they decide I'm of no further use to them. Do you have any ideas on how?"

The silence is deafening, but I wait for a response. He eventually speaks. "There is a means if you can overpower the guards. They are very lax sending only two guards to fetch you. Still, two-to-one. But you have the element of surprise. The door leads to a long corridor. Did you note your surroundings along the way?"

I wrack my brain, trying to think what I saw when they led me to the torture room. I had swollen and bruised eyes then. Closing my eyes, I try picturing the scene as I struggled with the guards walking through the passage. Several unidentified doors were on my left. Pictures hung on the right wall, and a doorway penetrated it but was filled in with brickwork. A sconce hung on the doorway's left and a picture on its right. No other features come to mind. I speak of what I remember and stop to let Abelard comment, opening my eyes.

"The bricked-in doorway is an entrance to the secret passages. You might think the sconce opens it, but it does not. That and the picture identify the entrance. You didn't notice, and I can't blame you, but two bricks of dissimilar color are on each side. Pressing these bricks will open the door and allow entrance to the secret passages behind it."

"But where do the passages lead? How does that help me escape?"

"One step at a time. I can't draw a map of the passages for you, so I will explain it and you picture it in your mind's eye — unless you have drawing equipment?"

I roll my eyes. "No, I don't."

"I didn't think so," the king says and continues by painting a map of the passages with words. As I absorb the words, I develop a map in my head, trying to remember everything that he says. It takes him half an hour as he has to stop twice when a guard walks in to check us and remove my eating utensils.

"I've memorized it now, and you've explained the way to the library. How will the library be helpful?"

"Many writings exist there, including an ancient manuscript describing the portal, not that it says much. But it appears to be reaching out to you, so I recommend you take time to study this text. You will recognize the tome when you see it. It is jet black, the color of the portal itself. A golden framed icon decorates the spine with the rune of a spaceship. That is the book. Study it with diligence. You never know how it may help you if you can access the workings of the device. You can ask the library questions and it will answer you."

"That sounds easy enough, but how does that help me escape?"

"Do I need to think for you? I don't know. But you're resourceful, you will find a way."

"And you?"

"I must stay. It's too dangerous for you if I escape with you. The entire palace would search for us. It will be dangerous enough with you on the loose."

"I understand."

"You can do something for me, though. If you escape and return to Adala, give her my love and tell her I am well."

"I will, I promise."

It turns out that I do not have to wait long for my opportunity. The same two guards come for me. Their casual stance betrays their laxity as if they know I can't escape even if I overpower them. They are foolish and don't consider my skills in hand-to-hand combat. They think I'm beaten into submission and that the disability of a broken arm renders me useless, not even bothering to cuff me. My opportunity comes as they shove me to the door leading to the corridor, one on either side of me. I turn my head to look for Abelard. He is looking at me, and I wink before I face forward again. I spring into action as the right-side guard opens the door. My good arm's elbow lifts with force, smashing into the solar plexus of the guard on the left, incapacitating him. I aim my fist at the other guard's temple as he turns to see what the commotion is, and it knocks him unconscious with one punch. That's a relief, as it means there's only one to attack now. He is recovering and gets in a kick to the groin before I smash my fist into his cheek, sending his nasal cartilage up into his brain. He is dead, wobbling for a second before toppling to the floor.

"Quick!" Abelard calls out in encouragement. "Others will come to investigate before long. Godspeed."

"I hope we meet again soon under better circumstances," I reply as I disappear through the door and into the corridor.

I rush to the spot with the bricked-in doorway and study it. Differently tinted bricks exist on either side, just as Abelard said. After placing my hands on them, I press with strength. Pain emanates from the broken arm, but I persist. They move and I hear a click just before the brickwork pulls aside, providing access to a dark passage behind it. After stepping through the doorway, the brickwork moves again, sealing me inside the passageway. Darkness encompasses me and I realize I didn't ask what I do for lighting, and Abelard didn't offer any suggestions.

As I recall the map from my memory, the library is to my left. Turning to creep in that direction, I get a fright as lights switch on in both directions for one hundred meters either way. I should have guessed such lighting existed after experiencing the same in Adala's tunnels. I notice something on the wall before I leave, covered in dust, so I brush the wall with my hand to remove it. The same map that Abelard made me remember is inscribed on the wall. I check it and confirm the library is in the correct direction. Shouts and voices ring out behind the entrance just before I leave. I chuckle to myself. *They'll scratch their heads for a while.*

I start walking to the library.

16

THE LIBRARY

I t doesn't take long for me to walk to the library entrance. Abelard has told me how I can find it. A replica map impregnates the wall's surface, a 'you are here' map. I look for the opening latch. The discolored brick is easy to see, and I press it. The door opens, just as I realize my blasé carelessness may be my undoing. Relief flows over me when I see that the room is empty.

The room is bare, with white walls, floor, and ceiling. The only variation is a bookshelf with a dozen ancient books, including the one with information on the portal, and two discolored rectangles on the doorway's entrance. These open the door. There is a door opposite, providing access to the palace corridors. Abelard warned me of the plain barrenness of the room and advised me to stand in the center and speak my inquiries. I feel self-conscious as I plan the words to speak to the room's walls. I decide on my inquiry.

"Show the library catalog."

Nothing happens until an opalescent light comes from the general room's space and coalesces into a hologram displaying a list in an unknown language.

"Display the catalog in Galactic Standard Language." The display becomes blurred and swirls like a primordial soup until it refocuses into a language I do now understand. How the library knows the language is a mystery to me, but I surmise they established it before the planet isolated itself from the rest of civilization. The catalog is now plain and divided into sections. I read the list. There are several categories of interest to me. I begin my exploration with the question, "Show me the palace layout."

The display swirls again, and soon a holographic model of the palace materializes. I am fascinated and start circling the image, finding landmarks and items of interest, especially a potential escape route out into the city. Studying the lower sections, I discover that one corridor connects to the caves I entered when I first arrived and leads directly to the portal. This amazes me. I note how to get there and memorize it. As I continue to study the image, I realize that my escape will be difficult, if not impossible. There are few unguarded places. The corridor leading to the portal recaptures my attention, and I spy a minor side corridor leading to a door directly behind the Brandenfälle Waterfall, a secret escape route in case of sieges of the main exits. I wonder why Abelard did not use it. Didn't he have the opportunity, or was he unaware of its existence? I spend another ten minutes studying the route from the library to this corridor to make sure I have internalized the map. I then study the chief palace defenses for potential weaknesses. Possibilities come to mind.

After reviewing the escape route again, I continue my interrogation. "Show me the catalog again in Galactic Standard." The list swirls back into existence. I look over the list and decide I need to understand the reason for the planet's isolation. I voice my choice, and a mass of text displays in the hologram, but it is too microscopic to decipher. Unsure of the correct procedure, I walk to the image and swipe both hands outward when they just touch the holograph. This has the effect of zooming the entire image outward, making the words readable. I can now read the text, and I start reading.

Helheim fell into a dispute with the rest of the galaxy over a mineral of significant value deposited only on Helheim. It could produce immense power. Helheim inflated the charges for the mineral until the galaxy grew intolerant of its greed. Several factions demanded the confiscation of the planet by force to improve the mineral supply. A war developed with a devastating and increasing loss to Helheim.

Much misery eventuated with the rationing of dwindling food and supplies. Many people starved, and the fighting slaughtered many more. The royal government was desperate to find a solution. It decided that its only choice was to isolate the planet from the rest of the galaxy. So, the government requested its scientists to develop a cloaking mechanism to remove the planet from normal space. In that way, it became inaccessible to outsiders. It was a mammoth task. An enormous quantity of the mineral was required to produce the cloaking field and support it for an indeterminate time until they considered it safe to rejoin the galactic civilization again. Once they established the cloak, they suppressed all science to do with the external environment until forgotten.

I break from my reading to internalize what I am learning. What is this valuable mineral? Why not say its name? Where is the cloaking device? How does the mineral still power it? Who is maintaining the machinery? What trigger will allow these people to rejoin galactic civilization? I have these questions whirling in my head like clothes in a washing machine. I read more ...

The government left one object installed by the outsiders, the portal, but left it buried deep within the palace environs. Local people could not access it because aliens had installed it. According to legend, when it was time for Helheim to rejoin the galactic society, someone from outside would enter the city and access the portal.

The person's qualifications are vague, except the text implies the person will come from elsewhere in the galaxy.

I consider everything that I have read and now understand why they do not have satellites. They do not need them. They keep their society contained so they can keep surveillance by other means and relay information without satellite coverage. I still don't understand why other common technology is missing. The commentary on an outsider coming to access the portal makes me uneasy. The text is deficient in what it does or why they placed it there. More information on it may be available in the library.

"Show me any information on the portal."

"Please clarify your question."

I think of what to say. "Show me information on the portal placed in the palace sub-terrain by alien beings." I shrug my shoulders, hoping that it understands my inquiry. A significant time elapses before a response comes with a text — one small sentence.

"Information on this topic is classified, but a tome sits on the shelf."

"... Who classified it?"

"... The library does not know the answer to your question."

I walk over to the bookshelf and search through the books on it until I spot the one that Abelard mentioned. I retrieve it, sit on the floor, and open it. It is essentially blank as if someone has redacted it. There is only one piece of information announcing that entry is available to those who can verify the truth, whatever that means. I replace the book on the shelf.

At a dead-end, I have one more topic for my inquiry. "Does the library have any information on the current crisis?"

"The current crisis is still in progress. So, no cataloging has occurred yet."

I am frustrated by the voice's evasiveness. "Tell me of the history leading up to the crisis."

Silence fills the room before the library replies, this time in the form of written text.

The society that eventuated after the cloaking settled into one of self-sustaining existence. The monarchy organized the rule to democratize the government without losing ultimate control. This policy worked well for an extensive period, except for one problem. The realm's military class had little to do after the war ended and, as a result, became restless. It lusted for more power and the ability to flex its muscle. The only victims of this aggression were the society they swore to protect, so friction increased between the military elite and the ruling royals. Successive kings managed the issue, but King

Abelard let his control over the issue slip when he suffered great losses in the deaths, one after the other, of his two wives. Speculation exists that the deaths were homicide, but no evidence ever proved any allegation. Over time, First General Egon increased his power in the kingdom until he could overthrow the king and seize control. He has a large popular following due to his promise of relief from a perceived state of repression and servitude. He holds tenuous control because his claim to rule is constitutionally invalid.

"What is First General Egon's history?" I ask. Again, more text:

General Egon came from a military family. He showed great strategic potential as he progressed up the military hierarchy and has amassed vast wealth by monopolizing supply chains, particularly military ones, which they still produce and improve, despite a lack of enemy to use them against, apart from the citizens of Helheim. He used his charisma and strategic thinking to gain promotion to First General through various means.

"Where are these weapons stockpiled?"

"The answer is unknown," comes the voice.

That answer doesn't surprise me. It is not information for a library. I recall another question. "Tell me of the political ethics of the royal family." A long silence passes until the library displays in text:

While the royal family enforced periods of great repression and dictatorial control, it tried overall to offer a democratic political framework, with its authority providing direction on any unresolved issue. However, King Wilmar, Abelard's father, was a tyrant who created great political unrest during his rule. Many political historians pin the source of the current problems to this period in the history of Helheim. King Abelard set out to correct the political power imbalance, but his personal problems diverted his attention from concentrating on the strategy he had determined to take.

That is an amazing snippet of information for me. I now understand the politics of the current struggle and why Egon is so desperate to capture Adala. His marriage to her will legitimize his rule. I pace the room, thinking over what I have learned but soon realize I must progress to the next phase and escape. I have a lingering thought, though. What is Chancellor Korbinian's entanglement in this? Why did he betray me to Egon but not divulge where Adala is? This and many other snippets of gained knowledge must wait. I must escape and decide whether I wish to, or have the courage to, help Adala recover her kingdom.

17

ESCAPE FROM THE PALACE

The library door opens to my touch, and I glance out into the corridor. I remember to be careful as I venture through the palace halls, which are not secret passages. It is quiet, so I step out and start toward the side passage and the exit behind the waterfall, alert to any noise warning me of others approaching. The corridors are silent apart from my footfalls. Before long, I arrive at the location, but the doorway is well hidden. I recall the signs from studying the map but can't remember the details. My palms become moist as footsteps echo through the main corridor, and I fight rising panic. They are coming toward me. My heart pumps faster at the unexpected complication in my plan. I search for a place to hide but find none. As I stand in a dead-end corridor, I consider that anyone following me must have a reason to. I resign myself to my fate.

The stomping reaches a crescendo and then recedes into the distance. I breathe again, grateful for my lucky reprieve, but I need to locate the door key before someone comes my way. My heart still pounds.

I continue staring at where the doorway should exist and scratch my head. The surface of the wall is smooth. As I lean against the opposite surface, a protruding nodule causes my back discomfort.

Turning, I spy the magnified image of what's in my memory and realize my mistake. I study the protuberance closely. Pushing it does nothing. I try twisting it and it moves clockwise until it clicks. The opposite wall opens into another tunnel, a faint light filters in from the far end. After passing through the doorway, the exit door closes behind me. I reach the end of the tunnel in five minutes and a deafening roar of cascading water greets me. A ledge to the right traverses behind the falls leading to freedom. No water lies on the ledge, surprising me. A force field must prevent splatter. I follow it, and moments later see the sun and the open countryside. The sun's brightness makes me squint.

My only thoughts are to return to my ship's safety, a known environment in which to hide and mend my arm with the vessel's medical kit. The grating of my broken bone becomes unbearable, the pain reaching a climax and then subsiding. After consideration, I decide it's wiser to wait until sunset before I begin the trek to my ship. To kill time, I retreat to the entry tunnel and doze as much as my throbbing injuries will allow.

When nightfall envelops the landscape, I start my return to the spaceship. After descending from the ledge to the plain below, a path leads around the lake. My pace is slow and stealthy until I am well away from the buildings, after which it quickens. I jog at a steady rate despite the pain it induces in my arm. Sentinel showed me a map of the city and surrounds when planning our attack of the security compound, and I recall only two rivers exiting the lake, my vessel having crashed between them. I realize I need to navigate the river to get to my ship. Several hours pass. When I reach the stream, I follow it, looking for a place to cross.

A ford shows up when I turn a slight bend as the waterway broadens into slow-moving turbulence. The water chills me as I wade across, the pull of the current tugging at my legs. The level reaches my hips before it subsides again as I near the other side. On reaching the other bank, I find a tree to rest. The day's exertion is catching up with me.

I wake with a start to the first light of daybreak. As I rise, I stretch my muscles to remove the traces of sleep from them. Hunger calls me to eat, but I must first get back to the spaceship. My grumbling stomach is my constant companion as I trot along the shore. After a full day's journey, I see the familiar river shoreline where I landed and collected water. The ship is nearby in the forest on my left. I pick up the pace as I enter the wood and after five minutes my vessel is in sight. But I come to a sudden halt. Two men are roaming in front of it. They belong to Egon's security forces by the look of their uniform.

I hide behind a tree, considering my dilemma. I thank fate that the dim light makes me hard to see, but I am surprised they didn't hear my approach. They must have assumed I was an animal in the underbrush. I overhear them talking as I sit and wait.

"What is it?" one asks.

"Dunno," the other replies. "The emperor just asked us to search for strange objects and report. This monstrosity is unusual."

"Someone's been living here, though. The canopy and fireplace and things."

"Yeah. You're not wrong there."

"Well, we can't do more here. We should return to the city and present what we've found."

"I'm getting hungry."

"Ha! Typical. You're always thinking of your stomach."

They both walk toward their scooter, get in, and leave. I see them fly overhead and disappear behind the tree canopy. A large blast and delayed explosion roar past me moments later. I glance around and realize it came from the scooter's direction. I rise to my feet and follow it, spotting the scooter's debris half-submerged in the river. There are no survivors. It worries me, as people will search for them, and it won't be hard to find my spaceship once they find the wreckage. My more pressing concern is, who fired the projectile that destroyed the scooter? Where are they? I search the surroundings but see no one. Losing interest, I return to my ship.

"Took you long enough to break your hiding," Sentinel's voice says from nowhere.

"Sentinel ... Where did you come from?"

"I knew you'd return here first. So, I've been checking. I came out today because I learned through my sources that Egon had ordered the search for your ship, and I followed those two."

"How long have I been away?"

"Three weeks."

I can't believe that so much time has passed. The solitude must've sped up time.

"Did you know they had arrested me?"

"Yes. Korbinian told us. He said a chance inspection caught you two having a drink."

"Did he now? You realize that is a complete lie. He arranged it. The security officers were looking for us. They only gave a cursory check of anybody else before coming to our table and taking me away. They even waited for Korbinian to confirm they had the right person. I presume he trusts I will never see daylight again, so he is safe with his story. What I don't understand is why."

"Oh, I've long known Korbinian is loyal only to Korbinian. I suspect he fancies his chances with Princess Adala and thought handing you over to Egon got the competition out of the way."

"You're kidding."

"No, I am not."

"Does he really think Egon would let him have Adala for handing me over?"

"I think he's arrogant enough to think he can manipulate Egon."

"How is Adala?"

"She's floundering on the military front, even with the injection you gave us, both with the extra weapons and the fresh approach. The generals are doing their best to keep the impetus going, but they're too predictable. They're set in their military logic; their tactics are too familiar to Egon ... and she is lonely." Sentinel adds the last comment as a hint that she's lonesome for me.

I consider telling Sentinel about the king so that he can reassure Adala her father is well but selfishly decide to keep the good news to tell Adala myself.

"Why did you kill them?" I ask, pointing toward the river and the wreckage of the scooter.

"I couldn't afford for them to report their discovery of the spaceship. Others would come out and they could have found you. You've caused a large commotion with your escape."

I glance at him suspiciously. "You have a good information network."

"Not everyone working for Egon is happy."

"Won't someone come looking for them?"

"Not after I am finished, not here."

We fall silent for a time. I wonder how he will make the scooter disappear without trace but am too tired to ask.

"How long before you come back?" he asks.

"How do you know I won't return at once?"

"You wouldn't have retreated here if you were reuniting with us."

As I wonder what my true thoughts are on the matter, I look away. "I must contemplate matters before I return, and mend this," I say, showing him my damaged arm. "I need to understand why I'm doing this and if it's worth my life."

Sentinel looks at me with discernment but without judgment. "You've accomplished much for us. I understand you may not wish to help us anymore. We will miss you, especially Princess Adala."

I blush both at the compliment and Sentinel's observation of the relationship between Adala and me. "Will you tell her you found me?"

"No. Not unless you want me to."

"No. Not yet. I don't want to give her false hope. Since I've only failed people in the past, I fear this turning into another defeat. And I don't wish that. I need to find what my true motivation is here. I thought I knew, but I am not sure anymore. Maybe I'm a coward at heart."

"I've watched you, Halwende, and I know one thing: you're no coward. I don't know your history. It sounds as if you've made a few mistakes you regret. Everyone makes them. And some mistakes take longer to heal than others."

"You own an abundance of wisdom behind that brash, stolid exterior."

"Ha! I wish. I have one aim. One only. Princess Adala must stay safe and alive on my watch."

My respect for Sentinel grows. He is an honorable man.

"I must return before they notice my absence. Things need doing," he says.

"Will you return?"

"If you desire it."

"I do. Who knows, I may return with you. Will I be able to enter the tunnels if I return on my own to the house Frieda and Sigmund used?"

"Yes. I will inform the person she can trust you but be careful if you do that. People are searching for you, and you're unfamiliar with the city and its dangers."

I ponder his warning. "You may be right. Return in a day or two. If I haven't decided by then, I never will."

"I will. Well, goodbye then. Till next time."

"Farewell and Godspeed."

Sentinel stares at me and my strange choice of words but says nothing. Instead, he wraps his arms around me in a gesture of friendship that I do not expect. I do likewise, and we part. He turns and blends into the trees before I know what has happened. I turn to my ship, shelter, and safety while I contemplate my future.

18

RETURN TO ADALA

I open and enter my ship, heading for my medical kit. After retrieving the trauma-repair sleeve, I wrap it around my arm and turn it on. A flashing red light indicates major damage that will take time to heal, so I sit and wait. The throbbing recedes as the repair progresses, and within half an hour the sleeve has healed my arm enough to relieve the pain. The rest will mend with time. I find food and eat it before closing the hatch to prevent any more inquisitive visitors from entering. No one can see me inside the ship, so I settle down to consider my alternatives. I then retire to my familiar bunk and slump into it for a well-earned slumber.

In the morning, I eat a hearty meal for breakfast and recap my ordeal so far. At the start, I believed the people and city were a case of me hallucinating. Now I am not so sure. How do you decide what's real or imaginary? Can you hallucinate your own pain? Your own death? Is that possible? Everything is so confusing for me at present, as my memories are returning, ones I thought I had buried long ago. The torture felt authentic to me. If true, why get mixed up in this political intrigue — royal family versus despotic dictator? The people's plight is horrible, but why is that my problem? I need to ponder these questions. According to the information in the library, life under regal rule wasn't rosy either. But I can't imagine Abelard, and especially Adala, sending troops around to summarily execute troublemakers with indiscriminate fervor, but how well do I know them? Adala certainly has a rapport with the rebels who follow her.

When night falls, I venture to the river to collect water. I note that the crashed scooter has disappeared. I'm bored and lonely cooped up in this metal pile of junk. I daydream of Adala and how intriguing she is. Her smile radiates with sunshine when she sheds the world's worries for a moment. I grin at the warmth of our affair. But how can it lead anywhere? What would happen if she regained control? She probably couldn't form a relationship with me even if she wanted to, her being royal and me being a nobody in her world. I worry I won't be able to protect her like I couldn't save my family during the failed uprising. It is time for sleep, so I bed myself in my bunk. My mind wanders to the portal as I doze, and a powerful urge calls me to return to the palatial tunnels to view it again. I'll consider it in the morning.

Sunlight greets me with a blazing warmth through the front viewports. I wash and have breakfast while I ponder returning to the palace and inspecting the portal, but then decide it is too risky at present. I realize that I have already decided that I will help Adala. Why? Because I must; I must redeem myself, even if it means death. I shall wait for Sentinel's return and have him escort me back.

I open the hatch and go outside for fresh air and sunshine. As I stroll to the edge of the forest, I enjoy the outdoor environs. A noise disturbs my peace and I curse to myself for not grabbing a weapon before I left the ship. I search around but see no one.

"Nice day," I hear Sentinel say from behind the trees. He shows himself straight afterward.

"You're getting sloppy. I heard you."

"Hmm. I'll have to train more then. Got a drink?"

"What sort?"

"Just tea."

"Sure? I have stronger stuff you've never tasted."

"Tea will be fine."

"Come with me." I walk to my ship, and Sentinel follows me. I enter the hatch, but he stops at the entrance. Turning around, I see him peering inside with suspicion. "It won't eat you."

"I know that. I was just checking my surroundings. One can never be too careful," Sentinel says with embarrassment.

I chuckle to myself as he enters. "Welcome to my realm. If you don't mind, I'll secure the hatch, so no one disturbs us." I press the button to close it, and it hisses shut. Sentinel looks around, taking in every detail. I stare at him with amusement, as I can appreciate his reaction to a novel experience.

We reach the ship's galley, and I make two teas. I gesture for Sentinel to sit, and I sit as well after placing our drinks on the table. "So, what has been happening?"

"The city is in turmoil searching for you. My contacts say that Egon believes you are in the capital somewhere, even though he can't figure out how you fled the palace. He's considered interrogating the king but needs him in prime condition so can do nothing on that front. He has been questioning his guards, though. And he thinks you could only have escaped with someone's help. Did you?"

"That is not important at present." I still don't want to tell Sentinel I met Abelard, not before I've told Adala.

Sentinel grabs his tea and takes a sip. He looks me in the eye. "So, are you returning with me?"

I lounge in the chair and stare back at him, stretching out my reply to create suspense. Why I don't know. Just to tease him, I guess. "Yes, I am coming back."

I hadn't realized it, but Sentinel was holding his breath. He lets out a loud sigh of relief. "Thank God."

"Things aren't that dreadful."

"I wasn't thinking of the battle."

I raise my eyebrows, questioning what he said, but he offers no further clarification. We sit and finish our beverages in silence.

"I'll just collect my belongings and we can be on our way."

"Fine. I'll wait here."

I pack food and a few other items in a rucksack and arm myself from my arsenal — I am well equipped with firearms if nothing else. After consideration, I select another maser, but I will retrieve my other weapons when I return to my accommodation in the cavern. I choose a personal protection field generator too. With a scan of the ship, to check I have everything, I return to Sentinel and say, "Let's go."

He rises, a smile on his face — a rare event for him — and gestures for me to lead. I look at him questioningly, but he offers no reason for his behavior. We reach the hatch. I open and close it after exiting, and we start our journey through the forest. After an hour's brisk walking, we come across his scooter parked in a clearing. We jump on it and Sentinel steers toward the city, reaching the outskirts in an hour, and arriving at the old woman's house soon afterward. Sentinel leads me into the tunnel and back to the underground settlement of rebels.

My tension mounts as we get nearer. I am nervous about meeting Adala again, but I don't know why. Word of our arrival must have gone before us because people are running, whispering, and pointing at me as we pass. We approach the entrance to Adala's residence and enter, heading for the throne room, and wait in silence.

Moments later Adala rushes toward me, tears streaking her face. "You are back!" she cries as she wraps both arms around me in a bear hug and squeezes tight. I realize I had been fearful she would not have missed me very much. Her greeting reassures me.

I turn and see Sentinel smile in private appreciation.

19

PRIVATE CONVERSATION

"I need to breathe sometime soon," I say after a few moments.

Adala realizes that her behavior is not proper for a princess in public. She lets go, wipes the tears from her cheeks and steps back, giving a more regal presentation to the audience – Sentinel – who doesn't care, his usual formality forgotten for the moment. I see her smile again, the smile I keep remembering, and I return it.

"Yes, I've returned, thanks to your father."

Adala's eyes bulge. "You saw my father? How is he? Is he alright? Did you know of this, Ranulf?" Adala spins around to him, and he shakes his head. He is interested in the news too, and a cog rotates, locating the correct alignment in his head. I see he's recalled my parting words the other day.

I motion for her to be calm. "He is well, confined but well. Although they should give him better accommodation. They incarcerated him in the cell next to mine, and he told me of things that enabled me to escape. He sends his love and says to keep fighting."

"Oh, thank you for telling me this. It means so much to me, Halwende. Please let us retire to more relaxed surroundings and eat. You too, Ranulf."

Sentinel looks at both of us. "With Your Highness's permission, I will take my leave. There are matters to organize."

I see a slight sparkle in Adala's eyes, and I sense Sentinel is deliberately leaving us alone. "Very well. But we shall discuss how you stumbled into Halwende in your daily activities later," Adala replies in a suspicious tone as if he is hiding things from her, and not for the first time. She doesn't appear very upset, though. "Come," she says, gesturing to me as she strides toward the exit. I follow.

As soon as we are out of public view, she slows to let me draw up beside her and wraps her arm around mine — the traumatized one. I wince in pain, and she exclaims hurriedly, "Oh, I didn't mean to hurt you. Are you OK?"

"It's alright. They tortured me on that arm, and it's still healing." I take the initiative, go around her to her other side, and wrap her arm in mine as she had intended. She smiles at me and leans closer. Minutes later, we are in the dining room. Adala orders the staff to prepare and deliver a meal to the garden, and we continue on our way.

Once there, we sit on a picnic bench. "Does it still hurt? Do you need treatment for your arm?"

"No. I ran it through a medical machine when I returned to my ship. Ergon's people shredded my forearm and broke a bone when they tortured me. The medical machine does ninety percent of the job, but the rest needs to heal naturally."

"That sounds terrible. Egon boasts of his torture techniques." A sudden panic grips Adala and she clutches my good arm. "They haven't tortured my father?"

"Not that I can tell. He was in high spirits when I was there, considering his predicament."

Adala sighs in relief.

We stop the conversation as the food and drinks arrive and are placed on the table. The servants step back and wait.

"You may leave us. I will inform you when to return."

"As you wish," the head servant says.

I select items from an antipasto plate and eat.

"Wine?"

"Yes. Thank you."

Adala pours a glass for each of us and hands me mine.

I take a sip. "You realize Korbinian can't be trusted?"

"Sentinel has told me many times, but he is so nice to me."

I nibble more. "He may have plans."

"What plans?"

"Protocol dictates you will marry one day, I presume. He might consider himself an eligible suitor."

Adala looks at me with an expression ranging from disbelief to disgust. "In his dreams."

"Well, it was obvious he organized my arrest. That means he has connections with Egon."

"But that makes little sense. If he betrays my cause and Egon defeats the rebellion, the first thing Egon will do is marry me to legitimize his rule."

"So, he's playing a dangerous double game. He may be jealous and want me disposed of, so I don't diminish his chances or undermine his power over you, as I did with the storming of the compound. He doesn't necessarily want Egon to win, but he thinks he can use the trouble with Egon to his own advantage."

"So, you are a contender then?" Adala asks in a seductive tone, more interested in that than my revelations about her chancellor.

"That's not what I meant," I say, flustered at how I expressed myself. I tell her candidly, "I like you. I like you very much. You have guts. But let's be honest, we hardly know each other, and I am not suitable for you to continue your regal bloodline. Your father queried me too, and I don't want him getting the wrong idea. I still value my life."

"Ha! You don't understand who is eligible and whether I adhere to protocol in these matters. My father would let me decide, anyway."

"That's what he said."

We fall into silence, musing on possibilities.

Adala glances at me, and I turn to her after I sense her movement. She blushes. "I adore you, though."

I smile, and my body fills with warmth.

"But you must have a family," she says.

My smile disappears as I remember my loss and the circumstances under which it occurred. I open to her. "I lost my family in a war on my planet."

"Oh, Halwende, I am so sorry."

"Well, that is the past now. We need to think of the future. Sentinel tells me things have been poor in my absence."

I've annoyed Adala by changing the topic, but she continues the developing conversation. "Everything is going amiss. Whatever we try fails, or we achieve our result with significant loss. What is wrong with my generals?"

"Nothing is wrong with them. They're just too used to thinking the same as Egon, so he has measures to counteract what you try. That is why the raid on the security compound succeeded. It was something unexpected."

"So, what do you suggest?"

"I don't know yet. There was a time when I considered withdrawing my involvement. But I realize that is not possible; I'm involved now, regardless."

"I am glad in more ways than one."

I look at her to understand her meaning, and I smile. "So am I, actually."

Adala raises her hand to my cheek and caresses it as she looks at me with eyes brimming with emotion. Our heads move closer, and we kiss. I caress her cheek too. We part.

"As much as I wish to continue, we don't have time for this," I say, disappointment coloring my tone.

Adala places her forehead against mine. "Yes, you are right." She pulls away, a wan smile covering her face until a look of mischief replaces it. "What to do now, then?"

"Ha! You ... I haven't decided yet. We need something big. Something that will make people notice." I face Adala. "I need to tell Egon that I'm back."

"You're just a child."

"Yes, I am ... aren't I?" I laugh at the thought. "But won't it be fun!"

Joy fills Adala's face, something absent until now. I've seen amusement, seduction, and many other reactions but not joy. It warms my heart. I sit thinking for a moment. "You don't own any troop movement machinery or heavy weaponry, do you?"

"No. We captured heavier equipment with the raid, but they keep the carriers and heavy weapons in the Heimstadt compound where they can protect it."

"It's the Heimstadt Security Compound, then."

"You're crazy. You'll never get in there."

"Every defense has its weakness — you just have to find it. Give me time and I will find it. In the meantime, don't tell anyone. Are there plans for the compound?"

"Ranulf has plans, but he will want the reason you require them."

"Send him to me. He is the only one I trust apart from you, and I don't mean any slight on Sigmund and Frieda or the generals. I just know that he can keep a secret to the grave."

"I agree. OK. I will send him ... tomorrow. Today you are mine."

"I like the sound of that," I say with a wide smile.

We eat and drink in silence for a while longer. I glance up as a swallow dares to sit on the table before us, inspecting its landscape. It doesn't display fear, despite its closeness. It spies a crumb near where we sit and darts to steal it before retreating to a safe distance again. I snigger at the similarity between the bird's actions and what I may plan to do with Egon.

"What's so funny?" Adala asks with a smile of joy on her face again.

"Nothing, just a private thought occurred to me as I watched the bird." I move, and it darts away in retreat, returning to the trees. My thoughts return to how to take the compound, but I force them from my mind. I wish to enjoy the time with Adala. She is becoming a part of me, and I can't understand my good fortune. We stay till late, until sunset overtakes the day, enjoying each other's company. "I had better go. I'm tired and need to prepare for tomorrow."

Adala sighs. "Yes, I suppose you must. I could sit with you forever, but we have our duties to do. I will send Ranulf."

"Ask him to come to my place with the plans."

"I will."

We rise and return to indoors. I say farewell and continue to my residence.

20

HATCH A PLAN

Sentinel arrives just after nine in the morning. I invite him in and close the door.

"I'm later than I intended, but I didn't want anyone following me, so I went on a mystery tour."

"You should've walked straight here as if everything was normal. Too late now. Drink?"

"No. I'm fine. Let's develop a plan to destroy this bastard."

I stare at him, impressed by the untypical earthy language. "You've been hanging out around me too long."

"Possibly."

I lead Sentinel into my little kitchen. He removes a folded piece of paper from inside his jacket, unfolds it, and lays it on the table. It's a map of the Heimstadt Security Compound, and we stand over it in conspiratorial contemplation.

"The entrance is *here*. A guardhouse on each side independently controls the gate and field and communicates to the primary control room *here*. We need to overpower both guardhouses and the primary control room to cripple the compound and cut the communication link," Sentinel outlines to me. "They store the equipment and heavy vehicles underground and bring them to the surface by these two elevators. There are separate personnel elevators." He points to the four other elevators, one attached to the control room. "There are watchtowers on top of each corner wall. These are manned 24 hours a day."

"We don't want to cripple the communication network. We just need to gain control of it," I recommend. "Outside personnel must think everything is normal, if noisy. What's the vast surface space used for?"

"Training of infantry troops."

"Are the guardhouses similar in layout to the other one?"

"Yes, exact copies."

"Good. Are there any hidden back doors along the rear wall?"

"No."

"Any underground tunnels people can move through to enter the compound?"

"Not that I'm aware of, unless Egon has recently constructed them, but my information says nothing has changed."

"Any other troops?"

"Barracks exist with a company of soldiers."

"You have any personnel carrying scooters?"

"No."

"Not even tucked away somewhere?"

Sentinel shakes his head.

"Hmm. Impregnable, isn't it?"

"That's why we have not attempted to break into it."

I study the plan, memorizing what Sentinel has told me. Afterward, I pace the floor, thinking. On coming back to the table where Sentinel continues to stand, I ask, "Does the force field cover the walls?"

"No. Just the entrance."

"And the top?"

"No."

I return to my pacing. Sentinel is watching me, expecting a revelation. The seed of a plan forms in my head. "How high can scooters rise from the ground?"

"Only 20 meters."

"But the troop carriers I saw rose much higher than that."

"Military vehicles can ascend to 200 meters."

"What's the distinction?"

"Commercial scooters have a built-in limiter that maintains a height ceiling for them. Military vehicles have it set to a higher value."

"Can you adjust the limiter?"

"They regulate the setting. There are severe penalties for anyone caught trying to tamper with them."

"But can you?"

Sentinel scratches his head. "No idea. I can find a mechanic and ask him."

I smile at him, schemes flashing from my eyes. "Get one for me. One that you can trust to keep absolute secrecy."

"Leave it to me. I will be back soon," Sentinel says as he leaves.

I continue studying the plan, devising an effective strategy to take over the compound. If I can execute what I intend, it may be as spectacularly unexpected as the earlier raid. There is a knock at the door. I don't know who is there, so I fold up the map and slip it into my inside jacket pocket. I answer the door, surprised to see Chancellor Korbinian.

"Hello, Halwende. I was only just informed you returned. Your escape from your incarceration is a relief." Korbinian has sly eyes that wander the room, spying for information.

I glare at him with contempt. "No thanks to you. You knew they were coming."

Korbinian pretends to be affronted at the accusation. "I didn't learn of the inspection before we entered the place."

I stare at him in unbelief. "What do you want?"

"I thought I saw Ranulf enter, and I wanted a quick word with him."

"He is not here."

"Pity. It was important. How did you escape?"

"My protecting angel rescued me. Now, if you don't mind, I'm busy."

Korbinian moves as if to leave but withdraws a gun from his jacket and fires at me. The bullet bounces off my protection generator field. He opens his eyes in surprise as I pull him into my quarters and slam the door shut, wrenching the piece from his hand as I shove him to the floor. He yells in fear as his rotund body rolls against a chair. I rush over and boot him in the stomach, making him curl into a fetal position and vomit. The stench fills the room, making me nauseated. "You pathetic excuse for a human being!"

Korbinian gasps for breath. "You will pay for this. I will tell the princess of your abhorrent treatment of me."

"Tell her whatever you want. I'll tell her you tried to kill me. I have the gun and the bullet to prove it. And I'm positive we weren't at that bar by coincidence. You set up the entire sting."

"That's a preposterous lie. Why would I do that? You gave us a significant victory with the confiscation of the weapons from the security compound."

"So why shoot me if you admire me so much? Am I gaining too much of Adala's attention? Or is Egon paying you to spy on her and keep him informed of her movements? I suspect both, although I can't figure out why Egon hasn't brought this rebellion to a halt if you can inform him of Adala's location. He wants that information the most."

"It is Princess Adala to you."

"She has given me leave to call her Adala."

Korbinian's eyes flicker with rage. He sits up and leans against a leg of the table. He's regained his composure enough to scheme how he might escape my presence, but I have no intention of letting him go now. He knows Sentinel and I are planning something, and I doubt he'll rest until he finds out, so he can get word to Egon. I'm undecided what to do in the meantime, though. Sentinel will return soon, and I don't want him to see the mechanic. That will only confirm his suspicions. I decide.

"How come you were not wounded by the bullet?" he asks, puzzled.

"Not your business." I retrieve the maser from the holster hooked on a stand nearby and place the power setting on stun. "Pleasant dreams." I fire the maser at him. He stiffens before slumping to the floor. What do I do with him now? I'll have to wait for Sentinel. He might suggest something. I sit and wait for Sentinel's return.

The wait is short. I hear another knock on the door and go to it, cracking it open. Sentinel has returned with a second person — the mechanic, I presume. I usher them inside. They both raise their eyebrows when they see Korbinian lying on the floor. "I see you're entertaining," Sentinel says, first glancing at Korbinian and then at me. "Is he dead?"

"No, only stunned. He suspected you of coming to my quarters and followed you. He then waited for you to leave because he came to assassinate me." I point to the gun and the used bullet I had retrieved and placed on the table. "He must be desperate to do something so rash. Do you have any suggestions on disposing of him? We can't allow him to get loose again until we complete our venture."

"I will tend to it. This is Guntram, by the way — one of the most devious mechanics I know."

"Just the person I want. Welcome to our little inner circle."

"My pleasure."

I glance at Korbinian. "We need to get him disposed of first," I say to Sentinel.

"Give me a minute then," Sentinel says and disappears out of the door.

We wait in silence until Sentinel returns with four others, who are pulling a cart with a man-sized box on it. They place Korbinian in the crate to hide him and haul him away. Guntram sits with an impish grin on his face the whole time.

"Where are they taking him?" I ask Sentinel.

"Somewhere out of harm's way until we decide what to do with him. It changes our tactics in how we were using him. Someone will ask questions."

"I'm sorry, but he was getting too dangerous. He'd have found out our activities, and we'll lose our element of surprise. And besides, I don't enjoy being shot."

"How did you come through that unscathed?"

"My little secret." I wink and look at Guntram. "Are you enjoying yourself?"

"It's not every day I get to see someone I loathe getting what they deserve."

I'm puzzled. "What is he to you?"

"Oh, really? He's as conniving and sniveling as they come, even before this started. Now, what is this with modifying scooters?"

I chuckle and Sentinel looks amused. "Sentinel believes you can change the height setting on them."

"Sure can, but how high? There's a machine limit, you know, and it affects other things."

"Like what?"

"Well, the higher you go, the slower the scooter is. We divert power from the propulsion drive to the lift drive."

"That makes sense, I suppose. The top of the cliff?"

Guntram breaks into a massive smile. "Easy, sir."

"Is it? And don't call me sir."

"OK, s ... well, I do it often — take a scooter out at night, adjust the height setting, and zoom up to the clifftop for business activities, then return and reset the limiter again. No one's the wiser."

I glance at Sentinel, stunned, and back to Guntram. "I don't need to know your business interests, but you're our man. So how long will ten to twenty scooter settings take?"

Guntram scratches his chin. "Half an hour, depending how many."

"Perfect."

"What's the go then?"

"I'll tell you when it happens. Just be ready for moonlight work soon."

"Will do, sir." Guntram cringes. "Sorry."

"That's OK. You can go. I presume Sentinel knows where to find you when we want you."

Sentinel nods.

"And I'm sure you'll keep this an absolute secret between the three of us."

"My lips are sealed. Pleasure doin' business with you." Guntram turns and leaves.

Sentinel puts his forefinger to his lips to silence me and walks to the door. He springs it open after a few seconds to reveal Guntram leaning by it, clearly intending to listen to our conversation. "Scatter, you tramp, before I put you away too."

"Don't get narky. Can't blame someone for trying." Guntram leaves this time, and Sentinel closes the door behind him.

I laugh at the comedy. "I take it you have experience."

"Yes, I have. Guntram isn't a gossip — but he does like to know things." Sentinel walks back to me. "I see you have a plan. Do you want to share it?"

"Not yet. I still need to develop it thoroughly, but you'll know first. And keep this secret from everyone but Adala for now."

"Will do."

21

STORMING THE COMPOUND

I gaze into Adala's eyes.

"Stay safe," she whispers.

"I will," I reply with pretended indifference. "And I will drive a troop carrier for you."

She laughs. "I want to see that."

We give each other a hug and I leave with the others to execute my plan, either with success or failure. I meet Sentinel outside Adala's residence, and we go off to join Guntram and the rest of the crew at the scooter assembly point. I've organized more attack personnel to congregate by the front gate at the designated time. We arrive at the rendezvous ten minutes later.

"How are we feeling?" I ask.

A general mumble of expectation for action reverberates throughout the group. "Are we doing this?" Guntram asks. "I wanna show you my skills."

I chuckle. "You'll do that soon enough. Let's move out."

Everyone gets into the scooters, and the drivers fly in formation toward the exit tunnel. I didn't realize that they had large scooter-sized tunnels to travel through until Sentinel told me. We go out to the surrounding landscape ten minutes later and speed away from the city, hugging the cliff face. The cool air is in my hair, and I lean my head back in delight at the feeling while thoughts of the impending challenge run through my brain. Doubts linger in the outskirts of my mind as sour memories flicker and intermingle with current expectations. My resolve clarifies as images of Adala cement my determination for the task ahead.

We stop and corral the scooters in a circle half an hour later. Guntram gets to work adjusting the limiters for the elevation. I pace the ground, working through the details of the plan, searching for weaknesses and improvements or options for when things veer off course.

"You'll wear your boots out before we get there," Sentinel warns as he walks toward me.

"Pre-performance nerves," I say with a tentative smile back to him when he catches up with me.

"That is understandable. What is on your mind?"

"Nothing, really. Just searching for shortcomings in the plan."

"It will be fine."

We stand together and gaze along the cliff and across the plain in front of it. Little obstructs the view. But cloud covers the sky, making it very dark. That is one reason we have chosen tonight for the mission. "Isn't this land used for farming or something?"

"No. It is reserve parkland. Property of the royal family. It is for public use, but they set aside areas for horses and other animals."

"Oh." I wonder if this charitable gesture continues under the current regime.

Guntram jogs up to us in the promised thirty minutes to adjust the scooters for the ascent. "All fixed, sir."

I roll my eyes at the 'sir' but decide not to reprimand him again. He's fixated on continuing the practice. "Good. Time to go then."

Sentinel and I return to the scooters, and the others get into their allocated machine. They start the vehicles, and we rise in the air, higher and higher until we reach the clifftop. As we move forward, we receive a slight jolt crossing the cliff's edge as the controls adjust for the changed ground level, but then speed up back in the city's direction. We return above the outskirts after another half an hour and to the cliff face overlooking the security compound fifteen minutes after that. The scooters settle out of sight on the grassy landscape, retreating from the precipice.

We disembark and congregate. "Do you all know your tasks?" I check.

They nod affirmation. "Well, some of us may not return, but I thank you for volunteering and for your bravery. Let's do it."

Three men approach me with abseiling equipment, including a set for me. I turn on the communicator that one of them hands me and switch it to the secured channel. "Testing," I say.

"Check."

"Check."

"And check."

"Check," Sentinel says.

"Can you set the gear up, including mine? I'll be over in a moment," I tell them.

I glance toward Sentinel, who is still with me. "You ready?"

"Yes. We'll be ready and waiting for your signal or before if the infiltration fails."

"Well, let's hope it doesn't come to that."

Sentinel points his eyes toward the cliff. "Have you done this before today?"

I give him a smug smile. "I competed in the sport on my world many times when I was young."

"You are not so young anymore."

"Look who's talking," I say, feigning to punch him in the stomach.

We both chuckle and glance at each other; the bond of friendship that has grown between us means we can say what's on our minds.

My abseiling partner comes over. "All set, Halwende."

"OK. Coming."

"Good luck," Sentinel says.

"Godspeed."

"... Godspeed."

I walk to where the other abseilers are and don my harness. After hooking the line to the anchor, I test the rigidity. It will support my weight with ease. The others have hooked onto their anchors and are waiting for my signal to start. Two will strike the far guard tower, and I with my partner will attack the tower below us. This is a risky drop. It depends on the guards in the front towers being lax and ignoring the cliff while we descend it. Fortune has blotted out moonlight at present, but lights still flood the compound, reflecting dim illumination up higher.

"Over we go," I say through the communicator and step backward over the cliff face, careful not to dislodge any pebbles or soil as I lean from the edge. I halt, facing outward from the precipice in a horizontal position. The others are likewise. "Drop."

We fall in unison, reducing the 70-meter distance at an ever-increasing speed until we are almost on the guardhouse roof. We engage our breaks and stop only centimeters from the roof. I nod to my partner, and we settle on the ridge. With the rope released, I retrieve the stimulator from my belt, swing over the side to the walkway below and through the guardhouse door, my companion two meters behind me. The two guards rise from their seats in surprise and their hands extend for their weapons, but I turn the stimulator on, and they drop to the floor, unconscious in seconds. We tie them up and take off our harnesses. Minutes later, "Clear," comes from the other crew. I breathe a sigh. So far, so good.

We both crouch and waddle out of the guardhouse, heading for the forward one. We are there within a minute. I nod. My partner opens the door and I incapacitate the guards. I get a similar, "Clear," from the others soon afterward. I retrieve my maser from its holster on my leg and my accomplice takes the repeating rifle from his back. Intent on leaving the guardhouse, I hear voices coming from the yard. "Stop," I command the others.

Two people are standing smoking cigarettes outside, conversing too softly for me to distinguish from this distance what they are saying. I can see the glow from the tips of their cigarettes as they draw in the smoke. It takes an eternity before they finish and return indoors. I breathe out my relief, and issue the command, "Go!"

My partner and I exit the guardhouse. He leaves to move to an elevator at the front by the near gatehouse. The other team, likewise, heads for the far gatehouse. I head for the control room elevator. After sending for the elevator, the door opens and I enter, preparing for the inevitable confrontation.

"Who the hell are ...?" one occupant roars before the stimulator beam drops the three guards to the floor. I tie them up and move over to the control desk. After finding what I'm searching for, I lock the elevator, preventing any surprises. "Secure," I say into the communicator and wait for the others, who are securing the gatehouses.

Soon after, the other team responds. "Secure." And another "Secure," from my partner.

"Start Overdrive!" Overdrive is the name we call the drop-off point for the scooters from the cliff. I glance at my watch. They should have assembled the ground forces by now, ready to storm the compound when the gates open. Five minutes go by before I see the gates pivot open. The others must see the scooters descending.

"What's going on up there? Why are the gates opening?" the desk communicator blurts.

I reply with the first words that come to me. "A malfunction. We're trying to rectify the problem."

"Well, get those gates closed a– What the hell are those people doing entering the compound?"

I cringe. They've discovered our surprise. "I think they want to collect something."

An alarm blares out over the yard moments later. The scooters descend to the ground, fanning out, creating a barrier around the perimeter. The invading rebels stream through the gates, racing to the heavy equipment elevators, ready to descend into the underground stores. They have brought the heavy artillery that we collected from the other raid. The gates close again once everyone is inside to prevent a surprise counterattack from that direction.

"Ready," I hear over the communicator. The strike forces are on the elevators. I make them both descend, watching them disappear below ground through the control room windows. Moments later, the first of the shots fire as the attack begins. I breathe out to relieve the tension and pray that casualties are low. A memory of disaster flashes back to me as I recall the events of my earlier debacle on my home planet many years ago, and I shiver when I consider the probability of a similar catastrophe. At least I'm resolved not to run like a coward this time.

"Incoming troop carriers."

I gaze up in reflex but see nothing. After frisking a stunned guard, I find his security card and exit the door into the compound, again searching for the inbound flyers. I watch them come, four of them.

I get my maser ready as they approach, placing the setting on maximum and aim. I wait until they come nearer and pull the trigger, disintegrating the closest one. The others veer for cover before I can take another shot. At least they have given up on entering the compound from above for now.

Intense fighting continues below, with the sound of gunshots and detonations spewing through the elevator openings at a constant rate. I should be there helping, but Sentinel refuses me, saying I would impede the training his people have internalized into their reflexes. Sentinel remains on the surface, so I walk over to him. "What do you think?"

"While fighting continues, both sides are still alive. Ask me when we hear silence."

"We should be with them."

"We have our jobs up here."

Moments later, an incoming rocket thunders into the compound and detonates in the center. Shrapnel and debris pierce the air, and we drop to the ground, hoping nothing hits us. Others scramble for the meager protection of their scooters after the conflagration, just before a second rocket explodes and careers with another spray of the deadly material.

"We have to stop this," I say.

"We can't do anything from here," Sentinel points out.

"What of the backup team?"

"They are grouping and hunting the enemy locations."

A massive blast resonates from the gates, but they hold for now. They are trying to blow the entrance so they can gain access without further losses from overhead. Another detonation rocks the doors. They have dented them. It won't be long before they have them open at this rate. I must do something. I get off the ground and race to the nearest elevator. On entering, I travel to the parapet above and search for the source of the assault.

Streamers emanate from a building nearby when another rocket discharges. I aim my maser and pull the trigger, stopping whatever was there from continuing with its attack. An instant barrage of bullets starts from another direction toward me, a bullet striking my arm. I scurry to a different location before I am annihilated. Peeking at my arm, I see it is bleeding, but it's just a flesh wound. I peer over the protecting wall to search for other attacking sites, particularly in the direction of gunfire. They launch another rocket at the gate with a flash from a space near that source. As I aim again, I extinguish another part of the attack. I move afterward, but not before another volley of bullets comes toward me. This time two lodge in me, one in my injured arm, the other in my shoulder. I castigate myself for not wearing my personal protector. Last minute distractions made me completely forget it. It's too late now. I slump to the parapet gallery in agony, knowing that I'm bleeding badly. Gazing back into the compound, I still hear fighting below ground. It sounds less intense, and I perceive with a smile that we are winning the battle. This was always a high-risk strike, but that didn't deter me. I sense we can win if we can prevent the outside troops from breaking in. I grow weaker but crawl to view the streets again. Gunfire starts in several locations surrounding the compound. Our forces must have located the regime's ones. A fierce fight starts. They fire another rocket at the gate. My vision blurs, but I take aim at that location and fire. That rocket launcher is no more, too. More bullets fire toward me but miss, all but one. That hits my chest as I crouch to leave, and I flop to the walkway, gasping for breath. I lie there unable to move, breathing with difficulty. My lung has collapsed from the wound. I cough and blood dribbles from my mouth. I can't do anymore, but I must for the sake of the mission. These thoughts continue to hound me as I lose consciousness.

22

RECOVERY

"Sir, we are under attack. What should we do?"

Sweat pours from my face as I see the troop movements and the slaughter that we are suffering. "I will return soon," I tell my adjutant. When I turn to my family, I say, "I must go."

"Yes, you go," my wife says.

I run off to the waiting vehicle and shoot into the sky to report to my headquarters.

As I crouch over my command console, I direct the forces into a coordinated counterattack. We appear to be gaining traction as the troops impede and repel the main spearheads of the enemy. I am regaining control.

"Who'll tell him?" I hear whispered behind me.

"Not me."

"I can't."

"Why are you two whispering?" I ask as I swivel in my seat to glare at my underlings.

They both look guilty and intimidated. One gains the courage to say, "We have grave news for you, sir."

"What is it? Don't leave it hanging there."

"Well … it's just that … People have informed us that …" The person gulps. "Your wife and daughter are dead, killed by a rocket attack, sir."

My world ends in that cataclysmic moment. I slump in my chair and rock my head as I cradle it in my hands. "No, not Genevieve, not Charlotte, no ..."

My brain fuzzes and distorts, and I sense a voice. "Halwende?" it asks, distress and weariness plain in the tone.

"Not Genevieve. Not my beautiful Charlotte," I whisper from nowhere.

My head clears and intense pain spears from my arm and chest. My eyes are closed. As I open them, I see Adala sitting by my bed. Her face is near to mine. She has red eyes as if she's been crying, and she looks tired.

"You look like shit," I blurt out before I realize it.

Adala looks hurt and then laughs. "You're not looking too good yourself."

"Where am I?"

"You are in our hospital."

I try rising but am too weak and flop back again. "What happened?"

"You have several bullet wounds and lost much blood." Adala caught her breath in sudden distress. "We thought you dead. Ranulf spent ages finding you after the fighting. He can fill in the details."

Panic rises inside me. "Did we succeed?"

Adala smiles. "Yes, we did. We retrieved the troop carriers and heavy weaponry, just as you had planned and wanted. We have hidden them."

"That's good. I am pleased. How many died?"

"Ask Ranulf, but fortune was on our side in the raid. Egon's forces suffered far greater casualties. Thanks to your efforts, I am told. But I talk too much. You need rest."

"I can see you're tired too, but please stay for a while. How long have you been here?"

Adala lowers her gaze and whispers, "Since they brought you in here."

"And how long is that?"

"Twenty-three hours."

"That long."

Silence floats between us again.

"Who are Genevieve and Charlotte?"

I stare at Adala in shock. "Why?"

"You were mumbling their names just before you regained consciousness."

I glance away in distress. "Genevieve was my wife, and Charlotte, my daughter. They died many years ago."

"Oh. I am sorry."

"I must have dreamed of them."

Adala brushes the back of her hand across my cheek and rubs it to comfort me. I return my gaze to her and smile.

"Was your little girl beautiful?"

"Yes, she was. She took after Genevieve." I release a grim chuckle.

"I'm sure she had your features too."

We are quiet again. After several minutes, Adala says, "You should rest, and so should I. I'm so happy that you are alive."

"So am I."

Adala rises to go. She bends and kisses me on the lips. "I will return soon. I'll send Ranulf to fill you in on what happened."

"OK." I'm suddenly exhausted as Adala leaves the room, and I fall asleep instantly.

I wake later with Sentinel standing in the doorway staring at me. Grogginess from sleep and the sedatives take time to dissipate. He is leaning against the doorpost with his arms folded, looking at me in the now-familiar stolid stare. "You gave me quite a scare," he says.

"Adala tells me I owe you for saving my life. I thank you."

"I thank you. Without you doing your deeds, neither of us would be here."

I gesture to the seat. "Come. Sit and tell me what happened."

Sentinel strolls to the chair and sits. He gathers his thoughts. "I had much to explain to Princess Adala. She was not pleased."

"Scared? Frightened?"

Sentinel sighs and smiles. "She was. You realize she didn't leave your side until you regained consciousness?"

"Yes. She told me. I hope she is resting now. So, tell me. What happened? I'm unsure when I passed out, but from my recollection, the backup outside was repulsing the attack on the compound, and the fighting underground was abating somewhat."

"You are right in your assessment. Trouble from outside ceased after the last firing of your weapon — and believe me, everyone knew when you fired it. The external party cleaned up the rest before they retreated. Inside, Egon's forces put up a strong resistance, and that is where we suffered our casualties. We overcame them and brought things under control. We retrieved the equipment we wanted and started rallying to move out. That is when I noticed you were missing. I told the others to retreat to the rendezvous point and leave me a scooter. It took me ages to find you. You were in a dire state and near death. I forewent any stealth and rushed you to the nearest tunnel as fast as I could so our hospital could treat you."

"That was risky."

"I know. No fallout yet, but it's still early. Adala isn't the only one with affection for you ... in my own way."

My heart melts with Sentinel's admission. I perceive that is not something he seldom admits, if ever. "I feel a deep bond of friendship with you too."

"Well, that's the course of events in a nutshell."

"And you've stored the equipment in a safe location?"

"Yes. They will not discover them."

"Good."

Sentinel stares at me, intrigued. "Why do I sense this raid is only the first part of your intentions?"

"Maybe because you could be right. But don't ask me what's next yet. I don't know myself."

"Well, it can wait. You need your rest before we consider any next stage."

"We mightn't have the luxury of waiting. Egon won't suffer humiliation without retaliation. No. He will strike back and hard."

"Let me do the worrying for now. You regain your strength. For Adala, if for no other reason."

I raise my eyebrows but offer no comment.

"I must leave." Sentinel stands up to go.

"I appreciate your coming to see me."

"You're welcome." Sentinel walks out, leaving me to my thoughts.

It took several days before anyone, especially Adala, would allow me to even think of getting out of bed. The day has now arrived, and I gingerly touch my feet to the floor. My chest and arm still hurt, but not too much. Clutching the bed's corner, I stand up, remove my hand from the support and start walking. My body is feeble, but I soon find enough strength in my legs to walk with confidence. I'm eager to be active again. Any gossip about Egon's movements interests me. I search for clothes to wear, but the wardrobe in my room is empty. That is a problem. I can't escape the hospital in my gown, not without people sniggering or worse.

I go to the nurse's station. "Can someone get my clothes for me, please?"

"Why? You aren't going anywhere yet."

"I am ready to leave. I have things to do."

"You're not going anywhere until the doctor says so."

I am frustrated by the brick wall confronting me. "We'll see what Princess Adala has to say about that."

"They were her instructions."

I stare at her. "Wait till I see her. She's not my mother."

"You don't have to wait long," the nurse replies with a smirk, peering past me.

I glance around, and Adala is there.

"Wait long for what?" Adala asks.

"You have no right telling them to keep me here."

Adala beams. "Oh, I don't? You know I am the princess."

"You are their princess, not mine."

Adala feigns hurt feelings and flutters her eyelashes. "I thought I was."

My heart softens and my frustration melts, looking at the goddess before me acting so innocent and fragile. "You're intolerable," I say, walking away in a huff as fast as my condition allows me. They laugh behind me.

"It's not funny," I grumble.

"I'd better mend his feelings," Adala says, and her footsteps catch up to me. "You're getting back to normal," she says when she gains my side.

"I hate being stuck in here. I need to know what's happening."

Adala becomes serious and says, "Let's go somewhere private." She leads me to a park on the hospital grounds.

Even though underground, it's lit with unique lighting to represent the sun, and the landscapers have designed the garden with artificial lawns and flowers. It's vacant at present, but I can imagine convalescing patients spending long hours here, basking in the artificial sunlight and the colorful landscape. It exudes a sense of peace and serenity almost as much as a real garden, calming my current frustrations. Bench seats stand in random locations. We sit on one.

I glance at her and perceive she has a matter on her mind. "What is it?"

"You have a price on your head. Egon is furious and wants you back. They think you were behind the raid on the security compound."

"He got that right."

"I am afraid for you."

"You don't have to worry. I can take care of myself. In fact, I've been thinking of the next step. I must return to the palace."

"What?" Adala exclaims in alarm. "You cannot. You will get captured again."

"No, I won't." I glance around to see if we're alone in the garden. We are. "Your father mentioned secret passageways, and I discovered a secret back entrance that no one knows of, apparently."

Adala looks puzzled. "Secret passages? ... secret entrances? Are you sure you're feeling alright?"

"How else do you think I escaped?"

"I'm going with you."

"No, you can't."

"Where is this secret door then?"

"No. Not yet. I don't want you getting any ideas."

"But, Halwende, how can I bear losing you again?"

"You won't. Don't worry. I won't be long ... as soon as I escape from here, that is."

Adala wraps her arms around me and hugs me tight before looking at me, pleading with me to reconsider. When she sees my resolve, she relents. "OK. Go then. But if you don't come back, I will never forgive you."

I hug her in response. "I must return to gaze into your magnificent eyes again."

She hugs me tighter at the comment.

We rise and go indoors. I am released from the hospital a day later.

23

THE PORTAL

Sentinel and Guntram stand before me next to a scooter in an underground workshop. Guntram has just readjusted the height limiter so I can rise to the cliff's summit again. I intend to travel to the waterfall via the clifftop with no eyes spying on me after dark.

"Are you sure?" Sentinel asks.

"Yes, I am. I need to go alone. Adala knows I do."

"It's just risky with no backup."

"Far better if I have problems. Only one of us gets into trouble then. Besides, I'm carrying my handy weapons." I tap the maser in its holster.

"I dislike it, but so be it then. Return soon and intact."

"I will."

I hop on the scooter and head for the tunnel exit. The door opens at my initiation, and I rush into the open air next to the cliff. I fly far away from the city before I rise to the mesa plain. After turning around, I go back the way I came along the precipice edge and 200 meters inland. An hour later, I pass over the river that supplies the waterfall. I cross it and travel alongside to the cliff edge. I then hover over nothing but the cliff base far below me. As I descend, I find the ledge leading to the escape tunnel. On traversing it, I enter the tunnel entrance, landing the flyer and hopping off it.

It is how I remember it. After walking to the door, I press my ear against it, listening for guards — a pointless exercise with the waterfall's thunder in the background. I get my maser out and press the concealed button that opens the door. It swings clear, and I dart through to the inside tunnel. The door closes behind me.

No one is in the tunnel, and I hug the wall as I slink along it to the intersection with the main trunk. As I stand hidden at the end, I listen to check for interlopers and to gain the nerve to peek around the corner both ways. There is no one there. After sneaking around the corner, I creep to the portal. It is only 100 meters away, so it doesn't take long to traverse the distance. It is as I remember it. A small entrance, ten meters square, and a smooth black slab in the far wall. I approach the portal, standing a meter away when I stop. I extend my left arm toward it.

"Who are you?" the ethereal voice asks.

"I'm Halwende," I say, interested where the conversation might go.

"Where is your origin?"

I am puzzled why it asks, and what answer it wants. I shrug and tell the truth. "I am from Eridu."

The portal suddenly shimmers and becomes translucent. *"Enter,"* it says.

I stare with amazement at the opening, anxious over what's inside and whether I will escape again. I shrug my shoulders. It is why I came here. I walk in and, as expected, the shimmer returns and changes to the opaque obsidian.

As I examine the cavern, a vast space opens before me with many machines humming with energy. I wander around, examining each machine, wondering what they are for and what powers them. At the back of the chamber, I discover a large panel, and I'm enlightened. This is the power source for the cloaking, but I see another panel that supplies power to the force fields protecting the palace and security compounds. Circuit breaker switches, with labels underneath them, project from the front of the panel. I see the one for the Heimstadt Security Compound and test my theory by swinging the lever to the off position. We should hear a commotion over the loss of their force field soon. I chuckle to myself. Won't they get a shock? I scan the board and see breakers for various sections of the palace. This gives me an idea for Adala to regain control.

I inspect the room more and sense I've seen this design of machinery before somewhere. I scratch my head and then realize that they are of Eriduan origin. Why is Eriduan equipment on this planet? They must have visited the planet before the inhabitants hid from the galaxy. They may have been the people who fought over the mineral. I search around and spy a glowing blue crystal substance in one corner. I go to it and hold one up to the light. It has a subtle elegance to it, but it bears no sign it might be a power source. If so, it lasts a prolonged period, as these machines have existed for centuries. I drop the crystal and search again, now understanding why they deleted this room's purpose from the files, but I don't understand why the portal permitted me to enter. It must unlock and open only for those of Eriduan descent. Logical, I suppose — if this equipment comes from Eridu. But what clue confirmed I am Eriduan? I can't believe it just trusted me. I must visit the library and check the records for answers.

The switch room has no more information I can glean, so I decide to return before Adala misses me. I fear I am becoming attached to her too. I just need to learn the door's opening mechanism. As I stand before the portal, I stare at it, wondering what to do. I reach out to touch it, and, as I do, it changes, as before, and opens. That was easy. It must keep a record of eligible users. I walk through and it turns to ebony again. After creeping to the end of the alcove, I listen for evidence of anyone else in the tunnel, but it remains silent. I scamper to the branch tunnel and hasten through the exit, out the external tunnel to my transport behind the waterfall. I breathe out, not realizing that I had been holding my breath, and mount the scooter.

The flyer lifts off the ledge and rises to the top of the precipice. I accelerate to top speed and head back. A commotion is happening in the Heimstadt Security Compound as I pass above, and I smile with satisfaction. As I approach the place of my intended descent, I become confused about where I had risen from the cliff floor. I must have passed it, but nothing is familiar as I travel. After judging I have already passed it, I fly to the edge. As I move from land to air, the engine sputters and dies. I panic. The scooter free-falls at increasing speed. What can I do? The engine won't start, no matter how often I press the start button. The ground is coming at me faster by the second. On realizing my inevitable fate, I relax and sit in the seat, waiting for the crash. What a way to end my life! Adala will hate me now. I promised her I would return.

Impact occurs. The scooter rips apart, and I fly into the air, jettisoning from the debris of the wreck. My body hits the ground hard and rolls ... and rolls ... and rolls until I blackout.

24

PRISON

"What have we here?" I hear a person saying as he kicks my ribs.

"Don't know," someone else says. "Must be an escapee."

"What do we do with him?"

"Better take him back. Don't want trouble, and there's so much paperwork when someone's missing."

"He's in poor condition. Looks like he's been in a crash."

"Can't you see? There are parts of a scooter strewn everywhere. It's not one of ours. He must have stolen one after he escaped and crashed it. Funny, there wasn't a report of anyone escaping." He shrugs as though he's already lost interest in the mystery. "He'll need to go into the infirmary when we return. He doesn't look too good. We'll say he got injured in the mine. They aren't interested in paperwork for that."

"What do you make of this? Looks to be a holster or something."

"Hmm. Can't see a gun that goes in it. Must have lost it when he crashed. We'd better remove it or there'll be questions."

One of them removes my holster from my waist and throws it away, but my maser is missing.

"Check his wrists. What are they ... and that thing?"

"That's a trinket. He can keep that but confiscate the rest."

They take my wrist lasers and I castigate myself for not hiding them, but I'm so sore. I wonder what's broken. At least I still have my protector field bracelet.

"OK. Let's get him to the scooter then."

My body is lifted, one set of hands under my shoulders and another under my ankles. Shards of pain wrack me as they manhandle me. They dump me into the craft. I open my eyes to put faces to the two voices. Men wearing security uniforms are standing above me.

"You'll be in trouble for trying to escape when we get you back to camp," the first one says when he notices I'm awake. He's obese and lax in his manner. I suspect he only does the job because it pays well. He is unkempt.

The other person is not much better. I wonder if they're friends from the same village and chose the job because it was easy with good pay and little harassment. They aren't menacing or capable of withstanding any resistance from attack. Unfortunately, I am too injured to do more, or I could test their resolve, although I see a taser baton on each of them. I have a quick scan on the ground before we leave to locate my maser, and I spot it lying in the grass nearby. Making a mental note of any geographic pointers for when I return to fetch it, I lie back and close my eyes again.

Their scooter rises, and we travel into a compound meant to keep people in instead of out. I must have grossly overshot my descent location and come within proximity of this prison, but I don't understand why the scooter just cut out the way it did. It must have had an engine fault. The gates close behind me and a brief time later, I am placed on a stretcher and hauled into the infirmary, where a doctor checks out my injuries.

"Nothing serious," he concludes. "Couple of broken ribs and concussion. He should be ready for work tomorrow."

"Good," the first guard says. "We don't want trouble."

It amazes me that no one has bothered to check my identity. They must receive so many inmates that keeping track is more annoying than it's worth. An escape plan is pointless at present as I wouldn't get very far with my injuries. Since I need to understand my predicament first and seek the weaknesses in the place's layout, I lie back and sleep.

Rough shaking wakes me sometime later. "Time to eat," a nurse says. I open my eyes to a rugged-looking woman, fatigued and unkempt as if she's run off her feet every day. Her demeanor is strictly official, and I can't find a smile on her anywhere. She is clearly tired of the daily repetitive tedium. I rise to a sitting position, and she places a tray of food and drink on a trolley that she maneuvers over my waist.

"Thank you," I say.

She looks at me strangely, as if anyone expressing their appreciation for what she does is a rare occurrence. She offers a reluctant, "You're welcome," and walks away.

I taste the meal. It is bland and uninviting, but it's food, so I eat it. Afterward, a bored official asks me how I received my injuries. I just tell him I tripped and fell, which he writes on a pad, satisfied a record exists for bureaucracy's sake. He stands and leaves.

The next day, they unceremoniously discharge me from the hospital and order me to return to the barracks, except I didn't come from one. I wander the camp until I am befriended by someone and told of a spare bunk in his hut, so I follow him and take possession of the bed, unsure of what tomorrow will bring.

25

THE MINE

An alarm blares before sunrise and I wake confused by the commotion. Everyone in the barracks is busy rising and readying for the day. I decide it is wise to copy them and start looking for cues. We rush to a mess hall where we get served the resemblance of food from receptacles containing mass-produced gruel and bread and not much else. The others are skin and bone, malnourished — something to expect if I get to stay here long.

I find a bench seat away from the main assembly to keep to myself. But others surround me before long.

One of them, sitting across from me, glances at me with curiosity. "You're new. Where did you come from?" He has a drawn face and a shaven scalp. Worn-out clothes hang on him.

I am confused about how to respond. "They caught me wandering nearby and threw me in here."

"Bastards. They don't care. I'm Panther. This is Rickshaw." He points to the person next to him who has an Asiatic face.

"Hi. I'm ... Hal," I say, deciding to give an alias in case news of me filters through from Heimstadt.

"You have a strange accent."

"Just a condition of mine. So ... what happens here?"

Panther chuckles. "You'll find out soon enough. You'll wish they hadn't caught you. We'll be going to the mine soon to collect the ore for them. Cheap labor. They just feed us, and they do little of that. I was thirty kilograms heavier when I got here. I'm nothing but skin and bone now. Still, I'm one of the luckier ones, thanks to Rickshaw here. He gets other supplies now and then. We'd better eat up before we have to move." He grabs his spoon and starts shoveling the gruel into his mouth.

I do the same.

A siren blares not long after I finish eating, and everyone rises and walks out in line. They deposit their dirty plates and utensils in a bin on the way, and I mimic the procedure to blend into the group. I stay near Panther and Rickshaw, as it's clear they know how to survive here. We segregate into gangs of twenty and head off out of the camp into the mine entrance's gaping mouth. Guards on either side deter anyone from escaping. The light decreases as we enter the mine adit; the tunnel is lit with artificial illumination of a design different from that in Adala's complex. Our group veers off to the left, the members swaggering as they go, clearly in no hurry to get to our destination, and the guards don't seem to care either. We arrive at the mine face. Everything is manual. They use no mechanical equipment. I can't believe the picks and shovels lined up to one side for us.

"Is this how you dig the ore?" I ask, holding up my pick for inspection.

"Yeah. What other way is there?"

"Don't you use machinery or explosives even?"

Panther and Rickshaw stare at each other, puzzled. "Never heard of mining machinery," Panther says, "and they wouldn't let us handle explosives. We might start getting ideas."

I shake my head.

"You're sure you're from around here?" Rickshaw asks, an investigative gleam in his eye.

"I had difficulties talking as a child. A speech impediment."

Rickshaw looks at me with suspicion but lets the topic drop.

"Come on, peasants," a guard calls, "get into it before we need to encourage you." He slaps his taser baton with his palm a few times for emphasis.

I glance at the others and copy the ones using the picks to attack the mine face. Perspiration comes quickly as the work increases my metabolism in the confined space and poor ventilation. The labor is hard and relentless, with breaks for lunch and to quench our thirst. They finally announce the end of the shift, and we congregate to trudge back to camp. It's such an inefficient means of extracting a small amount of mineral deposit. We barely dislodged a hundred kilograms for the day, although I've been told it's valuable.

I wipe the sweat from my brow as we walk. I am next to Panther and Rickshaw. "Who owns this mine?" I ask them.

"Egon, who else?" Rickshaw whispers.

"Why are you whispering?"

"We must say 'The Imperial Emperor' when we speak his name," explains Panther.

"What rubbish!"

"You," a guard shouts, "Less talking and more walking, or you'll get this." He waves his baton at me.

I nod and stay silent for the rest of the return journey to the camp.

We wash off the dirt and sweat, and the others don fresh clothes. That presents me with a problem as I only have the clothes I'm wearing. Panther sees my predicament and offers me some spare clothing of his, us being of similar size. I thank him and dress quickly.

"We'll get Rickshaw to source more for you tonight."

The evening meal is tasteless mash with a small serve of dried-out meat. I resolve to escape from here — if only to get decent food.

We stroll back to the huts in no hurry. A common room stands attached to the barracks, with an outside space furnished with benches and tables for inmates' use. I sit on one of the benches, and Panther and Rickshaw join me. Panther looks at me in a way that suggests I don't convince him of my identity. Rickshaw is similarly wary.

Finally, Panther asks the question that is on both their minds. "Are you a spy?"

"No. I am not."

"Silly question. You wouldn't tell me if you were. Destroys the purpose. Who are you then? You're not one of us. You're confused as if you've never seen this place, or you only use tools as a last resort. The blisters on your hands bear witness to your lack of experience with manual labor."

"That doesn't mean much," I say. "I could have been an office worker."

"True."

"And you? What's your story?"

"That is long and convoluted and boring."

"Try me."

Panther stares at me to discern whether I am genuinely interested or just a spy fishing for any suspicion of treason to the current ruling regime. "They captured me in a raid on the rebels several months ago. They determined I was of no propaganda or intelligence value, so they sent me here. Maybe you've learned of the rebels? The princess of the deposed king leads them."

"I know of them," I say warily.

"What is your allegiance in the matter?"

"I have no fealty," I say, which is fundamentally truthful.

"You must have an opinion," Rickshaw insists. "Is life rosier now or before?"

I glance away to decide what to reveal. They seem honest, but I need to exercise caution because of the reward for my capture. I'm unsure whether the news has reached here and what temptation it would present for these inmates. "I will tell you, but first answer my question, and then I'll consider yours. What is your allegiance and why?"

"That's two questions," Panther says, "but I'll answer both. I'm dedicated to Princess Adala and will cherish the day we're rid of the current rogue of a ruler. He's detestable. His interest is only in increasing his wealth and power. He rewards sycophants with luxury and leaves the rest of us to struggle. These camps didn't exist before he came to power. We're here to 'see the error of our ways.' Most of us die here from malnutrition and overwork."

I gaze at Panther, impressed by his earnestness, and perceive Rickshaw is also impressed. After glancing around to assure myself there is no one in earshot, I take them into my confidence. "You were right in your assessment of my origin. I'm a foreigner and I know more about the rebels than just hearsay. I am one of them. I crashed my scooter near here and the guards that found me brought me here. It seems it was less hassle for them to bring me here than undergo the bother and stress of reporting me."

"That'd be right, the lazy sods," Rickshaw says, nodding. "Can't upset their lucrative conditions guarding us."

"I'm fortunate that they are of that opinion and that they don't recognize me. There's a price on my head."

Both Panther and Rickshaw jump, surprised by the revelation, and their eyes widen.

"You're ...?" Rickshaw begins.

"... the troublemaker?" Panther finishes.

I nod but peer around. "Don't say that loudly."

"There's little to fear here. Most of us are rebels, but I get your point. It must not become general knowledge. We glean most of our information from overhearing the guards gossiping. They've been fidgety of late because of the main security compound raid. Rumor says it could change the power balance between Egon and the rebels. The word is that a mysterious beam destroys whatever it encounters. Is that yours?"

"Yes. I own unfamiliar types of weapons, but one's missing, and they removed the others from me when I crashed."

Panther whispers, "We'll have to protect you. Don't tell anyone else what you just told us. I'm not sure who we can trust to keep your secret."

"Now you tell me," I say with a grin. "But I need to return. Adala ... Princess Adala is relying on me."

"Well, good luck with that. There is a reason they located this camp here. It is too distant from anywhere to escape."

Depressed at this intelligence, I nonetheless resolve not to give up, not yet. There must be a way. "Can't we capture a scooter or something?"

"About the only thing they're particular about around here is keeping those scooters under lock and key 24/7. They're only used for ferrying guards to and from the camp. There's little chance of hijacking one. Others have tried and not lived to tell the tale."

"I'll think of something." I lapse into contemplation of how to steal a scooter. I will have to scout the parking compound over the next few days to find the weak points in their security. There are always weak points.

26

THEY'VE CAPTURED ADALA

The drudgery and routine in the camp have not changed since I arrived. I get the sense that they enforce the boredom so that we will lose our motivation to escape. The ore mining is a joke. The quantity collected is minute compared to what I understand of the energy requirements for the realm are. Hard manual labor is the aim, not an economic return, although Egon doesn't have to pay any wages or other overheads. The state takes care of us, being prisoners.

Ten days after arriving at the camp, I see Panther and Rickshaw whispering to each other, glancing at me furtively as if they know confidential information and are deliberating whether to share it with me. I push the issue and walk over to them. "What's the secret?"

"Nothing," Rickshaw says, a hint of nonchalance in his voice as if they were discussing the contents of the morning meal.

Panther is uncertain. "We've heard a disturbing rumor."

"What rumor?"

"A guard has told us they've captured the princess."

I focus my full attention on Panther now. "Princess Adala?"

"What other princess is there?"

"How reliable is the source?"

"He's usually right, and the guards have an air of optimism as if they think events are swaying in Egon's favor."

I pace back and forth for a moment, absorbing the information. As I return to Panther and Rickshaw, I announce, "We must rescue her."

Rickshaw gives a cynical humph. "Yeah ... right. We'll just escape, hop on a scooter, and rush to the palace."

I stare at him. "That's exactly what I intend doing. Thanks for the suggestion."

The idea agitates Panther. "How? You know what happens to anyone who fails."

"I'll think of something." I spend the rest of my day devising scheme after scheme for how I can escape. Each one has its pitfalls and is fraught with danger, but I must get back and rescue Adala from Egon's clutches.

The next morning at breakfast, Rickshaw strolls over to the table as usual. He has what, at first glance, appear to be earrings dangling from his ears. I lower my gaze to take another spoonful of the gruel they serve us for our meager sustenance. Rickshaw sits, and I glance at him again, my expression changing to an astonished stare as I recognize the ornaments.

Rickshaw is uncomfortable with the attention I am giving him. "What?"

"Where did you get those?" I say, pointing to the trinkets.

"I won them playing dice with a guard last night. Why?"

"They are mine, and they aren't earrings."

Rickshaw takes one of them off to inspect it more closely. It is a circular shape, the size of a wrist, my wrist. "They don't look special to me."

"Well, they are weapons. Fortunately, they only work when I wear them."

He removes the other wristband from his ear and looks at the pair of them, puzzled, still none the wiser as to their role. "And here I thought I could sell them for extra rations."

I hold out my hand for him to give them to me. He is reluctant but relents and hands them back. I place one on my wrist, looking around to check if anyone's watching. Nobody's interested in us at present. "Here ... I'll show you. See that mug?" A small metal cup sits on the table two meters away. Aiming the wrist laser at it, I project a quick burst of energy at it. The mug disintegrates before our eyes.

The spectacle amazes Rickshaw. He grabs my forearm. "Now what?"

"I don't know yet. But they could be our ticket out of here."

27

BREAKOUT

True to my word, I devise a workable plan for our escape and discuss the plot after a meal with my two accomplices. We decide to move the following evening under the cover of darkness. Panther and Rickshaw have convinced those they trust to incite a general disturbance in the prison when the time comes. The day proceeds at the usual boring pace, and we return to camp at sunset. We clean up and eat our evening meal, settling afterward as if retiring for the night soon.

I put my wrist lasers on and go to Panther and Rickshaw. I turn my protection field on, too. "Are we ready?"

"Ready as we'll ever be," Panther says.

Panther has detailed the camp and restricted zones to me where they keep the scooters and firearms. We meander to the scooter compound and wait for the furor. I am nervous and fidgety, wanting to start the action and worried that one of us, or all of us, will get hurt or killed in the escape.

An explosion shatters the silence, and everyone starts shouting and yelling. "That's our cue," Panther says. Guards run across the camp to the source of the commotion, and I have my chance. Using the wrist lasers as cutters, I cut through the wire into the secure zone.

No alarm has sounded yet, so the three of us thread through the fence and toward the scooters. The distance is short but cover to hide behind is scant with the compound's lights blazing the darkness away, so we crouch and waddle our way toward the gate. We are nearly there with no interference.

A guard emerges from nowhere. "What's happening here? You trying to escape? Is that the reason for the noise?" He points his rifle at Panther but can change his aim to any of us. It is doubtful whether he could shoot all three of us before we overpower him, but I don't take any chances. I point a laser and fire, a hole appearing in his chest where his heart once was. Panther and Rickshaw gape in astonishment, but we need to move before anyone else notices.

We reach the scooter's compound gate, locked as expected, and I blast our way into the enclosure. Guards notice the disturbance and start congregating at both locations to bring the commotion under control and check if it's a distraction for something more sinister, which it is. We dart to a scooter. Rickshaw tries to start it with no success at first. I search for an exit without encountering resistance. The compound sits on the outer edge of the camp, allowing us to escape by blasting a hole through the exterior fence for the scooter to fit.

Movement distracts me on the other side of the inner fence as investigating guards spot their comrade with a hole in his chest and then notice the hole in the fence. They start shooting indiscriminately at everything in sight.

"We need weapons," Panther says. "We need to get to the arsenal and arm ourselves."

"It's too far away," I say.

"We'll get slaughtered if we don't. You can't keep them at bay while Rickshaw starts the scooter. They will call the other guards soon and surround us."

"Where is the armory then?"

"Over there," Panther says, pointing to a building twenty meters from us within the scooter compound.

"What idiot has their arsenal in their transportation compound?" I say in disbelief. "OK. Get ready to dart over there."

We leave Rickshaw and sneak closer, using the other scooters as cover. When we can't get any closer, I say, "Ready?"

"Ready."

I aim both of my wrists and blast a hole through the building wall for Panther. He darts across amid shots fired from the guards now they have detected someone to shoot. Weaving expertly, Panther dodges the bullets. I search for the source of the attack and start my counter-offensive, driving them back and away from the compound with the lethal rays I fire at them. Impatiently, I wait for Panther to re-emerge from the armory and Rickshaw to start a scooter to flee the onslaught. I don't think we can withstand the army of guards for long, even with my superior firepower.

Rickshaw revives the scooter, and it throbs with energy for our escape. He is waving to me to mount the vehicle, but I must wait for Panther, each second torture. Finally, Panther's face emerges from the hole, weapons wrapped around him as if he is a gunslinger from an ancient western movie I used to watch as a child. I wave at him to hurry up and, at the same time, fire more laser bolts in the general direction of the guards to give him cover. He sprints over to me, and we backtrack to Rickshaw, who is hiding behind the scooter's shell to avoid being shot. Panther shoots his guns as we get onto the scooter, and I shoot a mammoth hole in the fence for our exit.

Shots hurl at us as Rickshaw gets into the driver's seat to make our escape. Both Panther and I fire back at the shooters. We hear yelps of pain as our aims reach their marks and reduce the resistance. When I glance back, I spot them retreating but circling for a better shot. "Let's get going, Rickshaw!" I yell.

The scooter lifts, rotates to the opening in the fence, and Rickshaw turns the throttle to full acceleration, threatening to throw both Panther and me from it. We dash through the barrier and away. I turn and notice guards emerging from cover, shouting for us to stop. Several are running toward the other scooters to give chase. I realize, too late, that we should have incapacitated them before we left. Before long, four scooters are on our tail and closing in on us.

"Move faster!" I shout. "They're catching us."

"This is as fast as it goes. I must've chosen the slowest one. Sorry."

"We might be dead in a minute if we can't lose this lot."

The guards on the other scooters fire at us. Panther and I take aim and fire back. I hit one scooter front on with my laser, and it careens out of control, rolling and splaying the guards over the ground as it comes to a stop. Panther shoots another driver's face, and the scooter careens and flips. The other two are catching up. I dispatch one with little trouble, but the other is dodging our shots. The driver has learned from the others' mistakes and swerves to make himself a harder target. The two with him fire at us, the bullets ricocheting from the scooter's metalwork. Our scooter momentarily skews, but Rickshaw brings the machine back under control. I take careful aim and damage the chasing scooter to incapacitate it. We speed off to the sound of yells and shouts of, "We'll find you!"

Panther and I sit and relax, regaining our composure as best we can. I am near Rickshaw and touch a sticky liquid as my hand rests on the floor of the scooter. I raise my hand to inspect it — blood. On searching for the blood's source, I see Rickshaw slump in his seat while maintaining his driving duty. "Panther," I say. "They've hit Rickshaw."

"It's just a flesh wound," a faltering and rasping voice from Rickshaw says.

I move over to him and find a bullet hole in his back. It must have just missed his heart and collapsed his lung. "Take over driving," I tell Panther, which he does while I lower Rickshaw to the floor.

"We did it," Rickshaw says, coughing up blood.

"Rest, Rickshaw. We'll get you to a hospital soon. You're needed where I am going."

"In case I don't make it, it was worth the risk to witness you fire those things and cause actual damage."

His comment reminds me of my lost maser. I desperately want to find it, but Rickshaw's condition worries me. We can't afford to look for it. But I search in the moonlight for familiar landmarks and recognize the crash site by the cliff face. "Can we go over there?" I ask as I point toward the cliff.

Panther looks at where I am pointing. "Sure." He steers the scooter toward the precipice and speeds there.

Minutes later, the wreck site comes into view. "Stop here." I get out of the scooter and search, sweeping wider as I seek my weapon. I spy the holster and maser a few minutes later, 50 meters from the wrecked scooter. I run to it and pick it up, strapping the holster to me and inserting the pistol into its pouch. I own another maser, but they're in short supply here, and I may need both before the fighting ends. I race back to the scooter and jump in. "Let's go."

Panther starts the scooter again; it levitates and shoots toward the capital. Lights appear ahead of us an hour later. Rickshaw's condition is poor. He has lost a lot of blood but clings to life. I attend to him as best I can while Panther keeps flying. No further pursuit comes from behind us. I raise my head from its reverie and ask Panther, "What is the risk that they radioed our escape through to the city?"

Panther considers his response before replying, "Small. They will want to make a thorough search themselves first and avoid any backlash for the slip-up, especially if they suspect they may have allowed such a valuable prisoner to fall through their fingers."

"Good. It may give us the time that we need. Can they track this scooter?"

"Rickshaw disconnected the beacon."

I sit back and minutes later, the city outskirts come into view. I direct Panther to the concealed tunnel entrance, and we fly to it as fast as we can go on the scooter. "We need to walk from here."

"And Rickshaw?"

I have a predicament. I wish to return to the rebels, but I don't want to leave Rickshaw unattended. He is not in a condition to travel on foot.

Guntram strolls around a corner. "About time you returned," he says, unfazed at the sight of us. He inspects the scooter. "That's not the scooter I gave you. It's a state one."

"Long story, Guntram. Panther, meet Guntram, our mechanic." They nod at each other. "Guntram, this is Rickshaw — he saved our lives, and I must save his."

"Leave it to me. I'll round up help and get him to the nearest hospital. In the meantime, you're needed elsewhere."

I look at him questioningly.

"You haven't returned a moment too soon. A major offensive is happening in the stronghold's two tunnels. Could use help from those," he says, pointing to my weapons.

The revelation alarms me. If the rebels fall, we will lose any hope of rescuing Adala and everything that she symbolizes. "Where should I go?"

"The main compound."

"Thanks. I'll be off then."

"And me?" Panther asks.

"Come with me and bring your weapons."

As we turn to go, I turn back to Guntram as a thought occurs to me, "What are you doing here?"

"Sentinel asked me to prep the scooters in case we need to escape. But don't worry, I'll get Rickshaw help first. With you here, we might not need to escape."

Panther and I rush toward the far tunnel that leads to the main compound. We hear sounds of a battle as we near the site, the noise of fired bullets reverberating through the tunnels. The anguish of injured rebels strikes my senses. We break through into the chasm that houses the underground town. Their resistance is crumbling as the state troops approach the two tunnels' entrances. "Cover me," I tell Panther as I run in that direction. I use my most destructive weapon first and lift my maser from its holster. I aim at one shaft and fire, making a mockery of the human flesh that had just existed there. Moments later, I do the same to the other tunnel entrance.

The shooting subsides as the rebels turn to locate the surprising extra firepower coming to their aid. They see me and an instant air of regained confidence fills the cavern as they return their concentration to the battle.

Panther stands still with mouth agape in disbelief at my destructive power. "I thought the rumors just a myth, but your beams of destruction really are beams of destruction."

I smile. "Come with me." Panther and I move forward. I meet someone in authority and direct him to concentrate his troops' defense on one tunnel entrance while I attack the other. He nods and trots away to relay my instructions. Panther and I approach the first tunnel with caution. We veer off to access it from the side, keeping to the protective wall. We inch to the opening, and I look around the corner. Destruction and devastation litter the site where I fired, but it's free of the enemy for now. Several obstacles placed throughout the shaft give us cover as we venture further through the cavity to the other entrance.

Panther has his gun ready to fire at anything that moves, but I caution him to be careful and act as my backup instead of taking the initiative. I don't want him accidentally killing rebels. I wield the deadlier firepower for the best impact on the intruders' psyche, and I know who the rebels are and so can avoid them.

We hear fighting further up the tunnel and make our way toward the noise with care. The action comes into view, and several rebels take a defensive position. I locate Sentinel in the thick of it, grime and blood covering his face and clothes and a defiant determination in his stance. The sound of several bullets fire past our heads as we approach his position. He turns toward us when we are ten meters away. A surprised smile of relief shows up on his face when he sees me. But I can sense worry, too, behind his eyes, which I have not seen before now.

We approach him. "Need help?" I ask.

Sentinel looks at me with an expression that suggests I've just asked the obvious. "We need those weapons of yours to get these vermin out of our tunnels."

"Happy to oblige." I look for the main attacking position and find a spot. As I aim the maser, I shoot, and the assault falters as the enemy comes to grips with what just happened. Sentinel's force takes advantage of the lull to advance, which pushes our foes further out of the complex. This continues for another hour as I fire, the opponent retreats, and we move forward completing the cycle. We reach the other end, and I finish the annihilation of the enemy arsenal in that fork of the attack. Soldiers run away and Sentinel's troops capture them and take them as prisoners.

On securing that tunnel, we drive to the other tunnel and start attacking their rear. It isn't long before their assault crumbles, too, and they surrender, licking their wounds.

Sentinel slumps to the ground from exhaustion. "You came not a second too soon. We were taking heavy losses. Where have you been?"

"Long story. Short version is I've been in a prison camp. Panther here and another injured in the escape helped me flee when we heard Egon has captured Adala."

A pained look slams across Sentinel's face and he looks guilty as if he allowed it to happen. "I failed her. I lowered my guard, and they knew she was there."

My sympathy reaches out to him, as he has told me many times that keeping Adala safe is his one and only mission. "We can't solve it now. Let's return to the complex and get cleaned up and refreshed. We'll discuss that and how we rescue her then."

A fresh sense of hope beams from Sentinel's face at my plain confidence, a confidence that I am not sure I can transform into actuality.

28

ATTACK ON THE PALACE

The remnant of Adala's cabinet assembles in her council chamber, minus Adala and General Tancred, injured in the earlier assault, and Chancellor Korbinian.

"We are pleased to see you," Frieda says with a serious face to suit the occasion.

"Yes, we hope that you have developed a plan for Princess Adala's rescue," Sigmund continues.

I am stunned that they look to me for ideas but realize I have a protective spirit toward these children, too, fate having unceremoniously wrenched them from their childhood into the present arena of chaos. I smile encouragingly. "Let's see what is possible."

General Ernst sits in silence, looking grave, and Sentinel appears drawn and tense.

"What's happened to our favorite Chancellor?" I glance at Sentinel.

"He is in our detention cells, and he is no favorite of ours," Sentinel responds.

"True."

"Were you able to find out how Rickshaw is?" I ask Sigmund, as I had asked him to chase up his whereabouts and health status, still hopeful he will live. I have given Panther leave to tend to his own needs while the meeting is in progress, much to his displeasure as he has assured me that he wants to be part of the action.

"He's having surgery today, but the doctors say he is stable and should survive."

"Good. I owe him."

"We need a plan of attack to rescue Princess Adala," Sentinel says, bringing us back to the reason for calling the meeting.

General Ernst shakes his head. "I have little hope of that. You know as well as I that the surrounding shield makes the palace impregnable."

"There must be a way. Can we dig a tunnel to it?" Frieda asks.

"That would take too long," Ernst says. "We have little time left now. My sources say that they have scheduled the wedding for tomorrow. Once that happens, it will end the war."

"Why?" I ask. "Surely a marriage under duress can't claim legitimacy."

"A marriage is a marriage in our law. Under the constitution, once a crown princess marries, her rights are shared with her husband — and once she is queen, he is king. We allow females to inherit ahead of younger brothers, but this is still a male-dominated society."

I fidget in my chair at the revelation. "We have little time then." The seed of a plan germinates, one that sprouted when I discovered the portal's purpose and the enclosed concealed room, but I hoped for longer to develop it for a better chance of success. We don't have that luxury now. "When is the ceremony due to start?"

"Regal weddings begin at three in the afternoon," Ernst states.

"That precise?"

"It is tradition, and we usually use the cathedral, but this one is being held in the palace for obvious reasons."

"Let's hope Egon adheres to one tradition then."

"It is likely that he will in this case," the general responds. "He is ruffling enough feathers without breaking this custom. That might change if he hears of a potential threat and brings the timing forward."

"Such as me returning to the battlefield?"

"Maybe."

We sit in silence. I survey the table and see faces prepared for defeat. I cannot delay any longer to polish my plan. Every minute counts. I give a conspicuous cough to gain their attention. "I have a way."

"You do?" everyone says in unison, looking at me expectantly.

"A rear entrance to the palace exists, one without shielding or guards."

"How do you know that?" Sigmund asks.

"How do you think I escaped? I told you I was in the cell next to the king. We had lengthy discussions while incarcerated. Through them, I found this back door." I leave out the private passages, the library, and the portal for now. I don't want to divulge too many secrets, especially since they remained hidden for so long and probably for an excellent reason. The kings over the years kept their secret, although I doubt that even they knew what lay behind the portal.

Sentinel mulls over the news. "How does that help? It won't be long before we're discovered if everyone enters through there. Few rebels will get inside before they're overpowered, and they'll kill us in no time."

I smile a conspiratorial smile. "I know. You'll storm the gates."

My calm statement causes a furor. Everyone starts talking at once, condemning my idea as an impossibility. Sentinel acts as speaker for the rest. "You have forgotten about the shields."

"Let me worry about the shields." I turn to the general. "I need you to marshal all your forces to attack the gates. Can you do that?"

"I can," General Ernst says doubtfully. "We have trained for it, but that training has never been tested."

"Let's put it to the test then. And you need everything we confiscated from the main security compound. This is a make-or-break offensive."

"I will make that my business," the general confirms with slightly more confidence.

"And what do you intend doing then?" Frieda asks.

I wink. "Shut off the shields, of course. A small group will do. Panther and two others."

"I am coming with you," Sentinel demands, ending any argument. "I'll find another trusted soldier for the mission."

"OK. We need the palace layout. Especially where Adala might be and where they'll conduct the ceremony. Who can help me with that?" I ask, looking around the group.

Frieda and Sigmund both pipe up, "I can." They blush in embarrassment. "We explored most palace areas growing up," Frieda adds, "much to our carers' frustration."

"OK. You two draw up a map of the palace as you remember it and show me when you finish. I'll tell you where I need more details."

Both Frieda and Sigmund are excited that we have included them in the preparations to save their sister.

"Let's get moving then," I suggest. "General, you have the most to organize."

"I have ample deputies to delegate the duties. I will be ready. When do we strike?"

I ponder the best timing for this assault. "I presume Egon will expect something to happen the closer the time gets to the ceremony. We need time to assemble ... and I need a diversion to rescue Adala and King Abelard. We set the attack on the gates at one tomorrow afternoon."

"That's cutting it fine. How will we know that the shields have shut down?"

"They will be. Let's get to it."

The others file out to complete their respective duties, all except Sentinel. I glance at him curiously. "What is it?"

"How well do you know Panther?"

"I know he helped me escape the confinement and return me to the city. He had my back. Why?"

"I haven't heard of him. I've asked around and nobody else has heard of him being in our organization either. It's just strange that he is so committed to our cause when he hasn't surfaced on our radar."

"He's been in prison," I point out.

Sentinel says nothing more. He sits in silence for a time.

I ask, "What exactly happened with Adala? How did she get captured?"

Sentinel winces at the topic but answers, "I lowered my guard. I failed her. She was frantic when you didn't return when you promised. We looked everywhere for you but found no trace of you. Adala ventured out on her own to search. She gave me the slip and the people guarding her were negligent too. She wandered into a part of the city that wasn't safe for her. It was foolish. Her face is identifiable throughout the kingdom, but she went regardless. She had heard a rumor. I told her I'd send someone, but she ignored me. From my information, it was a trap. Security guards stood ready to overpower her and take her to the palace." There is pleading and anguish in Sentinel's eyes as he completes his report to me.

I empathize with him. "You can't help it if Adala takes it on herself to do something without proper protocol."

"You don't understand, Halwende. She was in despair. You were her universe. She was counting on you, not just to save the kingdom and her father. You were her world. I could see it in her eyes, in everything that she did. She lost hope ..." Sentinel drifts away into a reverie of self-doubt.

Guilt accuses me also, even though I have no reason for it. Why do I feel guilty? Because I gave her confidence, offered everyone hope, and I am failing them, the same as I failed Genevieve and Charlotte, and the people relying on me on Eridu. I slump at the revelation and the responsibility.

Sentinel looks at me and understands where my thoughts are going. He shakes himself out of his despondency and, in a rallying tone, says, "This is not the time for doubt, for either of us. We are doing what we can. And you risk much more than we have a right to ask of you. Let's prepare for this mission!"

I nod and rise to leave. We both walk out and go our separate ways.

The time preparing for the attack passes quickly. Sigmund and Frieda draw up an excellent set of plans, and I combine them with my knowledge to devise a route to the Grand Ballroom, where the marriage ceremony will occur. It is fortunately not a circuitous route and easy to remember.

I grab a few hours' sleep before dawn and the start of my little group's part of the plan. We need to travel to the secret entrance before sunrise to reduce the risk of exposure. Guntram has prepared another scooter for the undertaking. I walk to the rally point where Panther, Sentinel, and a stranger greet me. I look to Sentinel for an introduction.

"This is Drago, one of my best deputies," he says.

I nod my acknowledgment. "Let's go then."

We mount the scooter and start out of the tunnel complex. Guntram has offered to ferry us and wait, which I accept gratefully after my prior journey's disaster. The city disappears as we speed away. Guntram has tuned the drive to its highest performance while he was doing his adjustments. We rise to the top of the cliff 30 minutes later and speed back toward the waterfall. On arrival, I take over the controls and maneuver the machine to the ledge.

We dismount from the scooter. "I will wait for your return," Guntram says.

"You do that," Sentinel replies.

Dawn breaks on the horizon as I lead the others to the concealed cave entrance. They gaze in amazement as they see this camouflaged access for the first time. We wait to synchronize with the attack on the gates. As we eat our provisions, each is in his own world of contemplation.

The time arrives for us to move, and we continue into the tunnel. I light the way to the entry door of the palace corridors. I prefer to hide my means of entry from the others, but I have no choice other than to ask them to look away, and that's childish, especially with Sentinel, so I just press the concealed button. The door opens, and we dart through to the passage. The others glance around to orient themselves.

"Follow me," I say. Eyes and ears alert for the enemy, I start walking along the internal tunnel. We reach the intersection, and I peer around the corner. There is no one in the vicinity. We need to progress to the Grand Ballroom, where I'll leave them, as I don't want them to see me access the portal and the chamber it conceals. Not even Sentinel at present. He is too valuable in setting up the assault from our end.

As I start toward the ballroom, I hear a muffled gunshot behind me. I glance around and see Drago on the floor, his life bleeding from him, and Panther holds his pistols aimed at both Sentinel and me.

"What are you doing?" I ask in disbelief.

"My job," Panther replies. "It'll please Egon to recapture you and with the information about the palace's secret entrance too. The news of the unknown weapons will be most welcome."

I grit my teeth in anger at Panther and chagrin at myself. Sentinel tried to warn me over including him in the group. "But you helped me escape."

"I had to make it look convincing."

"So, you staged that?"

"Oh, no. That was real. Nobody back there knows that I am the emperor's agent."

"And Rickshaw?"

"Just a patsy. It was unfortunate that I had to shoot him, but he was starting to suspect something. I couldn't have you suspect me. Inconvenient that I didn't complete the job, though."

I shake my head incredulous at the disclosure of his duplicity. Resigned, I chuckle at the luck that's following me. I can't take a trick anymore.

An opportunity to reverse our circumstances occurs to me, but I need to make sure Panther doesn't shoot Sentinel. I must position myself in the firing line. I'll play along with him for the time being and wait for my chance to jump him.

"Throw your weapons on the ground," Panther orders.

Sentinel takes his two pistols from his holsters and throws them to the floor. I remove my maser and place it on the ground too.

"And those wrist things."

I remove my two lasers and put them on the floor.

"Move away."

We step back three paces and stop. Panther moves forward and grabs the pistols, placing them in his belt while watching us with hawk eyes. He picks up the maser and wrist lasers and throws them back up the passage. I place my hand in my pocket and sidle closer to Sentinel. I will only have one chance to do what I intend, and it has a high risk of injuring Sentinel or worse, but I must try it if we are to rescue Adala.

Suddenly, Guntram appears behind Panther. Both Sentinel and I glance past Panther in amazement at the sight of him. Panther realizes there's movement behind his back and slowly half-turns while keeping a watch on us. I see my chance while he is distracted. I pull the nerve stimulator from my pocket and turn it on, aiming it directly at Panther. He is the only one in its path with no spill-over to Guntram. I move in front of Sentinel at the same time. Panther stiffens with a look of shock as his muscles cramp, but he fires a shot. The bullet hits me in the chest and bounces off with a blue flash where it has tried to penetrate the force shield. Panther collapses as the radiation takes full effect, and we relax in relief.

"I thought I told you to stay by the scooter," I say to Guntram.

"You're welcome for saving your ass."

I grin. "Yeah, thanks, but how did you open the door?"

"It's not that hard to find the opening mechanism. I'm a mechanic and a tinkerer."

Sentinel walks over to Drago to check if he is still alive and shakes his head. He goes to his weapons and retrieves them, picking up mine as well, and gives them to me. I place the maser in its holster and the lasers on my wrists again. "That was a poor start," Sentinel says to no one in particular.

I try to think about what this means to my plans. We need to inca-pacitate Panther for when he wakes. I don't want to kill him because he might have useful information about Egon if our mission is not successful today. I also need to move Drago out of the way. The blood is a problem, and we can't clean it up now. "Guntram, you need to return to the scooter and keep that ready for us."

"Ohh! But it's boring there."

"But we need you there, and we need you to watch him," I say, pointing to Panther.

"OK then," Guntram says in resignation, disappointed that he can't join us.

"Let's move these two outside," I tell them. Sentinel grabs Drago, and Guntram and I take Panther. We drag them up the tunnel to the exit door. I activate the opening, and we struggle through it back-ward, dragging our payload behind us. We deposit both bodies and return to the passage.

"You know how to use a pistol?" Sentinel asks Guntram.

"Yeah."

"Here, take this. I'll grab the other. Use it on him if he gives any trouble when he wakes up and don't be kind to him."

I frisk Panther to see if he has any other arms on him. Finding none, I tie him up with cables I brought with me. I was only expecting to use them on guards we might meet, but these will fulfill their task just as well on Panther.

Sentinel and I return to the palace through the door, leaving Guntram to retrace his steps back to the scooter. We head to the junc-tion. The blood lies congealing and darkening on the floor when we arrive.

"So, what do we do now?" Sentinel asks.

"Go to the ballroom and wait. I have something to do first."

"Is it wise to split up?"

"We must."

Sentinel looks at me as if about to dispute my decision but refrains. "I will wait at the side entrance wherever I can find a hiding spot."

"Good. I won't be long."

Sentinel leaves. I wait until he disappears from my sight before I set off in the other direction toward the portal room. I hear a noise behind me and start turning, but I'm struck on the head and sink into unconsciousness.

29

RUNNING OUT OF TIME

I come to, my head throbbing. My hands are free, so I gingerly touch the spot that hurts. Dried blood encrusts it, and there's a nasty raised lump. I groan and gaze at my surroundings. I'm still where I was but now sprawled on the floor, and Guntram is pointing a gun at me. "You just had to escape." His stance is casual, his tone laconic, as if he's in total control.

I drag myself into a seated position. "What are you doing, Guntram?"

"Why couldn't you stay in that prison camp until everything was complete? You had to break free. I didn't count on Panther. Nobody told me about him."

I groan again, not believing my luck. "Why am I jinxed?" My maser, wrist lasers, and stimulator lie on the floor near Guntram, too far away for me to grab. I still have my personal shield. He is unaware of it. At least I have minimal protection if he fires a shot at me, but I need to flee from him or everything I've done will be for nothing. "What will you do with me?"

"Others will arrive soon."

It worries me he has communicated with the palace. They will search for Sentinel. In silence, I sit and think. I'll never escape if I'm placed in prison, but I have little choice with no weapons. Guntram will shoot me if I make a move, but I wonder how adept he is with a gun. I try to stand.

"Stay seated."

I slump back to the ground. It's 'Plan B' then, and I wait for him to relax. He is glancing along the corridors, waiting for the others to arrive. As he looks up again, I swivel, tangle my legs through his and roll my body to unbalance him. He whimpers in surprise and discharges his pistol, but he misses me and falls to the floor. I move like a leopard and overpower him, wrest the gun from him and shoot him. With a sigh of relief, I stand and walk over to retrieve my weapons. My plans are unraveling around me now. People are probably hunting Sentinel, and they'll hunt for me soon too when they see that I have escaped from Guntram.

Footsteps pound up the corridor. I must move and quickly, but there's no time to reach the portal. My only choice is to retreat to the concealed doorway. That will leave me trapped outside, though. There must be another way. Markings on the opposite wall attract my attention. They are like the secret passageway entrance signs I used when I escaped from the prison ... maybe. I dash over to the fixtures and push them. The characteristic clip sounds and an aperture opens. I rush through, the door closing behind me. The sound of rushing feet penetrates the wall soon afterward. The people turn the corner and see Guntram dead on the floor. Viewports must exist in the passage somewhere; Abelard hinted at them. I search the surface as I walk along it. A small hole becomes visible, which I peer through, its lens providing a fish-eye view of the whole corridor.

The palace guards have rushed to Guntram and confirm he's dead. As they check up and down the passage, one of them tells the others to search for me. "He can't be far," he says. "There's nowhere to hide from us in here."

There's much they don't know. I wait, wondering what to do. Time is running short. It is almost one. The rebels will have assembled at the gate, ready for the attack. I pace my frustration into the floor. I need a distraction so I can reach the portal. I settle on a plan, not a wonderful plan, but a plan. As I sprint through the passages, I find an entry further along the corridors that is remote from the searching party and out of view when I re-enter the passageway near the portal. I can just hear them but sense that they are moving away from me. On opening the door, I fire my maser at nothing, just to make a resounding noise, one that must attract their attention. After re-closing the door, I stay until the guards run toward me, then hurry to the secret door by the portal. I listen hard but all I hear is silence. I spy a viewport — my luck might be changing. On looking through, I see the corridor is empty. I open the door, darting toward my destiny.

One o'clock is imminent, and I don't have the shield off yet. When I approach the portal, it surprises me by opening as if it's kept a memory of me. I stride through, the aperture sealing behind me, and thread through the maze of boards, searching for the palace door shield switches. It is past one. The attack on the gate has started, and they will soon speculate about whether I've led them into a trap. Sweat drips from my face as I search for the right levers. I finally locate them and pull them to the off position. As I survey other panels, I spot other switches that might be useful to turn off, so I do that too. I wonder what the security guards are thinking now. They must think gremlins are causing mischief. I snigger; they may be. I've done what I can here and must make my way to the ballroom since I cannot count on Sentinel reaching it. They may have captured him by now. I can't use the corridors to get to the ballroom, though. The risk of detection is too high. So, I decide to use the hidden passageways to the library and pinpoint the route to the ballroom. I listen for any noise outside at the portal entrance but sense nothing. Once it opens, I sneak out and hurry back to the entry point of the secret passages and enter.

Twenty minutes later, I arrive at the library. I must hurry. Time is pressing before the ceremony begins. "Show me a map of the palace," I command the library. A hologram of the palace materializes before me. I trace through the details and find the Grand Ballroom, but the secret corridor matrix is missing. "Overlay the hidden passageways." The network emerges, highlighted in red. It displays crosses at various places, and I work out they are passageway entry/exit doors. A passage threads behind the ballroom, and an exit point exists behind the dais. I surmise they will conduct the rite on the stage so, in theory, I could emerge from the door, snatch Adala, and re-enter the corridors. Great in theory, but too many holes exist for guaranteed success. It won't be so easy to tear Adala from Egon and the guards surrounding them, and they will spot us disappearing into the passages, revealing their existence. I must keep them secret for now. A branch passes along the side of the ballroom with another exit. But it's too distant for me to grab Adala without them whisking her away or using her as a shield for Egon to escape. It's the rear entrance, then. I memorize the route and tell the library to remove the image.

I enter the passages again, rushing to the ballroom. The sound of fanfare and music reaches me as I approach my destination. The ceremony is beginning. Although I hear other noises too — the clang and resonance of warfare, which makes me smile. The rebels must be inside the palace compound. I wonder where Sentinel is. The door comes into view now, with a peephole near it. I peer through.

Egon and Adala are on the stage, which is decked out in regal and wedding decor. The celebrant is with them. I can see Adala sideways. She is defiant, but defeat etches her features and despair clouds her eyes. It breaks my heart. A modest crowd watches from the auditorium. The rest of the crowd is made up of guards and soldiers, ready to defend their master. I move to the door after I spot Sentinel, captured, cuffed, beaten, and kneeling to the side of the others. His stature denotes utter failure. He has failed his charge. His head hangs low. I sense that, if he had a sword, he would impale himself as punishment for his failure. "Don't give up yet, my friend," I whisper.

Fear grips me as scenes from the past reappear in my mind's eye.
'Your wife and your daughter are dead.'
'What are your orders?'
I shake the images from my mind. But they have galvanized my resolve to succeed or die trying. I get the stimulator from my pocket and the maser from its holster. This will be spectacular if nothing else. After locating the lock mechanism, I push, and the door slides

open. I stroll through it into the ballroom. Time passes in slow motion. After aiming the stimulator at the left-hand-side soldiers and the maser on my right hand, I fire both devices. One set of soldiers drops like bowling pins while the others disappear into their dead constituent atoms.

Egon turns toward me, surprise and anger spread on his face as if I insult him by daring to disrupt his wedding. Sentinel's head rises, defeat changing to determination. And Adala ... I virtually stop in my tracks when I see her. Everything is for naught if I don't save her. The others will come out of their shock and overpower me. But Adala ... she turns, the elegance of the most glorious flower cannot match her, and the power of a true ruler is evident.

I turn the stimulator off and refocus my concentration on the task at hand. Another group of soldiers rallies in the rear of the ballroom. They take aim at me but hesitate for fear of hitting their leader. I must aim with precision to prevent slaughtering the innocent onlookers when I fire, but fire I do, and I wipe out another group of resistance.

"Kill him!" Egon orders the guards on the stage. "Kill him!"

He lunges for Adala, as I feared, but I am too far away to stop him, and he is too near her for me to shoot him. I curse myself. He grabs Adala's wrist and drags her away. She resists, but he is too strong for her.

I can't chase after them as I am being attacked. Bullets fire at me, one hitting my shield and bouncing off it. I place the stimulator in my pocket again and aim the wrist laser toward the nearest and fire. One at a time, I reduce the number of attackers as I try to gain access to Sentinel to free him so he can contribute to the battle. The guards are finding cover, so I have no easy shots anymore. I must do the same. A heavy wooden trestle stands nearby, which I upend with my foot and lunge behind. Using it as a shield, I pick it up and rush to Sentinel to protect him too.

"Hope I'm not too late."

"Never too late. But you could have arrived sooner."

I pant from the exertion of carrying a heavy wooden trestle. "We should work out how to pick more reliable members for our team next time, ones that don't betray us."

"Guntram?" Sentinel asks in dismay.

"Yes."

I retrieve a knife from a dead guard lying on the floor behind us and cut Sentinel's shackles. *They should have used material better than rope.*

Sentinel rubs the circulation back into his wrists. "We need to get out of here. It won't be long before reinforcements come." He grabs a gun from a guard and extra ammunition from his belt.

"Where is Egon taking Adala?"

"I presume into the lower halls, where the prison cells are. That is the most secure area. A path leads from there to the palace security compound, where they park the royal armored scooter. He will try reaching that to make his escape."

Tremendous explosions blast the doors of the ballroom open, and we see General Ernst burst through with his troops. The general's uniform and head are splattered with the blood and guts of battle, and he displays the fearlessness of someone winning the war. A smile of triumph plasters his face. The guards attacking us watch the detonations and flee.

"Let's go," I tell Sentinel. Leading him to the secret passages, I open the door, and we enter. Sentinel freezes in disbelief. "We had better hurry," I say.

He comes out of his trance. "Yes."

30

THE ESTATE

I guide Sentinel through the secret passages into the prison. My goal is the exit by the king's cell. I intend to rescue him first as I believe he may know the best way to the security section. We arrive at the location ten minutes later. I open the door and lead Sentinel to the cells.

We burst through to the prison block and take out two guards. I go to the king's chamber. He isn't there. Bugger! Where could he be? "They've taken the king," I tell Sentinel.

"Maybe Egon took him with him."

"Why? He has Adala."

"To convince her to cooperate."

"Do you know the route to the scooter park?"

"Yes. We had better dash. We are running out of time."

"Lead the way."

Sentinel strides back the way we came and up several levels. No one prevents us, as if they've called security elsewhere. Sentinel is in a hurry and starts jogging through the corridors. I follow. It amazes me he knows his way. The walls appear the same everywhere, but he must see signs, or perhaps he remembers from playing in them when young. I don't care, so long as we find Adala in time. After what seems an eternity, we reach a door.

"This is it. The parking is on the other side," Sentinel says. "Are you ready?"

"Do it."

He goes to open the door, but it does not budge. It's jammed from the other side. He tries again, placing his entire weight against it. It remains in place.

"Allow me," I tell Sentinel and motion for him to step aside. I draw my maser and blast the barrier out of existence.

We rush through to a vacant parking space. The scooter isn't there. Egon isn't there. His guards aren't there and, most important to me, Adala isn't there, nor the king. I stare in disbelief. How did he escape with such ease? How could I have failed Adala? I slump to the ground. The adrenalin and stress of the past events catch up with me, accusing my conscience, depressing me.

I spy Sentinel moving his arm and glance at him. "There," he says as he points to a retreating scooter. "That's them."

"Where are they going?"

"By the direction, one of his estates near the sea. He has them well guarded and he can stay there indefinitely."

"And running the state and his marriage to Adala?"

"He could communicate with the city. He will postpone the wedding until the current crisis is over, although he may use her as leverage to gain what he wants. Don't forget, many in the military support him."

"We need to rescue Adala. Let's go."

"Not so fast. I said it's well guarded. We must assemble a squad to attack the estate."

"No. We can't wait and, to be honest, we don't know who we can trust anymore. Consider Panther and Guntram. We must do this ourselves, and if you don't wish to join me, I will go alone. Just point me in the right direction."

"No. I must correct my mistake. I will help you, but this mission is dangerous."

"And our past missions haven't been?"

Sentinel smiles, acknowledging my point. "Where are you going?"

"Back to the scooter."

"There are excellent ones here, ones that are armored and armed."

"OK, then."

Sentinel leads me to the parking bay for the military scooters and selects an armored scooter that looks more like a tank with multiple accessory machine guns on top of the centrally mounted turret and a rotating cannon on the roof. An arsenal of firearms sits inside, enough to supply twenty troopers. He powers up the vehicle and lifts off, setting course to chase the other scooter. No one tries to stop us. That must mean the soldiers are attending to more pressing concerns. Good.

Sentinel opens the throttle to full speed, the city blurring away under us and disappearing, replaced by countryside and trees. He aims the flier toward the Brandenström River and follows it downstream. An hour later, I see the twinkling of the sun reflected from water on the horizon. Sentinel informs me it's the Ungestüm Meer, the sea encompassing this part of the country. The details of the coastline appear minutes later and become finer as we get closer. Sentinel points out a large estate to the right with a mansion covering several acres of land with a walled perimeter. There are guard towers protruding from the barrier at regular intervals, like parapets on a castle wall.

"Any ideas for breaking into the place?" I ask.

"I am unfamiliar with this property. He has fortified it. No force fields defend the estate, unlike the palace. The defenses are materials and guards."

"How many guards could he house here? It can't have been heavily guarded before he retreated from the castle. Did you notice any reinforcements escort him from the palace?"

"No. I did not."

I think for a moment. "These things fly over water, don't they? Let's check the defenses on the seaward side."

"Let's." Sentinel steers the scooter to the left and lowers it to skim the treetops and lower still, as the foliage gives way to marshland and water. We cross the coastline and head out to sea to reduce the risk of easy detection. Sentinel reduces speed and stops, facing the coast and the estate behind it.

I get my maser out and bring it to my eye.

"Are you going to blast it from this distance?" Sentinel asks, incredulous.

I chuckle. "No. This has a digital targeting telescope to see the layout and defenses." As I peer through the telescope, I focus it on the walls and buildings of the estate, activating the anti-shake feature to prevent a blurred view through the magnifying scope. Walls surround the property along the coastline, except in a small harbor where a pier juts out with boats at anchor. Behind the cove, a gazebo stands, and a multistoried mansion behind that. A lawn surrounds the gazebo extending to the jetty. I presume Egon hosts dinner parties there on balmy evenings to keep connected with his valuable contacts in society. Egon has parked the scooter he took from the palace on the grass. The walls on either side block my view of everything else.

Except for the walls, the defenses are sparse. There are only watchtowers at either end. I see nothing around the marina. That is a weak spot in the estate's defenses. But what then? Once we enter this gap?

"The harbor front is the obvious point of entry, but what next? How do we find Adala?"

"Why don't you do your usual trick and knock?" Sentinel proposes with a sardonic smile.

I laugh. "I could do that."

"I think we should do something soon, though, before he can gather more reinforcements."

"Have you attended a party here? Seen the guards' barracks?"

"I have." Sentinel thinks for a moment. "I recall the huts to the right. Buildings likewise stand to the left, but they are general-purpose ones for maintaining the estate. A small arsenal exists in the barracks building too."

"We have a plan then. We enter the harbor, incapacitate the barracks, and knock on the front door," I say with a wink.

Sentinel laughs his acknowledgment. "We have a plan." He starts the scooter's forward motion again and heads for the port.

I spy a shimmer across the two ends of the barrier just before we enter the harbor, "Stop," I shout to Sentinel.

He swerves and circles back. "That sly dog has found a means of installing a field here. I doubt it's large, though. It may just traverse the gap."

"Let's get rid of it then." I pull out my maser and blast the end of the right wall out of existence. "There goes our surprise." The shimmer disappears, and Sentinel darts through and lands on the lawn.

We hear shouts and confusion coming from various directions, especially from a building that Sentinel says is the barracks. I give that a volley and an extensive section disappears. I must have struck the arsenal because a series of secondary explosions occur like a cascade of fireworks. We jump from the scooter and sprint behind the gazebo and to the mansion's grand entrance door. Return fire comes from the house, emanating from windows in the top story. I aim my wrist lasers and fire. I think I hit one sniper, but I miss the other. We reach the cover of the entry porch.

"What do you want to do?" Sentinel asks.

I glance at him and consider the door. "Knock," I say as I blast the barrier out of existence with the maser.

31

RESCUING ADALA

We enter the doorway and search the room. A grand foyer with polished marble floors spreads before us, leading to a staircase rising to the upper levels of such magnificence that I gasp in amazement. Sentinel moves left, and I move right. We look for danger with our weapons drawn. It's quiet, too quiet. We both walk sideways, crablike, expecting someone to come out and attack us at any moment.

"What do you think?" I ask Sentinel.

"It's too peaceful."

"Agreed, but where do we find Adala?"

"I do not know."

"Let's make a noise then." I shoot at random doors peppering the foyer but realize the action is a waste of time. Where would he keep her safe? There must be a cellar somewhere. We need to locate the stairs leading there, but that leaves us open to being cut off by security from our rear. We'll handle that when it happens. I search for the basement entrance and see a doorway beside the stairs, one with double doors. It looks strong and typical of one designed for general use. "This way," I say to Sentinel, showing where I am heading. He follows me around the foyer, covering us both from any surprise assault, but none arises.

We reach the doors, and I try opening the latch but find it locked. I blast the lock with my wrist laser, deciding to limit the destruction I inflict this time. I glance at Sentinel, checking his preparation for an attack when we burst through the doors. He nods. I push one door open with my foot and jump aside, keeping both wrist lasers ready. Shots ring out from the darkened stairs below. Both Sentinel and I fire back, aiming at the flashes we see when they discharge the bullets. Grunts and groans of pain call out as our shots meet their marks, but more shots reinforce the first. They hold us up just outside the entrance, and I don't like it. We are much too vulnerable targets for anyone coming in from our rear. We keep shooting.

Bullets zip past us from the mansion entrance doorway. Half a dozen guards line up there, ready to kill us. I can't mess around, so I fire my maser at them and obliterate them. It saddens me to incur such a mounting toll, but I must. They don't realize they are fighting on the wrong side.

Sentinel works hard to free our path forward while I protect our rear, and the resistance ahead falters for now. He signals me to move through the door while he covers me. I comply and dash sideways when I am inside, my eyes requiring a few moments to adjust to the darkened atmosphere. As my vision clears, I can see at least five bodies on the ground; one still moves. I rush over to him and disarm him. I look around and see a wide stairway leading to the basement. Bracing for an attack in that direction, I say to Sentinel, "Ready."

He dashes in and closes the door to offer us protection. A heavy chest of draws stands beside the entrance, so he pushes it across the doorway. It blocks our exit, though. We can't have it both ways. It won't hold anyone back for long. I give the injured man my attention. "Where are the princess and the king?"

The question confuses him at first, pain overpowering his senses. His eyes come into focus, a plea for mercy in them. "The stairs and left." He pants from the strain. "Doors ... fifty meters along ... in there."

"Thanks." I look at his injuries. They are extensive and he needs urgent medical attention, attention that we can't offer him. I'm sorry about it but must leave him to die. The consolation may be that his information will reduce the number of future casualties. I move to the stairwell and Sentinel follows, standing back-to-back to me to give us the most coverage. I descend, braced for an attack from around the intersection of the basement.

Shouts come from above, and footsteps pound across the marble floor as reinforcements arrive. We need to hurry. I reach the bottom and glance around the corner to my left. Clear. I check the right. That too is vacant. "Clear," I tell Sentinel to let him know, as he is concentrating on covering our rear. I step into the passage and go left as the injured guard told me to. A set of doors pierce the wall on the right, 50 meters along, as mentioned. "Forward." I progress, and Sentinel follows. Our pursuers pound on the doors. It won't be long before they break through them. This is an unusual corridor. The only door along this passage is the one we intend to enter.

I approach the door and try the latch. It's locked. So, I blast that away too with a wrist laser. I work the door, but it still won't budge. I sigh and give it a dose of my maser, creating another doorless doorway. It is quiet ahead. As I glance around the corner, I spy another passageway with several doors leading off it, resembling a cell block. I slip into it, and Sentinel follows. The shouting behind us gets louder. They have breached the basement doorway and will arrive at the bottom of the stairs soon.

Sentinel looks at the scene in this corridor before giving his full attention to the one we just vacated. "Check. I'll hold them from here."

"They could trap us if an entire troop waits for us behind one of these."

"Yes, they could. But I don't think so. They would have attacked us by now if there were. Anyway, what choice do we have?"

"You have enough ammunition?"

"Plenty."

I turn to concentrate ahead. There are five doors. Three contain small slit windows and two are solid. I search the windowed ones first. On glancing through the closest windowed door, the chamber appears vacant. I test the latch and it opens. As I lunge into the room, I check the blind spots. It is empty. I search the next two windowed doors with the same result.

Shots fire at Sentinel from the other corridor. He fires back, but there's a stalemate, neither party making any progress in overpowering the other.

I have two doors to search, and what lies behind them is unknown. My palms become slippery from sweat. I lick my lips to moisten them and move to the first door. As I hug the wall, I test the latch. It's unlocked, so I shove the door open. No sound of movement comes from within, although I need to listen with care because of the deafening noise from behind me. I peer in. The room is larger than the others with furnishings — a table, chairs, and miscellaneous items. It appears to be a meeting room. I brace myself and lunge in, checking every direction as I go. The room is empty. I return to the corridor and check on Sentinel. He is resisting the attack at present. "One more," I tell him. "They must be in there."

"Go!" he says between shots from his guns. "But first reload those two."

Two guns lie on the floor where Sentinel has dropped them. I pick one up and restock it with a clip from his belt and place it within hand reach. I do the same with the other. "Here goes." I return my attention to the last door and walk to it. Just as I move to test the handle, a thud and groan echo behind me. I glance around. Sentinel is in pain but continues his vigilant defense. Blood drips to the floor. Someone has hit him in the arm. I must bring this to a fast resolve if we are to survive. He is leaning against the wall for support. I return my attention to the door and check the latch. It is unlocked. I push the door open and hear scuffles like mice hiding, but the noise suggests a much larger beast. The sound stops. I lick my lips and gulp, calming my tension for the assault to come.

I peer around the door frame. The space is large. It seems to be a torture chamber with many devices scattered around it and equipment large enough to hide behind. I freeze momentarily in indecision but then snap into a firm resolve. As I dash into the room, I turn to check my environment. Pain pierces my arm with a simultaneous thud against my rib cage. Stunned by the strike, I instinctively roll to the floor. Blood oozes from my arm where the pain throbs. Someone has stabbed me. Mid-roll, I see my assailant and blast him with a laser. Another attack does not come. I heave to breathe air into my lungs again after having had the wind beaten out of them.

Sentinel won't be able to hold the others off much longer. I must finish this. No one is visible, but shuffling and muffled noises come from the far corner. I creep forward toward the source of the sound.

I hear a noise behind me. Sentinel has retreated into the room. He can only use one arm now, although he still tries using the other. "We have little time," he warns.

"They must get past me first," I say to keep his hopes up, although mine are waning. I continue toward the noise and round the last obstacle to my view. Egon is there. He has Adala gagged, and his arm surrounds her neck with a gun pointed to her head. The king is slumped on the floor. I do not know if he is alive or dead.

"Stay where you are," Egon says. "You got through my defenses. You must be very resourceful with those ray guns of yours. I will own them soon enough."

Adala looks on in dread. She stares straight at me, and I sense that the fear is not for her own safety but mine. She is struggling as best she can, but Egon is too strong.

"You won't be alive long enough," I say. "Besides, they only work for me. I tailored them to my physiology."

"Pity. Well, you won't need them for much longer."

Doubt troubles me. "What do you mean?"

"That wound. They poisoned the knife. You'll be dead soon."

Alarm grips me now. I can't come this far for nothing, especially since I've led Sentinel into this trap of my making to save Adala. "Let her go!"

"No. And don't move closer, or I will kill her."

"You won't have a princess to marry then."

"That is a pity, but another exists. She is still young. Not pretty, but she will suffice."

I am light-headed and realize time is short for me. I can't use my maser to blast him. It is too coarse, and I can't chance the aim with my lasers from this distance. "Sentinel, throw me a pistol."

One slides along the ground toward me moments later. I pick it up, check it, blink the blurriness from my eyes and shoot Egon right between his before I collapse to the floor.

32

WHAT HAPPENED?

I wake in a soft downy bed, boronia scent in the air. My eyes stay closed as I luxuriate between silky sheets. Light filters through my eyelids, and I decide the time has arrived to open them and see where I am. An angel is sitting by the side of the bed when I gaze at my surroundings, worry lines creasing her brow and lack of sleep obvious from the drawn face. My memory of the past returns to me with a jolt of lightning. I try to sit. "Where am I? What happened?"

A smile of joy spreads across Adala's face. "You are in our hospital — again — and you are healing from the poisoning. Stay still. You need your rest."

I stretch out my hand and touch her arm as I lie back again. "Tell me what happened. Is Sentinel alive?"

Adala sighs in frustration at where to start. "Ranulf is fine and recovering in another ward. What occurred is a lengthy story, but I'll tell you if you promise to rest."

I smile. "I will but come closer first."

My summons confuses Adala, but she complies.

"Closer, I want to do something."

She comes closer until her face is only centimeters from mine. I rise and kiss her on the lips, her warmth flowing into me for a second before I collapse back onto the bed, a mischievous but contented smile on my face.

"You dare kiss a princess?" Adala says in feigned indignation.

"I dare."

She laughs a delighted laugh that fills me with warmth as much as the kiss did. The medicine of the moment is doing more for me than whatever else they have given me.

"No better remedy for one recovering from injuries incurred saving her."

She laughs again. "I think you have recovered."

That makes me grin too. "My recovery isn't complete yet. But please, what happened?"

"Well, I don't know what you remember, but you shot Egon right between the eyes. How you could have such great aim, with the confidence you wouldn't shoot me instead, astounds me. Of course, I did help you by twisting away to give you a better target. He died instantly, and you collapsed to the floor from the poison, although the knife wound was severe, and you lost much blood.

"With Egon killed, I commanded the shooters to stop because their master was dead and they were to take orders from the king and his family again, which they did. Ranulf was suffering from his injury too. It was good that you ended the struggle when you did, as his strength was waning. They then obeyed my demands and concentrated on tending to Father, Ranulf, and you. There was a medic amongst them. So, we loaded you three into Egon's scooter and rushed you to the hospital, and here you are."

"Is Abelard OK? He looked unconscious when I saw him."

The informal way that I refer to the king takes Adala aback. "Father is fine. He tried to rescue me but was no match for Egon, who knocked him out. The doctors say he is suffering from concussion. They have sedated him, and he is recovering. He remains here for the time being."

"He told me to drop the king thing, you know."

Adala produces another laugh and shakes her head.

"And retaking the palace? Did Ernst do that?"

"Yes. Once the shields collapsed ... you must inform me how you achieved that ... they overpowered the security. I am advised the remaining resistance collapsed not long after Egon fled with me, with you on his heels. Everything was in our hands by the time we returned. Many people died, though." Adala's mood becomes melancholy at the thought. "... On both sides. There is much healing to do."

As I gaze at Adala, my achievement makes me content. But I am mesmerized by her charm, and I wonder what will happen now. She has a kingdom to help rule, and I have a ship to return to and wait for unknowable rescuers.

She leans over me with a majestic smile. "Thank you." She kisses me with more passion than I could achieve. And I relish the experience, wishing the moment to continue forever. As she withdraws, she pours love into my eyes from hers, a love that I've missed for a long time, not since I last saw my wife.

I gasp at the realization but sidestep what it means. "That wasn't fair. I had nowhere to escape, trapped here in this bed."

Her smile broadens. "I didn't sense you squirming to get away."

"I suppose not." My grin matches hers. "How long has it been?"

Adala retreats into her chair, surprised by the question. "How long for what?"

"How long have I been here?"

"Oh ... two days."

"What did you think I meant?"

She blushes with embarrassment. "Nothing ... just that."

I do not want to push her on it anymore. She is too magnificent and innocent. "You should rest. You look tired. When did you last sleep?"

"I haven't slept since we brought you in here."

"Is Abelard that ill?" I say, alarmed.

Adala reddens. "He is fine. I've been here, sitting by you." Her eyes moisten at the admission.

I turn aside, unsure how to react to such dedication. A deep emotion stirs within me, one I cannot handle at present. "You should rest." I don't look at her again but hear her rise from her seat. I hope I haven't offended her with my sending her elsewhere. She rises to leave the room and I turn my head towards her again. "But return when you're refreshed."

She has reached the door of my room and turns her head, a smile breaking out at the invitation. "I will."

It takes a couple of more days before the doctors allow me to leave. Adala visits me each day. I want to leave the hospital, but I don't, too. Here in the hospital, we can be together; outside, I don't know what our future holds or if we even have one. Something keeps attracting me to Adala, and it will be so hard to leave her.

I sigh as I pack my belongings and go, intent on returning to the place where I stayed underground and collect my few possessions there before going back to my ship. My work here is complete. They wanted me to help them, and I did, and in doing so, my cleansing of the guilt and torment from my soul has begun. In one way. My long years of isolation are over, but I can't return to that galaxy to redeem myself, not before someone answers my distress beacon.

The journey to the underground feels slow and lonely. I wander through the tunnels with no purpose, but I continue. The cavern housing the accommodation and Adala's temporary seat of power appears before me, deserted. After collecting the items that I wish to take with me, I sling the bag over my shoulder and make to leave. I gaze at Adala's residence and remember the garden she loves. I must return there now, sensing its therapeutic value for me. So, I walk into the palace building and trace my way to the park entrance.

Passing through the doorway, I survey the serenity of my surroundings, the lush green lawn and the flower beds, flowers blooming in their glorious splendor. The waterfall cascades to the pool below before disappearing to other regions. A lone figure sits on the bench seat watching it. A quantum of melancholy leaves me when I spot her, replaced with a sense of partnership and union as if we should be together but a barrier exists to prevent us.

"I knew you'd show up," Adala says. She turns and smiles, the sun radiating from her. But a subtle air of uncertainty lingers, too. It's as if she is as lost in her direction as I am in mine. "Come. Sit with me, please."

I walk over and sit. "A princess need not say please."

Adala chuckles and her eyes glisten with joy as she looks at me. "It depends on to whom she speaks." We rest in silence before Adala speaks again. "Were you just going to leave?" A sadness spreads across her face as she considers such a tragic ending.

I shrug. "I've done what you asked. I helped overthrow Egon as you wanted. You have demands to attend to in re-establishing control with a stronger government than before this happened. I can't help you with that."

Adala places her palm on my forearm, the warmth and softness of her skin giving me goosebumps. "But your task has only just begun, if only you listened."

I stare at her, confused. What is she saying? I have been listening, haven't I? "What do you mean?"

She moves her hand to my chest. "What is your heart telling you?"

I gulp. "My heart tells me I have a long way to go to redeem myself, but I've started."

She takes her hand back and looks away. My words were not what she expected. I lower my gaze and dig deeper into my most secret thoughts, and I meditate on the past weeks since I have known Adala. A spark ignites the kindling of a fire within me that grows as more understanding unfolds. It's like she is placing more wood on a young fire to give it life and strength. I remember the first moment I saw her — the amused smile and the shafts of lightning from her eyes mesmerizing and joining us for a moment. A warmth infuses me from within and the fire builds in power. A sudden jolt breaks the shackles of my internal prison as the full realization of her devotion comes to me, and a bolt strikes as I glance up again.

Adala is looking at me, studying me, fear and hope connecting her to me as my fire takes hold and now needs to jump the gap between us. I smile. "You're right — my work has only just begun. But what will you have me do?"

A supernova of a smile explodes on her face as I wrap my arms around her and she wraps hers around me, our lips meeting with passion as the fire threatens to run out of control, but we contain it within the bounds of both of our hearts. We part.

"I wish to see your ship again."

"You've been there. There isn't much more to it. It's broken."

"I want to see it again. I want to glimpse your past life. We were busy, and I didn't get a chance last time."

"I suppose. I'm going back there now."

Adala pulls away. "Why? What for? You have a place at the palace and ... elsewhere ..." She turns aside, keeping the privacy of her innermost thoughts. "And you must show me how you deactivated the shield on the palace gates. It's still not returned, and no one knows how to switch it on either."

I give a mocking sigh and pull her back to me, feeling the warmth of her cheek against mine. "I had better obey the princess then before I get my head removed."

Adala giggles at my words. "Yes, you had better, and I'm happy you know the order of things."

I laugh at her mocking stance of superiority with me, and we hold each other in silence for a long time, enjoying our closeness.

33

THE SHIP

We both leave the garden and return to the palace. Her guardians have waited patiently next to a scooter for our reappearance from the underground tunnel. There is a hubbub of work as we enter the palace gates. People are busy trying to repair the damage and clean up the mess caused by the fighting. They look up as we emerge from the vehicle. A few people gesture at us; others give a cheerful welcome as they recognize me. We walk, holding hands, through the palace doors and toward a conversation in progress.

Adala motions me to enter, and she follows behind me. Sentinel, his arm in a sling, glances up as we enter the room. He stops talking and approaches me. King Abelard is there too, and General Ernst and General Tancred, busy studying and discussing notes displayed on the table. They glance at us as well, the generals nodding.

Sentinel stands before me. "It is a joy to see you again, friend," he says, in the solemn tone of his normal demeanor. "Forgive my not hugging you in greeting, but my incapacity prevents me."

I break out in a laugh. "Oh, stop it, Sentinel. You're embarrassing me." He frowns, affronted by my mocking, so I wrap my arms around him and give him a welcome hug instead. I see a smile when we part. "I'm glad to see you again."

Adala moves closer and wraps her arm in mine. She gives an adoring gaze back when I glance at her, acknowledging the rightness of her familiarity in this setting.

Abelard rises from his seat and shuffles toward us. His imprisonment has wearied him, and he will take time to recover. "Welcome, friend." He holds out his hand to shake mine. Adala releases me so that I can return the handshake but reclaims my arm straight afterward.

"Your attention and familiarity embarrass me since you're the king."

"Ohh ... rubbish. We shared prison. That gives you a right to intimacy if nothing else." His gaze reaches over to Adala, showing that he is aware of the blossoming relationship between her and me, and he approves.

I blush but stay quiet.

"Halwende is giving me a guided tour of his ship, and then he will show me how he turned off the shields," Adala announces.

I open my mouth to speak but can't think of any words in reply, so I close it again.

"That intrigues me too," Abelard says. "But have your tour. We have matters here in hand."

Adala pulls me from the room. "We had better unload your things first." She leads me through the corridors into a residential wing. It has a regal but tasteful opulence, with golden gilding covering much of the architectural fittings. It presents a subtle display of their wealth without overbearing ostentation. I appreciate the humility in the decor's layout, despite the family's status in their society. She gestures to my apartment, and I enter.

The chamber's spaciousness overwhelms me. The bed is monstrous with a canopy over it. "I'll lose myself in that," I say, pointing the bed out to Adala.

She laughs. "I must come and find you then."

We both cease joking as we realize what she has said, passion rising in both of us. I wrap my arms around her and place her face near mine, whispering, "Yes, you will." We stand embracing, content in each other's arms until I reluctantly pull away. "I better show you the ship."

She lowers her gaze in resignation instead of disappointment. "Yes, you should." A smile returns to her as she gazes at me again.

We leave and stroll to the scooters' parking enclosure. A protection detail awaits us. Someone must have arranged them. There are four scooters ready, one for us and three more for the guards, overprotective of their princess. I go to mount our assigned scooter when a head pops out. "Want a lift?" It's Rickshaw.

"You have recovered!" I grin and step over to hug him. "How on earth did you get here?"

"I'm Rickshaw, remember."

"Yes, I remember. The slipperiest person I have ever met."

"I'm insulted."

"No, you're not."

"Well, why are you waiting?"

Adala has been standing aside, watching our banter with a smile. She's happy for me. I hope that at least one person in my life doesn't turn out to be a traitor.

"You were right to be suspicious of Panther," I said.

"Yeah, but I didn't act quickly enough. There was always something about his story that was unconvincing, but he could have just been a petty criminal of some sort trying to big note himself as a supporter of the rebels. And then when he was so eager to help you escape, I thought maybe he was okay. He had me fooled, too — although this bullet in my back shows he didn't know he'd fooled me. Anyway, that's history now. Let's move."

"Why have they assigned you to travel with Adala and me?" His reminder of Panther's treachery makes me protective of her.

"Has nobody told you? I am one of Sentinel's agents. He planted me in the camp because he suspected there were traitors in our midst. I didn't exactly cover myself in glory there, given that I didn't expose Panther."

I glance at Adala for confirmation of the truth of what he is saying. She nods her head in agreement.

"Let's leave then," I say, and hop on the scooter. Rickshaw and Adala follow, Adala staying near me.

"Shall I drive?" Rickshaw asks.

"No. I know where my ship is, so I won't need to give you directions."

"So be it. I'll sit back and relax," Rickshaw says and sits contentedly on one of the vacant seats, reclining with one arm draped over the rear of the seat beside him.

Adala moves to sit next to me.

I start the scooter, and we lift off the ground. The other three do likewise and maneuver into close formation in a triangular pattern. We speed out of the city and toward my ship. I see it appear on the horizon in 50 minutes, and we land nearby soon afterward. The security detail files out of their scooters and sets up a perimeter around the spot.

I lead Adala and Rickshaw to the hatch and open it. Rickshaw stares in astonishment as he sees the ship's shiny metal exterior.

"You go up there in that?" he asks, pointing to the sky.

"Yes, though it isn't space-worthy now. It needs repair work after the crash landing." We enter the dimly lit interior. I lead them to the cockpit. "This is where I sit to fly the ship."

Adala walks into the space and looks around, fascinated with the various instruments and devices arranged throughout. She touches each one, careful not to press a button or pull a lever. "This is where you sit?" I nod. She moves and sits in the pilot's seat. She stares at me, her eyes glistening with wonder like a child opening a present and finding a toy beyond her wildest dreams. "How do you navigate?"

I move over to the astrogation station and activate it. Star charts appear on the screen, and I show her where we are and the surrounding stars. I show how to chart to another star and lock it in place. "It's that easy. I just need to start the propulsion systems and the ship's drives fly me there."

"I wish I could go there, but it's so unbelievable. Our science says nothing is out there; it's just tapestry painted in the sky above us." She frowns. "Why spread such lies?"

"From my study, they wanted people to forget the galaxy to protect themselves."

"Study? Where did you read that?"

I realize too late that I may have said too much, particularly with Rickshaw within earshot. "You should talk to your father."

Adala looks at me in defiance, as if she will challenge my withholding of information but relents instead. She changes the topic. "Can you fix it?"

"I don't think so. You don't have the technology here. I can try working on it now that I have resolved your situation."

"Situation?"

I smirk. "Yeah. That's how the children phrased it, and it didn't take me long to fix it."

She tries to hit me but is too far away. "I'll give you a situation." She smiles.

"What's this?" Rickshaw says from behind me.

I turn around to see what he wants explained, just in time to see his hand extended toward a lever. "Don't touch that!" I shout, alarmed. "That is the drive power supply. You could cause an explosion if you activate it, with the state of the drive machinery."

"Oh," he says and drifts away from the equipment as if he never had an intention of touching it.

Adala stands. "Let's explore the rest of the ship." She wraps her arm in mine. "Lead the way."

"There isn't much else." She looks at me as if to say, "Show me," and I sigh in submission. Am I already submitting to this woman? I lead her to the galley and point out the gadgets there to make food and prepare it, then my sleeping quarters and the cargo hold. "As I told you, little to see."

"What's in here?" Adala is standing at a door that I have locked with a biometric lock, although she is unaware of the locking mechanism.

"Nothing."

Adala looks at me, demand in her demeanor.

"Sorry, I must keep a few things secret. I'm sure you have things you hide from me."

"No, I don't."

"Really ...?"

"Well ... maybe."

"Let's leave it at that then. That's it."

Adala's in a huff over my reticence about the locked door, but she recovers from her mood quickly. "I wish this ship could fly. Oh, to explore another world!"

"There's little chance of that unless someone notices my emergency beacon and decides it's worth investigating. They won't find me anyway since your people cloaked the planet."

"Well, I order you to fix the ship so it can travel again," Adala says in a mocking regal tone.

I play along with her. "Your wish is my command," I say as I bow.

Adala laughs at the comedy, and we both hug and stare into each other's eyes.

I can sense Rickshaw rolling his eyes at us, but all he says is, "We should return."

I pull my attention over to him and disengage from Adala. "Yes, we should."

We emerge from the ship and get into our scooter again. The guards withdraw from the perimeter and mount theirs too, and we ascend and return to the city.

34

CELEBRATIONS AND ANNOUNCEMENTS

We reach to the city within the hour, and Adala and I enter the palace not long afterward. She escorts me to my room. A change of clothing sits on the bed, formal attire.

"What is this?" I ask.

"There is to be a dinner tonight. As we invite you, you are to wear that. Be ready at six."

I shrug. "Looks formal."

"I'm sure you will enjoy it. See you at six."

"See you then."

Adala disappears from the doorway. I glance at the chronometer, and it's just on four in the afternoon. With an hour to kill, I fidget, bored with inactivity. On strolling to the window, I gaze out to get my bearings. I am on an upper level of the palace, with a lakeside view that includes the waterfall. It is very picturesque. A rainbow shimmers in the mist generated by the cascading water as the droplets waft westward. Wreckage from the fighting lies below me, and people are busy cleaning the rubble away. They need time to restore the damaged palace to its former orderly condition. After moving away from the view, I inspect the mansion near my location and generally fill time before preparing for the dinner.

When the time comes, I shower and dress, studying myself in the mirror once finished. I have transformed into someone half-respectable. The provided clothes, a black uniform with a white shirt and emerald cummerbund, fit me to perfection and grant me a cultured guise. I might even pass as a prince in this outfit. The only item I insist on wearing, not handed to me, is my maser, which I tuck away in an unobtrusive position.

A knock disturbs me, and I open the door. The sight takes my breath away. Adala stands there, the image of a goddess. She has arranged her long hair in a cascade of curls, and a tiara sits on top, resplendent with diamonds. She wears an emerald-green dress that matches her eyes and my cummerbund to perfection and flows to the floor in ripples of fabric, hugging her upper body, accentuating her figure. A gold necklace adorns her neck, dropping to her cleavage with an emerald hanging from it as large as an egg. "Are you ready?"

I open my mouth and close it again, then say, "You're fantastic … beautiful."

Adala blushes in delight. "I am required to wear this clothing on these occasions, but tonight I made a special effort … I wanted to … impress you."

I gulp. "Well … you did that."

"Shall we?"

"Yes," I say as I step out of my apartment and lock arms with her, content for her to lead me to the banquet. It feels so natural as we stroll to the dining room for the celebration dinner, exchanging small talk and banter.

We arrive at the room, and the ushers attending the doors open them to allow us to enter without obstruction. The congregation inside is producing a loud hubbub of conversation, which stops when they announce us — yes, announce. I see King Abelard there with Sentinel and Sigmund and Frieda, General Tancred, and General Ernst, and many others including many women, but when we enter, the crowd falls silent. I do not know why, but I suspect Adala has orchestrated the effect, and I don't care.

King Abelard walks forward. "Well, you two are a handsome couple."

I blush, but I see that the compliment from her father delights Adala when I glance at her.

"Ladies and gentlemen," Abelard says in a loud baritone voice, "may I present the reason for tonight's celebration: Adala's persistence in returning the kingdom to its rightful rule and Halwende, who unselfishly risked his life to help us. They exemplified bravery in risking their lives for a righteous cause. Let us raise our glasses and toast our gratitude to Adala and Halwende."

"To Princess Adala and Halwende," the crowd responds as they raise their glasses and toast us.

I stand speechless, both honored and humbled. If they only knew the secrets that I have buried within me. "It is only one step that I have made in redeeming my past mistakes," stumbles from my lips. Pain etches my face as I say it. I don't want to project this mien, but it happens regardless.

Adala catches the expression and squeezes my arm in support. I glance at her and mouth my thank you. A server approaches and provides us both with a glass of champagne. "Shall we mingle?" she asks.

"Do I have a choice?"

"No." She releases my arm, and we walk over to a small section of the crowd, joining in with the general conversation.

After 15 minutes, the chief steward announces dinner and asks everyone to sit. Adala sits next to her father, who is at the head of the table, and I sit beside her. Sentinel is on my other side, and Sigmund and Frieda are opposite us. Sentinel has dressed in formal attire too and has styled his hair formally in plaited braids.

"I never contemplated seeing you in any clothes but a fighting outfit," I say to him in jest.

"Nor I you," he quips back.

They serve the meal in its various courses, and we wash it down with copious amounts of wine of our choosing. The stewards clean away the food and plates, and the guests continue talking and drinking until King Abelard stands and waits for us to coast to silence.

"There is one more topic I wish to bring to you tonight," he says. Adala looks puzzled, but he continues. "I have ruled this kingdom with justice and fairness for forty years. You may or may not agree with that assessment, but that is mine. My body is wearing out, and my recent confinement has not helped. So, I intend to abdicate my throne–"

A cacophony of confusion arises in the room. I glance at Adala to learn what Abelard's announcement means, but she's as bewildered as the rest of them. She looks to her father, questions in her eyes, and then lowers her gaze to her lap, perplexed and emotional, clasping her hands tightly until they whiten. I'm unsure what I should do, so I touch her arm and squeeze it to give her reassurance.

Abelard waits for the noise to abate. "... I have had my day. It is time for fresh blood to take you forward to the future ahead, and I sense that our destiny is beyond our expectations." Abelard glances at me before his gaze returns to the group. "In abdicating, I name my firstborn Princess Adala as my successor, as she has proven herself well able to carry out the duties of a monarch."

Adala looks at her father, tears in her eyes, shaking her head, not wanting this to happen.

Sentinel stands and then kneels before Adala. "You have my fealty forever, Queen Adala."

I stare at Sentinel and back at Adala, sorting through my own thoughts. As multiple emotions rush through me, I realize that I want nothing more than to serve Adala in whatever capacity I can for as long as I live on this planet. So, I stand and kneel too.

Adala looks at Sentinel and me. Her emotions break, but she pulls herself together to face her new challenge. After wiping the tears from her eyes, she stands and stares at the guests' expectant faces and then at Sentinel and me. She smiles and bends to take my hand, gesturing me to stand. "Father," she says, "this announcement is unwelcome and unexpected. I have so many things still to achieve and experiences to have before being called upon to undertake my royal duty, contingent on the realm's desire. But I acknowledge your tiredness of the past months and the deprivations you have endured. So, with reluctance, I accept your nomination and will strive to accomplish even a small fraction of what you accomplished in your time ruling this great nation." She pauses and then, holding her head in regal dignity, adds, "I wish to request one thing that I have no right to ask." She turns to me. "I wish you, Halwende, to stay as long as you wish, to guide me as best you can."

Mesmerized, I stare at her, speechless. I want to run, but her power enchants me, and her charm overpowers me. Somewhere deep inside me, I know that my destiny is with Adala. I gaze around the room, and everyone waits for a reply. I gulp, look back at Adala, and kneel once more. "Nothing would please me more than to counsel you to the best of my ability, Queen Adala."

Adala breaks out in a radiant smile, her sparkling eyes outshining the milky way on a cloudless night, and the depth of her elegance and capacity for love overpowers me. I let out an involuntary sob and bow my head to hide my emotions.

The guests rise from their seats and raise their glasses. King Abelard says the fateful words, "To Queen Adala."

"To Queen Adala," the rest respond.

A few moments later, I get a tap on the shoulder. "You can sit now. You're embarrassing me."

I stare up at Adala, and she has an impish, teasing smile. I glance around and see Sentinel has taken his seat, so I stand, straighten my uniform, and sit too. "This is most uncomfortable," I whisper to Adala.

"What is?"

"How do we have fun now, since you're the queen?"

Adala giggles at my dilemma. "I'm sure we'll find a solution, and besides, I'm not the queen yet. We must conform to protocol."

"Yes ... protocol."

She laughs again. "Stop it." She taps me. "You're making fun of me now."

I give her an innocent expression but then sigh and grin with content. "I will never mock you ... without your permission ... but I will stand beside you as long as you will have me."

Adala bites her lip, emotion overpowering her as she looks deep into my eyes. "And I you."

I have no reply but to grab my glass of wine, gesturing for Adala to take hers. Our glasses meet and we sip, while I hold her eyes in the depths of my soul and she holds mine in hers.

We both return to reality after our intense moment and spend the rest of the evening conversing with the guests. At the end of the evening, they leave, even Sigmund, Frieda, Sentinel, and finally Abelard. Adala and I are alone and exhausted from the day's emotions. They have drained her of strength, and we both need rest, but I can't bring myself to leave her for my room's isolation.

Adala sighs. "It has been an exhausting day." She looks at me, still with fresh charm despite her tiredness. "Let's retire to the balcony," she says, motioning to the terrace that extends from the banqueting hall.

"Is that a command?" I ask with a wry grin.

"No. A petition ... a wish."

"I will comply regardless." I rise and help her do the same.

We wander over to the balcony doors and open them. A balmy breeze meets us, and the aroma of newly opening blossoms tantalizes our senses. It is sensuous and alluring. We stroll to the balcony's railing and embrace each other as we gaze out over the city, our shoulders touching and heads brushing against the other.

"It has been a big day for you," I say.

"Yes. It has. I never expected Father's announcement. He gave no hint that it was coming. He has not prepared me for it."

After I consider her words, I say, "I disagree. I think your father has been preparing you for it your entire life. The events of the last months have convinced him you are ready."

"Maybe. Why do I feel so unprepared, then?"

"It would worry me if you didn't feel that way."

Adala giggles and then returns to her reticence. She finally asks, "Did you mean what you said?"

"What was that?"

"That you'd stay with me."

"... Yes, I did."

"So did I."

As we gaze into each other's eyes, we move our faces closer before we brush our mouths together in passion for an eternity of bliss. We part again but pursue our passion as much as we can in a public place. We then retire to Adala's room to continue.

35

THE PORTAL ROOM

Over the next few weeks, everyone is busy preparing for the coronation of Adala as queen. The city is abuzz with work and celebration as the troubles of the past years fade, replaced with joyous events and preparations for the upcoming festivities. No expense is being spared.

I'm a hindrance, unconnected with the city's fever, and regress into myself, although Adala and I meet at least once a day. It is problematic, though, as she is so busy. Catching her alone is becoming increasingly more difficult. I use my time to explore the palace. I am particularly interested in the portal room. I need to discover whatever else is there. The room admits me at once without question, unnoticed by anyone. Everything is as it was when I left it. I do not turn the gate shields on, as no one has requested me to.

As I walk along the rows of switches and equipment, I read the labels that describe what each switch or item is. A row of unfamiliar levers come into sight, although I must have seen them before when I studied the chamber. I realize these devices control the cloaking of the city, people, animals, and even the planet. It shocks me that the machinery in this room controls the cloaking — and that I could deactivate it. I'm tempted to do just that, but it's Adala's decision, not mine. I must show Adala when I bring her here, whenever that will be.

There is a seat in the corner, and I sit on it to regain my composure. Why locate the controls in this crypt? Who were they? From my understanding of what the library and King Abelard said, they installed the cloaking device to prevent the planet from being annexed for a particular mineral deposit, valuable as an energy source. The only ore I'm aware of is the blue crystal lying on this room's floor, the same stones I helped dig up at the mine. But they're not rare, albeit special to Egon and presumably others on Helheim.

An apparition unexpectedly materializes before me as I sit and ponder these thoughts. A robed man, familiar from ancient times, in holo-movies of antiquity, and in the museum on school field trips, stands staring at me. Astonished, I try to understand what is happening. Why has this vision appeared?

"Welcome, fellow Eriduan."

I jump in surprise at the voice. Unsure what to do, I say, "Hello. What can I do for you?"

"I am the custodian of this room. It has been eons since an Eriduan has graced me with his presence. Did you find the room's key in the library?"

I bristle at the query. "The library gave me no message."

"You can't have asked the right question or given the correct information."

"Yeah, right? Why have you appeared, anyway?"

"I am the custodian of this chamber. I have been waiting for a true Eriduan to arrive to release me, as the prophecy promised. The room and portal supervision is yours, and I can now rest."

"Not so fast. What do I do with it? I don't understand this room and why it's here."

"The answers are in the library."

"But I don't want it. You can't make me. You're just a recording or something."

"That is not my concern. I have fulfilled my duty and now hand control over to you." The specter fades away.

"Wait ... What do you mean 'It's not your concern'? Why is it my concern?"

It's useless talking to nothing, and I propel myself from the chair in disgust. What do I do now? This makes no sense. Why is this responsibility placed on me? I'm a nobody, a trader who lost everything because he was a coward. This is too much. I must escape and think, and my only haven of safety is my ship. I rush from the portal room and along the corridors. Fortunately, because of my status, I am not asked to explain what I am doing or where I am going, so I dash to the scooter pool and borrow one. After lifting off, I travel through the gates and out of the city at speed, reaching my vessel a half-hour later.

I smile, pleased to be back. I'm home again in my wreckage of a ship. After opening the hatch, I enter and rummage for a bottle of my favorite rum, happy I still have a good supply. The top pops off with practiced ease, and I gulp a copious quantity of the fiery liquid, spiraling into a drunken stupor, staggering to my bunk to rest, where I devour the contents and forget my worries and responsibilities.

I wake with a hangover I haven't experienced for a long time. I definitely need to drink more. Noises come from outside, but their meaning fails me. I try to focus with bleary and bloodshot eyes, but I give up and fall back on my bunk, my eyes shut. I try once more to raise myself to awareness but descend into a semi-consciousness hungover sleep instead.

Banging from the hull reverberates through my brain like a pile driver's percussions. I must stop it before my head splits. I swing from my cot with the ease of my many years of practice and stagger to the hatch and open it. "Will you please stop that?"

Adala and Sentinel stand before me, worried until they see me.

Sentinel's expression changes to a smirk. "You need a rest."

I try glaring at him, but the light intensity is too bright for my eyes to open and give the right effect. "Yeah, well, I had to get away." On turning, I retrace my steps through the ship to the galley and a table with bench seats and sit on one. The others follow me. As I gaze at Adala, I see she is not happy. She presents a face to me that she never has before. It's as if I'm a young child being reprimanded with silence. "What?"

Adala remains standing even though seating is available. Her face colors. "You scared me. I thought you were injured, or you ran away and deserted me after you promised ..."

I'm a jerk. As I rub my eyes, reducing the pressure of the hangover, I blink and peer at her. "Sorry ... I discovered something ... something happened, and I needed time to think."

"What? What happened?"

"Will you sit? I feel like a schoolboy being chastened." My face colors as I realize Adala hasn't earned my harsh words. I take a big breath and calm my mood. "Please ... sit. I deserve your displeasure."

Adala softens and comes over to the bench I am sitting on, sitting near me. She extends her hand to one of mine and caresses it. "What happened, Halwende?"

I sigh. "A room exists ... under the palace. The shielding controls are in it. That's how I deactivated the gate shield. I went into it again yesterday, trying to understand what else was in it. I encountered something I didn't want to know. It gave me a responsibility I don't want."

"What is it?"

"I can't tell. Not yet. I need to find out more first. I need to go to the library."

"Can I come with you?"

"Aren't you busy ... with the coronation and everything?"

Adala looks at me, assessing my demeanor, and decides. "I have been neglecting you too much ..."

"No, you ..."

As Adala lifts her hand, placing a finger on my lips to silence me, she continues, "... Yes, I have. The excitement and planning have diverted my attention from you. I have forgotten what is important. Please, the library is an essential place. My father has only just informed me of it, that it has a wealth of knowledge of our kingdom and our origins. I must learn this, beginning now."

My mind swirls with indecision. I prefer to be alone when I try to understand what the apparition in the portal room told me, but I want Adala by my side, too — her comfort, the protective aura she projects onto others. "OK. We will go together."

"Hmm, hmm."

Both Adala and I glance at Sentinel.

"What is it, Ranulf?"

Sentinel shuffles, a movement unnatural to him. "Begging Your Highness's pardon, but we should be returning. We said we would not be long."

"Oh, Ranulf ... enough of that," Adala says, her irritation showing. She looks at her chronometer and sighs, "You're right, though. We should return." She glances at me. "Will you come with us?"

"Yeah, OK. Let me clean myself up first."

"Can I help?" Adala asks, an impish grin on her face.

A grunt of annoyance slips from my mouth, but a lustful thought escapes from my eyes as I ogle her, and she giggles in delight but stays where she is while I step away to use my bathroom on board the ship. Minutes later, I'm ready to return to the city. We walk out, and I lock the hatch. I go to the scooter I borrowed.

"I'm going with Halwende," I hear Adala tell Sentinel.

"As you wish. I will follow."

I turn and stare at them. Sentinel nods, accepting the arrangement, and Adala strolls over to me and wraps her arm around me as we both stroll to my scooter. We get on board. I start it up and program it for the palace. We both sit, and I lean against Adala's shoulder, feeling her softness and warmth on my cheek as my head tries to control its anger from the chemical storm wreaking havoc within it.

The scooter lifts from the ground and speeds back to the city, Sentinel following close behind us.

36

BACK TO THE LIBRARY

I arrive back in my apartment as they whisk Adala away to another appointment. She promises to see me soon so we can visit the library together. Sentinel goes to follow her in his dutiful manner, but Adala orders him to stay with me.

"You know a cure for a hangover?" I ask him.

Sentinel chuckles. "I've had one or two in my life. Come with me."

We weave our way through the palace corridors and reach the kitchens, where utensils clatter with a buzz of enterprise. My head pounds in protest. "This is your remedy?"

"Wait." Sentinel disappears for a few moments and comes back with a glass filled with liquid. He gives it to me. "Drink."

I stare at him, not knowing whether I can trust his intentions. Is he playing a trick on me? I smell the contents of the glass and it smells drinkable. Raising it to my lips, I take a taste and almost spit it out in disgust. "Are you trying to poison me?"

"Drink. You will feel much better," he says with a smirk.

For an insane reason, my brain trusts him, and I consume the rest. Growls of protest churn my stomach for a few minutes while digestion starts and nutrients trickle into my bloodstream. My mind clears and the headache dissipates within a few more minutes. I glance at Sentinel. "You must give me the recipe for that."

"Someday. Let us return before Princess Adala does."

We retrace our steps, returning to my room. "Now what?"

"We wait. Princess Adala won't be long."

I try to keep busy, doing little, until I realize I am still wearing the clothes I had on yesterday. "I will have a shower and change if you don't mind."

"As you wish. I shall stay outside the door." He leaves.

It comforts me to know he's standing guard. Sentinel is an enormous asset to Adala, and I realize he has become a close friend to me, too. I hope that never changes. Undressed, I soak up the warmth under the shower with the water cascading over me. Minutes later, I turn off the spray, dry myself and peer in the mirror. I look like a derelict with an unkempt beard. A shave is in order, so I comply. My hands stroke my smooth face afterward with approval, and I search for clothes to dress in. An array of choices I could only dream of hangs in the wardrobe. I decide on a soft mint shirt with black pants and a matching black jacket and shoes. I stand for a moment, inspecting myself in the mirror.

"Not bad."

I jump. "Where did you come from?" I say as I see Adala standing in front of the closed door.

Adala laughs in delight. "I didn't think you had any vanity or modesty in you."

"Well, I don't ... and I do," I say annoyed, but aroused. "You shouldn't be here."

"I'm to be crowned queen. I can be wherever I want to be," she says as she approaches me.

"You know what I mean." My discomfort shows as she stands in front of me.

"Yes, I do ... and I am sorry if I make you uncomfortable." Sparks of delight and love emanate from her eyes.

I can't stand it any longer. Her allure overwhelms me. I grab her around the waist, pull her to me, and give her a kiss of passion. She reciprocates. We break, gasping for breath, not sure what should happen next. I push her away gently. "We should go."

Adala is flushed but takes a few quick breaths to compose herself. "Yes, we should. I sent Sentinel away so we can go to the library together, just the two of us."

We leave together hand in hand and wander through the palace depths to the library.

"How did you find this place?"

"Your father told me where it was."

"I wonder why he never told me. Why did he tell you?"

"I don't know. I needed to know to escape the palace ... or I'm more trustworthy than you," I say, grinning.

"He trusts ... ooh, you just wait." Adala tries to grab me, but I evade her efforts and laugh as we near the library entrance.

I touch the opening mechanism. The door opens and we enter. I glance at Adala, and she stares as she takes in the room, fascinated.

"There aren't many books, only those shelves," she says, as she points to the bookshelf. "How do you access information?"

"Those books contain information, but normally you just query the library, and it responds. Sometimes it can be reticent in providing the answer. I think that's because you haven't asked the right question. But I believe it decides on whether the person asking needs to know."

"So ... what are you going to ask?"

I contemplate my approach, considering the trouble I had last time when I asked imprecise questions. I start by showing Adala what she can find out. "Show us a map of the palace."

It displays a hologram of the palace compound in the center of the room moments later. Adala stares in awe at the apparition. She looks at me. "Where are the secret passages?"

"Ask the library."

She creases her brow in thought like a child trying to decide how to ask how boys are different from girls. "Show ... me the secret passageways."

"The map shows them," the library declares in its ethereal speech.

The response annoys Adala. "Highlight them," she commands in her regal tone.

The corridors illuminate in a soft red color.

I snigger. "You need to be precise, or it won't give you the information you want."

"So, I see," she says, studying the image to comprehend the design of the passages and their extent. She peers at me. "You worked out your route into the Grand Ballroom from here?"

I nod in acknowledgment.

Adala stands straight again after hunching over, inspecting the map. "I will need days to absorb this. I can return later, now I know the room exists. What information did you want?"

"Answers to more fundamental questions."

"You had better continue then." Adala steps back as a sign that I have the floor to speak.

"Who built the portal room?" I ask, looking up at nothing.

There is a moment's silence. *"I am not at liberty to divulge that knowledge."*

My blood boils with the cat-and-mouse game that the library plays whenever that topic arises. "Listen, I am now custodian of those controls. If that doesn't give me permission, what does? Now tell me immediately!" I smile at Adala with a hint of vanity. She rolls her eyes but looks impressed.

Its silence is prolonged this time, but a reply eventually comes. *"The settings have changed, and I have verified your claim."* If the library's voice were physical, I'm in the mood to punch it, but it's not. *"You are the chamber's custodian now. It has released more intelligence to me. The Eriduans constructed the chamber."*

The hint that there may be even more information than I was expecting intrigues me, but I will let the revelations unfold as I thread my questions through the maze of responses that the library might give me. "Who from Eridu built the room?"

"Emperor Alalgar had the room built when the prevailing wars over the planet's resources threatened to overthrow his position of power on Eridu.

He wanted to calm the escalating frenzy of greed and removed the material from everyone's grasp for a time. His son, Alulim, stayed on the planet to restore order."

Adala gasps at the name.

I turn to see what has startled her. "What is it?"

"Alulim was the first King of Helheim. He is my ancestor."

"Small galaxy." I scratch my chin. Something puzzles me. The names are familiar to me because they originate from my home planet, but that isn't it. "Tell me more about Emperor Alalgar."

"Emperor Alalgar reigned in the empire of the Rigelians four hundred years ago. He had two sons — Alulim, who stayed on to rule Helheim and Dumuzid, who succeeded Alalgar when he died."

It is my turn to be astonished in more ways than one. Not only do I remember Dumuzid as my ancient forefather, but that means that Adala and I originate from the same bloodline. I stare at her as if I have just met her for the first time.

"What is it?"

"We have the same heritage."

"That is impossible. You do not come from here."

"Dumuzid is my ancestor. Dumuzid and Alulim were brothers."

Adala's eyes widen as she understands what I am saying. "No wonder I admire you so much," she says with a cheeky grin.

"I don't know; you are different, not my type of woman."

"You'll pay for that."

We both laugh.

"What now?"

"Not sure ... Library, how long was the cloaking meant to exist?"

"It was uncertain, but they programmed the portal to preserve the cloaking until another came from Eridu to remove it."

"You see what that means, Adala? It has mistaken me for that person."

"How do you know it's a mistake?"

"You kidding me? I'm just a trader, one that has disgraced himself and runs, a coward."

"That's not the person I see. I see someone of honor and courage. No one in my realm would have gone to such lengths to save me from Egon, apart from Sentinel."

"That's different."

"Is it?"

I recognize we are at a standoff in our argument, and I realize I must go away with this fresh knowledge and digest what it means. As I gaze at Adala, I sigh. "I can't decide what to do. I need to think. We may as well go back. I got the information I wanted." I consider one last question. "What powers the equipment?"

"The design and room details are in the designated tome on the library bookshelf."

I stagger in disbelief. That's what the book holds. I rush over and pull it from the shelf. It opens and I flick through the pages. Documentation, drawings, and diagrams now exist where there were only blank pages. My new status must have unlocked the contents of the book. I realize I can't digest its contents now, so I put it back for later. "Let's go."

Adala nods in agreement and moves over to me. She grabs my hands and raises them, bringing them up to our chins, and squeezes them, "Remember, Halwende, I am here for you, and I hope you will always be here for me." The sincerity in her eyes scares me, but I sense an element of fear there too.

She might fear I will run away from her like I did yesterday — and like I ran years ago. I'm ashamed that she cannot trust me in that, and I turn away. That is cowardice. I turn back and gaze into her eyes again. "I will try. Give me room to learn and time to warm to the idea. It has been a long time."

"I will. Now, let us go. I have a surprise for you."

I raise an eyebrow in query, wondering what she has up her sleeve. She has arranged something. She lets go of one hand but maintains her hold on the other, pulling me through the library door and to the palace's upper levels. We weave our way through the corridors until we enter a courtyard that opens onto the lake with a pier projecting into it. A boat sits next to it, rocking as the waves pass by underneath. The boat, recognizable as a yacht with a tall, majestic mast towers above us. The royal flag of Helheim flutters at the top. I am intrigued. "What do you have planned?"

"We are going out onto the lake for lunch and to relax for the afternoon."

"Who will steer it?"

"I will. I am not just a pretty face."

"Most definitely."

Adala huffs in indignation.

"You are Athena personified."

Radiance emanates from her at the compliment.

"Still, I hope you can handle this. Who taught you?"

"Father. Enough talking. Come."

"Where is everyone?"

"What do you mean?"

"We are going alone?"

"Why not? Don't worry. Ranulf will make sure nothing happens to us."

I glance at her, skeptical, and search to locate Sentinel but can't. An afternoon alone with Adala is to be treasured. I intend to enjoy the tryst and walk happily to the sailboat as she draws me with her. We climb on board, and Adala pulls away from me to attend to the job of disembarking from the pier. I feel useless but spend the time watching what she does, impressed by her skill. I can see she has spent significant time on this boat. I am content to relax while she does her tasks. I walk over to a seat at the rear of the yacht and sit.

The boat floats away from shore as the zephyr of a breeze catches the sail Adala has rigged. It gathers speed as it progresses to the center of the lake. The wind catches my hair, and I sit back in the chair enjoying the sensation. Adala stands at the helm, steering the yacht toward its destination, whatever that may be. She is in intense concentration as she looks across the expanse of the lake. The warm humid air raises her mane from her head as well, and I can see her unmistakable cheekbone structure, which I have become accustomed to admiring. As I search the lake, I see a flotilla of other craft following us. Her security detail. She is too valuable to be far from sight outside the palace. Sentinel stands in the lead boat, and I wave to him. He waves back.

"Where are we going?" I ask.

"I thought we might pass by the waterfall and anchor nearby for lunch," Adala says, turning to me with a smile.

"Great. I wish I had a hand-held camera at this moment."

"Camera? Why?"

"To capture an image so we can reminisce later."

Adala shakes her head. "I don't think so."

"How else do we remember this time?" I get up and walk over to her, placing my arms around her waist as she steers.

She arches her spine to lean back on me and her warmth seeps through me as we gaze forward toward the cascading waterfall looming larger as the distance shortens. Only the boat's bow slicing through the lake disturbs the calm surface. Spray from the fall is creating a rainbow of color as the sunlight diffracts through it. I sense true peace, a feeling missing for many years, and know I belong here.

"Credit for your thoughts."

I jump as I mentally return to the yacht. "Nothing. Just thinking how I'm enjoying this."

"Maybe it's the company."

"No ... don't think so."

Adala shoves me with her rear as punishment for the comment. I laugh and squeeze her tighter, brushing my lips on the side of her neck. She closes her eyes and parts her lips in erotic response, leaning her head back against my shoulder, and I have trouble stopping myself from progressing any further in my sensuous teasing, but we are not alone. Nearing the waterfall, I presume Adala will have duties to attend to before we lunch. I am right.

Adala opens her eyes again and smiles, sparkles of light reflecting from her pupils as she turns around to me. "I have to weigh anchor."

Reluctantly, I let her go to do her tasks, returning to my seat again.

She furls the sail and releases the anchor, the chain rattling as the weight speeds toward the bottom of the lake. With the boat anchored, Adala goes to a cupboard on board and pulls out a basket and rug. I get up to help, and she hands me a bottle of wine. "Here, open this, please."

"Where are the servants?" I tease.

Adala peers at me. "I can do without servants sometimes, you know. Do you really want servants here disturbing our serenity? *They* are bad enough." She points to the other boats floating nearby but keeping their distance.

Acknowledging her point, I busy myself by opening the bottle. She lays the rug on the deck and sits, legs to one side, unpacking the basket afterward. I sit cross-legged across from her, grab the two glasses from the hamper, and pour a glass of wine for each of us. We sip our drink and gaze at each other. I consider her, and she me, each wanting the other to start the conversation. "This is a magnificent sight," I say, gazing at her.

"Yes. I came here often when I was younger, before the trouble started."

"I wasn't talking about the scenery."

Adala looks away and blushes. She looks back. "Thank you."

"You're welcome." We sit in silence for a moment. "How are you feeling about becoming queen?"

"It's so unreal, and I don't think I am ready for the responsibility." Adala looks at me, earnest. "I think Father has made a mistake."

"Have you ever considered your father might have had the same feelings when he became king? He wouldn't have abdicated if he thought you couldn't rise to the occasion. And, from watching you lead the rebels, I know you'll make an exceptional leader."

"But I had a talented team of people around me to support me and give me advice — Ranulf, Sigmund, Frieda, the generals ... and you."

"Nobody can rule in a vacuum. Assemble that same team again, and anyone else you trust. That is what leadership is." I wonder where I stored that gem of wisdom.

Adala turns away, gazing at the water tumbling from the ledge above us. "You are right. I suppose I will have to have more confidence in myself." She looks back, gives a faint smile, and busies herself with the food.

I keep watching her for a moment and then join her in finding morsels to eat. After a brief pause, I say, "You're fond of this — being alone, in charge of your own destiny, having no outside interference — aren't you?"

Adala looks at me, eyes sparkling. "Yes, I am. I enjoy being free, something I fear losing with my new responsibilities."

"Even monarchs need time off to refresh and rejuvenate themselves. You need to set aside time in your schedule."

"And you?"

"What of me?"

"You talk as if you will be leaving. You promised me you would stay, to be with me."

"I won't leave without your consent. But I am confused. There's a craving in me, but I'm unsure for what. I gaze at the stars and itch to travel there again, but this existence is so peaceful, and I enjoy your company."

"I enjoy being around you too. Did you not promise to show me these stars I still can't believe are there?"

"I have no ship. I am not going anywhere."

"No, you're not." Adala looks absorbed but doesn't share her thoughts.

We complete our lunch without saying much more, and I move to sit beside her, draping my arm around her as she leans against me. We both gaze at the lake and waterfall as the sun descends the western sky. It is so peaceful here. I feel that my buried troubles are healing in this serene place, and Adala's love soaks through me. The boat's gentle rocking lulls me to sleep, and Adala bumps me to wakefulness more than once with giggles of delight.

Adala sighs. "I guess I had better get us back."

"Do you have to? I could stay here forever."

"So could I, but I am sure they will not allow it."

I chuckle. "Aye, aye, Captain," I say in mocking fun as I prepare to lift myself from the deck.

Adala does the same, and we repack the picnic basket, which Adala returns to the cupboard. I help her raise anchor, and she rigs the yacht to return us to the palace docks and the business of life again.

37

CORONATION

Coronation Day arrives with great fanfare. The entire city is astir as people jostle for a glimpse of their impending new queen. The streets between the palace and the cathedral are filling with lines of spectators on both sides. I take all of this in from a vantage point high in the palace as I wait for transportation there myself. Sentinel is with me. Adala will be in the Royal Scooter with her attendants. I will travel with Sentinel, Sigmund, and Frieda in a separate scooter. My attendance at the ceremony in an important position makes me uncomfortable, but Adala insists. My uniform is scratchy, and I fidget to get it in a position that doesn't irritate me.

"Relax. The ceremony will finish before we know it."

"It's just that this outfit is so annoying. It's itchy."

"The burdens we bear," Sentinel says as he pats me on the back. "Come. We leave soon. We are to be in the cathedral before Princess Adala arrives."

I follow Sentinel as he walks away. "You know she hates formality."

"Ha! Old habits die hard. I do it for my sake, to remind me I am protecting her and not being a loving uncle taking her to play or to a familial event, as I used to when she was young."

He has piqued my interest in Adala's past life. "What was she like as a child?"

Sentinel chuckles. "She was a real brat on occasions. I had to inflict harsh punishments, at the king's pleasure, for her behavior, but there was never any malice in her. She was always full of energy and inquisitive for knowledge." He becomes somber. "She grieved her mother's death bitterly, as we all did. Apart from her father, it hurt her the most, though. She closeted herself away for days, not wanting to talk of it."

"How old was she?"

"She was seven, mature enough to understand what was happening. Still, she came around to acceptance in time, and I believe she became a stronger person for it."

We walk the rest of the distance to the scooter in silence. I ponder Sentinel's comments and place them in my memory vault for later thought. The craft sits in front of us as we round the corner. Sigmund and Frieda are waiting impatiently to get going.

"Greetings, sir," both Sigmund and Frieda say to me.

"Greetings to you too. We meet rarely of late."

"You've been too busy with another person," Frieda says with a snigger, one of the first displays of childish behavior I've seen in her. It pleases me, as they should both be able to enjoy their childhood.

Sigmund has a cheeky smirk too, and I see him break into a grin.

I appreciate the banter and smile. "Yes, I have. But please remember you are always welcome to visit me when you can, so long as you don't surprise me as you did when we first met."

"That is most gracious of you," Sigmund says.

"Shall we?" Sentinel says as he points to the scooter.

We get in and sit. Moments later, we lift off and travel to the cathedral where attendants usher us to our seats. We sit in the front row on the right of the central aisle. Sentinel sits on the end, Sigmund and Frieda are next, and I am beside Frieda. No one is to my right. My clothes still itch. I shuffle to find a more comfortable position but can't manage one. We wait for the building to fill and for Adala to arrive. I scan the audience occasionally as the pews fill and notice the crowd overflowing outside the entrance.

An enormous pounding reverberates throughout the cathedral, and everyone quietens. Dignitaries enter from a side entrance, including King Abelard, and stand at the front, facing the crowd and the cathedral's doorway. I see Abelard smile as he gazes in that direction, so I glance around and see Adala at the entrance resplendent in a white dress reaching the floor, covered with a regal blue robe that has gold trimmings and an emblem on her right breast — a lion, the insignia of the royal family. The garment has a train flowing behind her, which is being tidied by her attendants in preparation for the long walk down the aisle. She smiles but looks nervous. I smile but don't expect her to see me. I presume she has too much turmoil in her head to scan the audience for me.

Music plays from a huge pipe organ in the back of the choir, the sound resonating throughout the cathedral. The piece is familiar to me, a coronation tune on my home planet. Adala strides toward the front with measured steps, looking straight ahead at her father. As she nears where we stand, she glances to the side toward us, spotting me, and her smile broadens as I grin back and give a nod of encouragement. She turns her head forward again and halts her march as she clears the seating. The music ends.

"King Abelard, Ruler of Helheim, please state your intentions," a robed dignitary intones. He is clearly someone of importance, but I am unaware of his role in government or society. The acoustics of the cathedral amplify his strong voice.

King Abelard then pronounces the all-important words, "I hereby abdicate my right to rule Helheim and hand authority over to Princess Adala, heir to the throne, if she will accept the responsibility."

"Princess Adala, heir apparent of Helheim, do you acknowledge King Abelard's abdication?"

"I do," Adala says, her voice not betraying her nerves.

"Do you hereby intend to rule the kingdom of Helheim to the best of your ability, for the good of the citizens of Helheim, protecting them from foe and enemy, internal and foreign, using your best endeavors to lead them to live in peace and prosperity as long as you rule?"

"I hereby intend to rule the kingdom of Helheim and swear to protect my subjects, using my best endeavors so that they live in peace and prosperity, as long as I am permitted and agree to rule."

The dignitary takes a crown from a cushion carried by a page. "By the authority empowered upon me by the state, I declare you Queen Adala of Helheim." He places it on Adala's head. He picks up what I presume is the royal scepter and gives it to her too. She holds it with both hands.

Adala turns to the congregation, and we all chant in unison: "All hail, Queen Adala."

The nervousness of before has subsided, and she blushes with pride. Abelard descends from the raised dais, stops in front of her, and kneels. She touches his head with the pommel of the scepter. He stands again and steps aside. Sentinel leaves his seat and does the same, as do Sigmund and Frieda — Frieda curtsies with head bowed. Adala acknowledges them.

The royal staff advise me to do likewise, but I freeze. Adala glances toward me, and my feet start to move, my face reddening at my unintentional delay. Standing in front of her, I make to kneel, but she stops me with her scepter and places the pommel on my right shoulder and then my left. Murmurs come from behind me, but I don't understand what just happened. I glance at Adala with a questioning expression.

She beams and whispers, "I've just given you the greatest honor in the realm."

I still don't understand. "I haven't accidentally gotten myself married or something?" I quip.

Adala just manages to stifle a laugh and looks at me, twinkling delight in her eyes. "No, you haven't, but I can arrange it ... In the meantime, you are my Grand Chancellor."

I stumble from surprise and shock but regain my composure quickly.

I step aside with Adala still trying to control herself.

"Not here," Sentinel whispers.

I glance at him.

"Next to her."

I stare at him again, blinking as I try to comprehend his words. "What?"

"Beside her ... over there," he says, pointing to Adala's left side.

I look to where he is pointing. My feet are leaden, but I move them and step to my correct position. "You could have told me," I whisper to Adala.

"What, and spoil my fun? Walk with me and stop complaining."

As I stare at her, I prepare to give a retort but reconsider.

She starts her march along the aisle, and I shuffle to mimic her rhythm, finally pacing in unison with her. The assembly bows their heads as we pass their position in the cathedral. I glance behind me and see that the others, including Abelard, are following us. We reach the cathedral entrance and descend the steps and into the royal scooter, Adala's attendants arranging her train so that it doesn't catch in obstacles. The vehicle is open to the air, and we still stand so that the crowd can see us. Two men sit up front in the piloting seats, attired in a costume akin to ancient regal coachmen. We relax and scan the crowd. The people cheer and wave, enthusiasm and excitement etched on their faces, eager to be acknowledged by their queen and creating a memory they can tell their grandchildren one day. It's not every day they see a new monarch crowned. Most didn't see the last one, and they may not see another in their lifetime. The scooter rises above the ground and travels at a steady pace toward the palace.

"What am I doing here?"

"As my Grand Chancellor, you are escorting me back to the palace."

"You just wait till I can get you alone," I say.

Adala is waving to the crowd but looks at me with a mischievous smile. "I can't wait."

I huff. "You know what I mean."

"Stop whining, will you, and enjoy yourself. Every man in the realm would give their soul to be in your shoes."

"Well, I'm not every man." My annoyance subsides, and I stretch myself straight, deciding I may as well enjoy myself as Adala suggested. I glance at her and smile. She is so radiant and graceful in her regal attire as if made for the position. Turning my head, I stare at the crowd. "Am I supposed to wave as well?"

"Of course. You will upset your queen if you don't."

"That's not acceptable." I start waving.

Adala looks at me with a smile but gives me a dig in the ribs with her elbow.

I search the surrounds and spot the others in a scooter behind us. We continue waving for the entire return trip to the palace, where the scooter stops at the Grand Ballroom entrance. They have decorated the ballroom for a large celebratory dinner with the dignitaries and important nobles of the realm. We alight from the scooter and, to show my good faith and because I wish it, I raise my hand with Adala's on top of mine, leading her up the steps, escorting her as a gesture of honor.

She looks at me, sparkles of appreciation in her eyes. "That is much better."

I smile back with an impish grin, my annoyance forgotten. "I take it being the Grand Chancellor has advantages when it comes to taking liberties with the queen."

"Ha! That he may. He may have his head removed too."

"You wouldn't," I say.

"Only if he doesn't obey my every desire." A momentary flicker of lust escapes from her.

"We can't have that." I chuckle.

We reach the top of the steps and turn. The crowd still lingers at the gate, eager to get one last glimpse of their queen. We wave for their sake, turn, and walk inside and to the awaiting feast.

38

A PROMISE AND A DECISION

The day has been long and exhausting. Adala and I now sit on a bench in the small, secluded garden just outside the residential wing, accessed by French doors from Adala's private study. We sip sweet liqueur wine. Adala has changed from her regal garments into casual clothing, and we gaze out, admiring the ever-changing colors of the magnificent sunset that nature has provided for the evening.

Her body's warmth soaks in as she sits next to me, and I place my arm around her when a slight chill breeze wafts past us. She snuggles into me and rests her head on my shoulder.

"I am sorry about putting you on the spot. Truthfully, I was in two minds whether to make you my Grand Chancellor without discussing it with you first. I only decided when you went to kneel. It just felt right considering how you helped us."

"It was a shock. I am not part of your society, so I don't understand why you did it. Sentinel's a much better choice."

"He already warned me he would decline if I asked him. His life mission is to protect me, and he has sworn to do that."

"Typical Sentinel."

"Besides, it gives me an excuse to always have you near me."

I glance at her and, raising my hand, stroke her cheek with the back of my forefinger. "Sneaky."

Adala smiles. "Yes, I am."

We sit where we are, contented, for a long time. The sun is dipping below the horizon, and darkness encompasses us as the stars replace the fading light.

"What will you do if someone comes looking for you?"

"I don't know. It's unlikely at present. No one knows there's a planet here, so why would they investigate, even if they pick up my distress beacon? If they do — one part of me aches for the freedom of space travel. But another part has found immense happiness here, a joy I've lacked since my family's death. I could grow used to it."

"I must make sure you do." Adala looks into my eyes and closes the distance between our lips until they lock together in passion. We separate and she withdraws, panting. "You must pledge me you will take me with you if you ever go."

"You have a kingdom to rule."

"I will abdicate."

"I don't have a ship. Let's worry over that if it eventuates."

"Promise me." Her eyes are pleading in the dim light.

She will not contemplate rejection. "I ... promise." We kiss again.

Adala parts and stands, pulling me up with her. "Come, I have a gift for you."

I stand and follow, holding her hand as we enter the house and her rooms.

THE DAYS PASS QUICKLY. I'm kept busy helping Adala organize her cabinet and the business of running the kingdom as she wants it run. I pity Sentinel. He doesn't have a minute's rest, but we get the opportunity, at last, to go to his favorite bar for a catchup.

"Adala is working you like a horse," I tell Sentinel.

He laughs as he takes a sip of his beer. "I enjoy being busy, and

Queen Adala is happy. She has a natural talent for ruling, don't you think?"

"Yes, she does," I say, smiling at the correctness of his perception.

"She has never been so content. I'm unsure whether it's the added responsibility or a particular person in her life."

I blush and take a draft from my beer. "It's the added responsibility."

Sentinel roars with laughter. "Yes, it must be." He downs the rest of his glass and requests two more.

I gaze at him and ponder the changes he's undergone since we first met.

"What are you analyzing now?"

"I was just considering how much you've changed. You were serious and distant. You're relaxed now and sometimes a pain in the ass."

Sentinel grows thoughtful. "Things were desperate when we met. I was unsure I could keep my promise to protect my princess, but I knew I would die trying. There was no cause for cheer, and when Sigmund and Frieda presented you, I despaired of our plight."

"Thanks for the vote of confidence."

"Do you forget you refused to help us at first? They are good judges of character, but I thought they erred. But when you offered your aid, and I saw the joy that you gave Adala, I saw the strength within you. You say that I've changed. So have you. You have unburdened yourself of a great load. A burden of defeat and immense sorrow weighed heavily on you when you arrived. That disappeared when you rescued Adala from Egon's clutches."

I turn away, not wanting him to remind me of my past, but I realize that what Sentinel has said is true. This experience has lifted a weight from me.

We sit in mutual silence until we join in with the rest of the bar's raucous atmosphere, drinking well into the night. With our staggering return to the palace, arm in arm, singing whatever songs come to mind, we arrive at the residential section, where we are to part company and retire to our respective bedrooms.

"Good shing Adalash not here."

"She might give you a good shpanking."

I stare at him with bleary eyes, wondering if he realized what he just said. "In my dreamsh."

We both guffaw and leave, weaving our separate ways to our rooms.

I emerge the next morning, a thumping headache and bloodshot eyes accompanying me to the dining room for breakfast. Adala sits there, studying me with disapproval.

"What?" I ask.

"Have any spanking dreams?"

My face reddens as I recall the parting conversation Sentinel and I had last night. I lower my head in repentance and shame. "No, I didn't ... and I'm sorry."

Adala chortles. "It is OK. I'm pleased that you and Ranulf could relax for a change. You've been working too hard, both of you." She lowers her voice to a whisper, "But it's no way to talk about your queen."

"No, I suppose not," I say, relieved that I haven't offended her too much. "How did you find out?"

She laughs again. "The entire palace heard you two when you returned last night."

"Oh." I redden further. "I didn't realize we were making such a racket."

"Well, eat breakfast and tidy yourself. We have matters to discuss later."

"When?"

"When you are ready. I shall be in the study, reviewing boring reports, so you'll be a welcome break from that drudgery."

"OK."

Adala rises and comes over to me, places a hand under my chin, raising my face, and kisses me gently on the lips. Moving her mouth to my ear, she whispers, "We may discuss that spanking afterward, though."

I laugh in delight. "We will, will we?"

She winks and walks away.

I busy myself with breakfast and return to my room to dress. Two hours later, I walk to Adala's working study and am given permission to enter by the person guarding her. After a knock, I hear "Enter." I open the door and step inside the study.

"Halwende. At last. I'm going insane with these damn reports." Adala stretches back in her chair. She rises, pressing a button on her desk as she does so.

An attendant enters the room moments later. "Your Majesty?"

"Can you please bring refreshments? We will be on the terrace."

"Yes, Your Majesty." The servant disappears.

"Let us enjoy the sunshine." Adala leads the way, opening the double doors and striding onto a small patio furnished with a table and chairs. I follow and we both sit, the sun warming us with its heat. The humidity is low today, so it's pleasant basking in the warmth.

As I gaze at her, I notice she has something on her mind but wait for her to start the conversation. She doesn't hasten to relieve my curiosity. The servant comes with a coffee tray laden with the sort of biscuits she knows Adala and I enjoy, pours us a coffee each, and discreetly retreats from our presence.

I grab a biscuit and take a bite, staring at Adala as I chew, wondering what she's thinking.

She takes a sip of coffee and glances at me. "I've been pondering the contents of that room — the portal room. You must show it to me."

"I can do that. Any reason?"

Adala sits in silence for a moment. "... It has been centuries since we cloaked and segregated ourselves from the rest of the galaxy. Maybe it's time to lift that cloaking and rejoin civilization. From your descriptions and studying the gadgets on your ship, I believe we will profit by reintroducing ourselves." She glances away and back at me. "We have you to moderate any potential conflicts and negotiate exchange agreements we may wish to make."

It is my turn to avert my gaze as I consider the implications of her words. This is a mammoth decision, and she needs to get it right. It will be disastrous if removing the cloaking causes the old problems to resurface. There won't be a second chance to re-cloak the planet once she has opened this Pandora's box. "I'm sure I don't need to list the risks you and your people face," I say, returning my eyes to her. She nods in agreement. "You must have considered the ramifications a thousand times before even suggesting it to me. Tell me, did that blue crystal caused the original conflict?"

"I cannot tell you. It is too distant, and when I query the library, it remains silent on the matter. It has answered me on every topic other than the portal room itself."

I scratch my chin in thought. The machine's energy source is a mystery. The scooters' power source is very primitive. We abandoned that method eons ago, so it's likely that whatever the galaxy was fighting over no longer holds such value, or they found other sources and its rareness reduced. "I can see your point in wanting to rejoin the galaxy. Life would become much easier for you ... your military could focus on more productive activities than its persistent infighting. They must re-educate themselves, relearn space warfare tactics. And renew their hardware to current galactic standards."

"So, do you agree I should do it? Will you aid us?" Adala says, a pleading, earnest look in her eyes.

I gaze at her, my heart melting as her grace dazzles me. If I agree to help, there's one more commitment keeping me here, although here is a pleasant place to be. There is much I can contribute to Adala's plans, and they involve off-world trips once I repair my ship or get another vessel. I could buy an entire fleet of them for the royal house. The more I consider her request, the more I warm to the idea. "If you're sure of this course of action, I will help you as best I can."

"Thank you. You do so much for us, and we can't repay you as you deserve."

"If this pans out and someone answers my beacon, you can compensate me by fixing my ship. I'll need to re-establish ties with the outside worlds, starting with my home planet. Although, I prefer it here." I wink at her.

Adala laughs. "I want you here."

"When will you do this then?"

"I will announce my intentions to the cabinet this afternoon and make a public announcement over the coming week. We will uncloak ourselves after that."

"Fair enough. I can enjoy looking at you in the meantime. Now, let's discuss that spanking ..."

39

THE CLOAKING LIFTED AND THE BEACON ANSWERED

The week rushes to completion with Adala absent, as she is busy with publicizing the event, but she then announces the time to me, and I wait outside her study, ready to escort her to the portal room. The door opens, and Adala comes out.

"Ready?" I ask.

"Yes."

"Let's do this then." I hook my arm so that she can place hers around it, and we stride off together.

We walk to the lower levels and through the passages leading to the portal, reaching the obsidian door blocking the room's entrance. The door fades as I approach, but a voice sounds moments later. *"Who is your guest, Custodian?"*

"My guest is a fellow Eriduan, although she was not born there, and you are to give her permission to enter."

"As you wish."

We enter the room, and Adala's eyes bulge in amazement at the machinery inside it. "I never realized this existed."

"Nor did I until I saw it."

She strolls along the aisles studying each piece of equipment, trying to match the name with the physical location in the city. "Do you know what needs deactivating?"

"I have a reasonable idea. Come ... I will show you." We walk to the chamber's far side. "This is it."

Adala grabs me, the stress of the decision now hitting her as we approach the point of no return when I flick the switch.

"Are you sure you want to do this?" I ask one last time.

Adala looks at me with uncertainty but takes a deep breath and straightens. "Yes, I'm sure, for good or ill, we must."

"Well, here goes then." I reach for the lever that will isolate the planet's cloaking and move it to the off position. The lights on the equipment that it powered wink out. Several other switches cloak sections of the planet, so I isolate them too. "Well, that's it then," I say once I've checked that I have de-energized every cloaking switch.

"Now we wait and see," Adala says.

"Yes. Now we wait and see."

EVERYTHING CONTINUES as usual for some time after we turn the cloaking off, and the prospect of an imminent visit starts to fade from our minds. Everyone is more concerned with daily life. Even I think of it less, too busy conducting the affairs of state that Adala has given me. As Grand Chancellor, I am busy reviewing a plan to improve the economy of the kingdom.

One day, a commotion outside my study disturbs my concentration, and I lift my eyes. It's difficult to hear what the fuss is about, so I rise and stroll to the window. People are pointing toward the sky, and I gaze in that direction. My heart skips a beat. A spaceship is descending. Watching it for a moment, I realize it's heading for my vessel's crash site. It must have come in response to the distress beacon.

Someone knocks on the door, and it opens. "Halwende, have you ... I see that you have," Sentinel says as he pokes his head through the doorway. He enters and walks over to me. "They're going to your vessel."

"Yes. We must go meet them. Just you and me. I don't want whoever they are to come to the city until we understand their intentions. Has Adala been told?"

"I do not know. I came straight here. We must tell her before we leave."

"You don't need to," Adala says as she walks into the room. Excitement, tinted with fear, lights her face as I turn to her.

"Sentinel and I will greet them. Check their credentials."

"You had better hurry then," Adala says, gazing out of the window. "They will land soon, judging by their speed."

I stride over to a cabinet and open a concealed door, extracting my wrist lasers and two masers in holsters. I give one to Sentinel, whom I have instructed on its use, and I reset it to his metabolism. We strap them on, and I place the lasers on my wrists. "Let's go." I walk out with Sentinel close behind me.

"Godspeed and stay safe," Adala calls after us.

"We will," I call back.

Sentinel and I hurry to the scooter station and requisition a speedster. He drives, being more experienced in the art. We speed out of the city and toward my spaceship, with the descending ship preparing to settle near my stricken vessel's location. We arrive half an hour later and meet two men talking and walking around my ship, trying to find a way inside it. They stop when they hear us approaching, turn and gaze at us as we land. I notice they bear arms like ours. Sentinel watches them with wary eyes, but I approach them with a friendly smile.

"Greetings, strangers. I take it you came in answer to my distress beacon."

"So, you sent the distress beacon? Yes, we did, and you are ...?" one man asks.

"I'm Halwende. Pleased to meet you," I say as I extend my hand in greeting. "And Ranulf, but I call him Sentinel."

Sentinel shakes hands but stands back again, watching.

The man who responded eyes Sentinel, assessing what level of threat he might be. "He looks true to his name. I'm Balashi, and he is Udama."

We stand in silence, unsure who should speak first.

"How in hell did you end up out here?" Balashi finally asks.

"Long story. I was running a quick trip to Santori and bumped into an asteroid I didn't spot. I found this planet and crash-landed. But I didn't understand why it was not in the astrogation charts. What brought you this way — apart from the beacon?"

"We were doing the same Santori run. We spotted your beacon and came to investigate, as the law requires us to do. It's put us behind schedule."

"Well, I can make it worth your while, if you can stay and talk."

"I don't know, Balashi ... you know how bitchy the trading houses are when we're late."

"Sure, Udama, but it won't hurt to listen to him. The fresh air will do us good, and we may placate the trading houses if we like what they tell us here." Balashi turns to me again. "Does this place have a name?"

"Helheim, the locals tell me."

"Never heard of it."

"Nor had I until I crashed into it."

"Are they native to the planet?"

"They originated from elsewhere, but a long time ago. They removed themselves from the galaxy but are now interested in rejoining the rest of us."

"I see. Well, lead the way."

"If you travel with us, we can take you into the city to meet our leaders."

They follow us onto the scooter, and Sentinel retraces our route back to the city.

"Any local talent?" Udama asks.

I look at Sentinel to figure if he understands what Udama means. He has the slightest trace of a smile on his face. "I wouldn't know," I say. Sentinel's smile becomes more obvious but doesn't give any hints.

"You're a strange one. How long have you been here?"

"Six … seven months."

"And we're the first to pick up your beacon. Just our luck."

"There's a reason for that, but I won't go into it now."

We sit in silence for the rest of the trip back to the palace. The visitors crane their necks to take in their surroundings. The craft lands at the palace scooter pool 40 minutes later, and we disembark and follow Sentinel into a palace meeting room. He leaves us to tell Adala of our guests. Ten minutes later, both Sentinel and Adala enter the room.

"I thought you said there wasn't any talent," Udama blurts out without thought when he sees Adala.

As I cringe in shock, I glance at Adala to watch her reaction. He has embarrassed even Balashi by the outburst, and Sentinel struggles not to pull his maser out to disintegrate him for such an insult to his queen.

Adala turns her visage to the source of the comment and gives him a gorgon stare. "This talent is far above your grade, isn't that right, Halwende?"

Udama turns to stone, unable to dig a hole deep enough in which to hide.

I struggle to not burst out laughing, but manage not to, albeit with an enormous smile. "Yes, you are... Queen Adala."

Balashi stares in shock at the introduction and stiffens to attention. "Please pardon my partner, Your Majesty. He sometimes speaks before he thinks."

Adala smiles, accepting the apology. "No harm done. Your friend might mix with *the talent* while he's our guest — if he lives long enough. Let's forget our little misstep and start with introductions. As you may have gathered, I am Queen Adala, Queen of Helheim. And you are ...?"

"My name is Balashi from Eridu, Your Majesty." Balashi bows his head to acknowledge her status, and in return she acknowledges his deference.

"And your embarrassing friend?" Adala turns to face him.

"U-U-Udama, Your Majesty." Udama's face has turned as red as a cherry.

Adala takes pity on him and refrains from making any further terse comments. "Let us sit and have a free discussion on topics of mutual interest." She strolls toward the table and sits in the central seat. I sit on her right and Sentinel on her left. She gestures for Balashi and Udama to sit opposite us, which they do. Servants arrive with pots of tea and coffee and finger food, placing them in front of us. They pour the drinks and leave. "Now, I don't know how much my Grand Chancellor and Trade Minister have discussed of our circumstances." Balashi and Udama look at me in astonishment. "But we can now reengage with the rest of galactic society after centuries of self-imposed isolation. So, I wish to re-establish relationships, trade and diplomatic, with the galaxy. And Halwende and yourselves can contribute to those aims. Are you interested in assisting me with this?"

Udama moves to speak, but Balashi stops him by raising his hand. He takes his cup of coffee and sips it thoughtfully for a moment. "We can't help you on the diplomatic front. Your ... Grand Chancellor may be in a better position for that. But on the trade side, I'm sure we can help you, as long as it's worth our while."

I laugh. "Spoken like a true trader."

"Come now. You'd say the same."

"Yes, I would, but please continue."

"Yes, well, as I was saying, if we agree on terms, I could help you establish contacts with our sources."

Adala takes in his comments with a considering expression. "I take it that your contacts are legal and of a standing to negotiate with a sovereign state?"

Balashi looks at me and back to Adala. "I assure you we run a legitimate business. You can have your Gr... Halwende confirm our credentials, and the people we can put you in contact with, as to their legality and ability in handling large contracts of various commodities and other merchandise."

"Good. I will let my Grand Chancellor handle the details from now. You are both invited to dine with us tonight." Adala looks at Udama. "I may even invite talent for social intercourse with you."

"You are too kind," Udama says.

"It's an honor to join you," Balashi replies.

Adala rises. We rise too. "I'll meet you again this evening." She walks out of the room.

We re-sit and start serious discussions, working out details for mutual profit.

40

LEAVING HELHEIM

I enter Adala's private rooms two days later. She has been crying. Rushing over to her, I wrap my arms around her. "What's wrong?"

She sniffs. "I do not want you to go."

"But I must."

"I know, but it doesn't make me feel any better."

Looking at her, I stroke her hair to soothe her, and I realize it soothes me too. "I will be quick as I can and return to you. I promised, remember?"

Adala nods her head.

"I'll buy a ship suitable for you and take you into space, as you wish."

Adala smiles. "Yes." Her eyes glaze with dreams of adventure.

We stare into each other's eyes for an eternity. I don't want to lose this feeling. Our heads move toward each other, and we kiss long and passionately.

"I love you," I say before I realize it.

Adala beams with delight. "I love you too."

It strikes me at that moment that I have forgiven myself for my past sins and can now move forward in my life.

The End

The story continues with Halwende's Resurrection (see next page)

Get the next book in the Halwende's Legacy Series - Halwende's Resurrection.

Type https://books2read.com/Halwendes-resurrection into your browser.

Thanks for reading this book. If you loved the book and have a moment to spare, I would appreciate a quick review on the site that you purchased the book from, as this helps new readers find my books.

Subscribe to my Newsletters and receive three free episodes of The Chronicles of Gatacus Todd.

Type http://subscribepage.io/g4r4f8 in your browser.

ALSO BY JOHN WEGENER

Books

Reach For The Stars Trilogy

FTL

Centauri

Ceti

Reach For The Stars Box Set (Books 1-3)

Loki's Fall

Zodiac Series

Scorpius

Libra

Halwende's Legacy Series

Halwende's Redemption

Halwende's Resurrection

Halwende's Reincarnation

Halwende's Legacy Box Set (Books 1-3)

Solar Dawn Series

Lunar Rift

Other Stories

The Dark Ages

SAGI

Short Stories

The Love Particle

ABOUT THE AUTHOR

John Wegener grew up in the Adelaide Hills of South Australia. He now expresses his imaginative dreams by engaging in writing after a 34-year career as a Chemical Engineer in the steel industry, which has taken him to many countries and allowed him to experience many cultures. John currently lives in Wollongong, Australia with his wife and children.

Click on johnwegener.com to find more of my books or read his blogs. Type subscribepage.io/g4r4f8 to subscribe to my emails for more stories and information.

f